THE
DARK
LIGHTHOUSE

Tales of speculation and the fantastic

DAVID R. GRIGG

ISBN: 978-0-9872654-7-0
2nd Edition

Published by Rightword Enterprises,
Melbourne, Australia, September 2014

www.rightword.com.au

Cover design by the author, based on an image licensed from
CanStockPhoto.com.

For Sue, without whom I could do nothing.

Contents

The Dark Lighthouse

At the Dark Lighthouse

ANNE STOOD AT THE WINDOW OF HER BEDROOM, looking out into the night. There was still a light on in the curate's cottage; if he was looking out he would be able to see her window.

She turned and adjusted the flow of gas to the mantles of the lights, making them as bright as she could. Then she returned to the window and closed the curtains slowly, then opened them again. Closed. Opened. Again and again. Surely he must see? Surely he must understand?

She'd had the dream again. It had woken her yet again in a flood of terror. There was never a night now when it didn't recur.

She is standing on the cliff above a rocky shore. Her long hair, unbound, blows out in a long stream behind her. Waves lash high, filling the air with foam, and the wind screams. It is night, but behind the storm clouds, the moon glimmers from time to time. Out at sea, a ship pitches and heaves, all but one of its sails furled, as it struggles to keep its head turned to meet the waves.

The curate had come to visit again yesterday. For her part, Anne would not have let him in, but her mother greeted him politely, and so they had tea together. Anne had been silent except for when she must speak or else be openly rude. Her father, of course, was not there, was away at the factory, making yet more money. Her father would have thrown the curate out, or worse. Her father... her father knew how to be cruel.

As she watches the ship, it is driven closer and closer to the shore. In a panic, she looks up at the tall lighthouse. But all there is dark. There is no light! There is no warning for the imperiled vessel. She begins to run towards the tower.

She had begun to hate her father in her childhood. It had been slow coming. He was always busy at his business, and she did not see him very often. She was usually in bed before he returned, and still asleep by the time he left. Only on Sundays, when the family went to church together, the better to be seen in their private pew, did she see much of him. She soon learned to dread that holy day. After church, there was always some incident to arouse his wrath or his cruelty.

One Sunday, when she was only eleven, she had stumbled into the stone-lined washroom to find him drowning kittens, picking up the little mewling things one by one, then holding them underwater as they struggled, until no more bubbles came and the kitten was still. When she had realised what he was about, she had screamed and burst into tears, but he had just looked at her with a stony gaze. "No need for these," he had said. "One cat is enough to catch the mice. Everything has to have a purpose, Anne. We'll have no waste in this house."

She fumbles open the door and runs into the body of the lighthouse. It is dark, but there is enough light from above for her to see the long, long spiral of the staircase. Lifting up her skirts, she begins to climb as fast as she can manage, her breath coming short, her panic rising. The staircase seems to go on forever.

It had been on a Sunday, of course, when she had first seen the curate. At church. Assisting the vicar at the service. He had looked across at her with his dark eyes, and held her gaze for a moment, a moment too long for decorum, perhaps. His face was thin, with a long straight nose, and he had dark hair, like her own. In women, it was unfashionable these days to be dark, but in a man it was attractive. Beneath his cleric's black gown, he seemed a strong, well-built man. Then, blushing, she dropped her gaze, hoping her father had not noticed.

The curate first came to visit their house on the following week. She had been happy to see him then, before she understood the way it was to be. Her mother, always with an eye to what was expected by village society, welcomed the curate in and talked at length about local affairs. He had smiled at Anne, and she had smiled demurely back.

Up the stairs she runs, gasping, her legs an agony, every new step a torment. Up at last to the top of the tower, until she can see the lantern room above her. Staggering a little, she climbs the final flight of steps. Glass surrounds her, and she can look out on the storm-wracked sea. And from here she can see the ship, coming ever closer to the deadly rocks.

There had been some further visits by the curate over the next few weeks. Her father had been busy, and at first did not know about the visits. But when he discovered them, he had flown into a terrible rage, picking things up at random and smashing them on the floor. Her poor mother was in tears as a clock and one of her precious vases crashed down. But then he had taken control of himself.

"My daughter will not marry a penniless priest!" he had said grimly. "I've got better plans for you, my girl. If you marry at all, you'll marry who I say you'll marry, and when I say. If that black-frocked bastard comes here again, he'd better watch out."

There had, of course, been no talk of marriage from the curate, no hint of it. Just the curate's polite visits, a shared smile once in a while, that was all. Her father's fury had been out of all proportion.

Why is there no light? Why does the glass not turn, and the warning beacon not sweep out? She runs down the steps again into the service room and sees where the great lamp and its wick can be reached. A packet of lucifers is there. She strikes and the lamp flares up. On the wall is a mechanism with a lever. She hauls at it and it moves. The lens begins to turn.

Anne could not understand why her mother still permitted the curate to come. Surely she saw the peril? But polite society dictated that the curate be received. To ban him would have caused comment. How could they ban the curate's visits when the vicar and his wife were still welcomed?

So Anne tried to discourage the curate's interest in her. But there was never a moment when she was alone with him to speak her mind. She was as silent as she could be, tried not to look at him. She knew that he had sensed the difference in her. Alas, he seemed to think that it was due to maidenly modesty, indicated an increased interest from her, not a lessened one. She found it hard indeed, when her heart had begun to yearn for him, not to look with longing at him in church from time to time. Despite her earnest efforts, her father noticed.

The beam swings out across the ragged sea. "Oh, keep away," Anne cries in futile agony, "keep away!"

Surely the ship must see? Perhaps it does, but it is too late now, too late. It cannot change course, cannot but be driven upon the stony teeth awaiting it. She cries out in horror as the ship comes closer and closer, and then, in an instant, is smashed all to pieces in a foaming cataclysm of timbers and brine.

One Sunday afternoon when her mother was out, her father seized her by the arm and dragged her into his study. Mounted on the wall was a gun, a shotgun. He pulled it from its mount, broke it open and showed her the cartridges inside, then snapped it shut.

"What's mine is mine," he said, holding the weapon at his side. "I don't like other men craving what is mine. You are my property, no less than any machine in my factory. I don't like the look of that fellow, don't like his creeping ways. One day I shall find a way..." He fell silent, but by his grim smile she knew he was relishing some terrible deed. Had he *enjoyed* drowning those kittens? With an awful dread, she knew at last that he had.

She runs down the interminable spiral stair, down, down, down, until at last she can run out into the moonlit night, and down to the terrible shore. Timbers surge and smash against each other as the waves beat against them and force them further upon the rocks.

Heedless of how she is becoming soaked, she struggles out against the waves. Something not a timber is floating there.

And so, dream-awoken, she stands now at her high window, hopelessly signalling with the curtains, her own dark lighthouse.

She reaches the floating thing, and knows it is a man. Sobbing, she pulls it toward the shore, half-tumbled by the waves, until at last she reaches a level place beyond the water's reach. Falling to the shingle beside her burden, she stares up at the tormented clouds, then turns at last to look at what she has found.

Drowned and dead like one of those pathetic kittens, the curate's face stares up at her.

"Oh keep away," she cries at the window, "oh, keep away!"

October 2012

Rear View

BRIGHT LIGHTS IN HIS REAR-VIEW MIRROR. Too bright. The driver behind hadn't bothered to drop his high beams. Carl cursed a little, and flipped the switch on the mirror to dim the reflection.

He was weary, bone-weary, and there was a long way to go before he reached the city again. And he didn't much like driving on this particular road. It was along here somewhere that Marie had died, and he hated having to think about that. It hadn't seemed so bad, having to come this way, when he had driven up to the wedding during the bright daylight. But now, driving down the long black tunnel of the night, it was giving him the creeps.

The headlights behind him were quickly coming closer, still annoyingly undimmed. Well, they would probably go around him soon enough. They were traveling fast. He was keeping pretty close to the speed limit himself: he'd been picked up speeding a couple of times recently, and couldn't afford to lose his license. That's why he'd been cautious about how much he drank at the wedding, too. And there was plenty of room for the car behind him to pass. This country 'highway' had only one lane in each direction, but at this late hour, there were few other vehicles.

Closer came the lights, and closer, until the following car was right on his tail.

"Come on," he said irritably, "go around me."

But instead the car behind him edged closer and closer, until it was so close that its headlights started to drop out of sight behind the rear of his own car. Carl swore. Dickheads! Some teenagers trying to get a rise out of him, most likely. Only one approach would work. He took his foot off the gas pedal and allowed his car to start slowing down. He couldn't actually brake, the vehicle behind him was so close that they would rear-end him in a flash.

As he slowed, Carl expected the driver behind him to get annoyed and swerve around him. Instead, they slowed in pace with him, dropping back a little more so that he could see their headlights clearly again. Carl tried putting on a sudden burst of speed, but that was a predictable game: the vehicle behind just sped up to match his own speed. He went back to gradually slowing down, becoming more and more angry. If it came to an argument with these kids, he thought he could handle himself, provided there weren't too many of them. He was a big enough guy, pretty fit. He just wished that he didn't feel so tired.

Together, the cars drew to a halt. The edge of the road here was pretty rough, so Carl didn't pull over much, but remained on the asphalted road surface.

It was only as they came to a complete stop that Carl started to think something was odd, but he couldn't place it at first. Then he had it. The headlights behind him were very bright, glaring, in the mirror, but didn't seem to be lighting up the inside of Carl's car. Perhaps they were tilted down at the road? Dismissing this puzzle, and shaking his head in annoyance, he opened the door and got out, ready to give the kids behind him a tongue-lashing they wouldn't forget in a hurry.

There was no car there. The road was empty in both directions.

Astonished, Carl looked around. Had the other car gone off on some side road he hadn't seen? Surely not. Dropped back at the last minute and turned off their headlights? But, though the skies were cloudy the moon was peeping out and gave more than enough light for him to have seen the other car if they had been anywhere near.

Baffled, he stood there for a long minute until finally he shrugged and climbed back into his car and started off again. Could he have dreamed it? He *really* needed a coffee, then. There would be a town somewhere up ahead with a gas station or two. He'd stop as soon as he saw one.

The wedding he'd attended had gone on far too long, too many damn speeches. And he'd been disappointed. There had been a good looking girl he'd been chatting up nicely, but she'd ended up dancing with a much younger guy and had vanished before he could catch up with her again. Maybe he was getting past it? But he was still only in his thirties. Was that over the hill these days? There had been a time... but that started him thinking about his wife Marie again. He shook his head, gripped the wheel tightly, and forced himself to concentrate on driving.

A few minutes later he saw headlights behind him again. The same car as before? No way to tell. But again, the car behind him was coming up fast, too fast. This time, though, it didn't sit behind him, but without indicating it moved smoothly into the other lane and started to overtake him. Started. But instead of passing him, it drew level, closely matching his speed, just edging a little forward from time to time, then dropping back again.

Really alarmed now, Carl looked quickly across at the other car. The driver was the only person in it. He couldn't quite make out the driver's features without taking his eyes off the road for too long a time. But it looked to be a woman, not some young teenage lout. A woman? Carl frowned, his pulse quickening. What was going on here? He put his foot on the brake and quickly pulled to a halt. As he did so, the car alongside matched him, keeping freakishly level, moment by moment, until they both came to a standstill, side by side in the road.

The moon came out from behind a cloud, and for a moment Carl was able to see the other car more clearly. A powder-blue Toyota sedan. What felt like an electric shock ran unpleasantly through him. It was familiar. *Too* familiar. Marie had driven a car like that. Hands shaking, he pressed the button to wind down the window so that he could call out to the other driver.

As the window slid down, the image of the other car simply slid away down with it, like some magic trick. Beyond the open window was nothing but the night air.

He sat at the wheel trembling, trying to rationalize what was happening. That wedding... it had been pretty wild. Maybe someone had slipped him something, something which caused hallucinations? Possible. Very possible.

Whatever it was must be working on his memories, bringing to the surface things that he had long tried to forget. Marie had died in a crash somewhere along this road. He'd never visited the exact spot, though he knew that some of her friends had. He hadn't been able to bring himself to do that, hadn't wanted to re-kindle the pain. The drug he'd been given must be bringing those feelings of regret and guilt to the surface, that was all.

He should stop driving, pull over somewhere and sleep it off. It was too dangerous to keep going. But he couldn't just leave his car just sitting on the road here. He had to find somewhere safe to pull off. Reluctantly, he started up the car again and moved off slowly, looking for a spot.

Lights in his mirror again. His stomach clenched. That car again? No. The headlights were different. In a few moments he could see that it was a massive freight truck, lit up like a Christmas tree. It raced up behind him and then swerved around, its deep horn blaring in fury at his slow speed. If he hadn't started driving again, if he'd still been at a halt, it would probably have smashed into him, and they would be picking up the pieces for a month. He found that his hands were shaking on the wheel with the thought of it. But at least it hadn't been *that* car, that power-blue Toyota.

Finally, there was a slight bend in the road and an open, level spot where he could pull the car off the asphalt. He got out, taking long deep breaths of the cold night air.

The moon came out again from behind the clouds, and as it did he noticed something pale hanging half-way up the trunk of one of the trees. He hesitated for a moment, but then walked closer. It was a bunch of flowers, tied around the tree. He reached up. Plastic flowers. And a card with something written on it in large but faded black letters.

"R.I.P. Marie. We love you."

He gave a little cry of shock. Right here, then. It must have been right here where she'd crashed, two years ago, on the way back from visiting her parents. Now he could make out the scar on the bole of the tree, the bark only partly healed. He felt dizzy. What were the odds that he would stop right here? It was crazy.

He turned back to his car, intending to put down the seat and sleep until time and daylight could blow away this madness.

His car was gone.

It wasn't there any more. In its place stood the powder-blue Toyota, dripping with condensation as though it had just emerged from a cold fog, emitting the faint pinging sounds that engines make as they cool down.

He stood silent, staring, unbelieving.

It was too dark to see inside the car, but after a long pause, the passenger door clicked and swung open a fraction. The interior light came on.

Marie, his dead wife Marie, was sitting in the driver's seat.

One step, two steps. Almost against his will, he found himself stepping closer to the car, to this mirage. Marie didn't move, didn't look at him, just stared forward into the night, her hands on the wheel.

Another step, another. Half-expecting the blue car to vanish again, step by step Carl came close enough to touch it. He reached out tentatively to put his hand on the roof, expecting his hand to pass right through it. But instead it met his hand solidly. Solid and wet and cold. Very cold.

Hardly daring to do it, conscious of his heart racing, he slowly bent down to look at Marie. She still sat unmoving, her gaze distant, not looking at him.

Surely this was some kind of mistake? Surely it was the drugs which were making him imagine his wife instead of the woman actually driving this car? But then she did turn to look at him, or at least, in his direction, though her gaze somehow still did not connect with his. It *was* Marie, there was no doubt about it. She looked exactly as she had done the last time he had ever seen her. She reached out and pushed the passenger door further open, a clear invitation.

Bewildered, he opened the door fully and got in beside this impossible woman. "Marie..." he said, but she turned away to gaze forward again. The car started with a sudden jerk, throwing him back in the seat with a gasp. The open door slammed shut at his side. Gravel spun beneath the wheels.

Fumbling, he strapped on his seat belt as the car swerved onto the roadway and started forwards. "Marie..." he said again, but she did not speak or look at him.

The car sped up, and in the dim moonlight he could see trees and fences flashing by.

"Marie..." he cried out, "What's going on? Tell me what you want!" But she was silent. As silent as the grave.

Then, as the silence stretched on for long moments, something even crazier happened. There was a beep and a vibration from his phone, stashed in his pocket. Not sure whether he dared take his eyes off the road, off Marie, he managed to pull the phone out from his pocket and glance down. A text message.

im on the road

It had been sent from his wife's phone number. A phone which had been destroyed in the crash. Carl had never removed her number from his own phone's contacts, feeling that to do so would be a final betrayal.

He looked up at her. She still gazed fixedly at the road ahead.

There was another beep and a shake.

wanted to let u know i found yr phone last week

He gave a little gasp. These were the very same text messages she had sent him two years ago. The messages he hadn't let the police know about. The corner had concluded that Marie had simply fallen asleep at the wheel. But if they had known about the series of texts...

u should b more careful

The car veered suddenly, and he gave a yell of terror. Then it straightened back onto the road. Was that a faint smile on Marie's lips?

u should clear out yr texts more often

He put out his hand and touched her arm. Cold, so cold. As cold as the car had felt. As cold as death.

Beep. Shake.

seems u have a little friend called tania

"Marie," he said, "I'm so sorry. I always wanted you to know that I was sorry." But the texts were relentless, and Marie did not take her eyes away from the road.

i dont hav to ask if shes pretty cause she sent u her pic. nice boobs!

The car was speeding up, the trees were flashing by even faster. He began to be very afraid.

she wasnt the first tho. i know about the others too

Had Marie been texting these one-handed as she drove? She must have. He looked desperately out of the car. Could he open the door and jump out? Why had he ever climbed in?

Beep. Shake.

but ive had enough carl, had too much. cant bear it any more

He didn't really need to look down at the phone. He knew that string of texts off by heart, had many times replayed them in his mind, feeling the regret.

so now im going to make an end

"No, Marie, please!" He clasped again at her arm, trying to reach her, trying to make her stop. But her arm was cold, cold; like steel, unmoving, relentless.

letting go now

She looked at him then, directly in the eye, and this time her gaze connected. He sat frozen as she took both her hands off the steering wheel and pumped hard on the gas pedal.

There was a bend in the road up ahead, but the car did not take it.

October 2012

This story was published in the December 2012 issue of eFiction Magazine.

Faces

Stephen lived amidst a crowd of faces.

There were faces everywhere he looked. Faces in the pattern of a dress; faces in the cracks in a brick wall; faces in the clouds, the trees, the grass. Oh, and of course, almost as an afterthought, there were the faces of people.

He had started seeing the faces when he was very young, so long ago now that he could not remember the beginning of it. He could only remember being afraid of the faces in the wallpaper of his bedroom, of his screams when the light fell on it in a certain way, and how the faces leered at him, threatening. Then it had been the carpet, its loops of colour turning into the faces of animals or demons or nameless horrors.

In the end, his parents had taken him to a child psychologist. He had been given what he now knew to be a Rorschach test. In every random pattern of ink he had seen a dozen faces. He had only been five and he hadn't understood the doctor's diagnosis. Later, though, his parents had told him what had been said.

Stephen, it seemed, had a hypertrophy of that part of the brain which recognises faces. All humans tend to see faces in random patterns, but for some reason, Stephen had that tendency to an alarming degree. Everything in which a face could possibly be imagined was, to him, a real, living face, little different from the faces of his parents or of his playmates.

His parents stripped back the wallpaper in his room, painted it white, pulled up the patterned carpet and replaced it with a plain colour. It helped, but not much. The moonlit shadow of leaves falling on his wall was enough to start the screaming again.

As he grew older, he eventually learned not to fear the faces he saw; learned to suppress his reactions when he saw new faces in the drizzle of rain down a window pane, in spilled ink, in a pile of rubbish in an alleyway. He couldn't stop seeing the faces, but he could learn to ignore them.

By the end of his teens, managing to live what most would call a normal life, there was an incident which revealed a new side to his disability. He discovered that his disability was also a talent.

Walking down the street one morning, on his way to college, a woman a few metres ahead of Stephen screamed and began to struggle. A hollow-eyed teenager wearing a hoodie was pulling at the woman's handbag, trying to get it away from her. As she continued to resist, he pulled out a knife and slashed the straps, but she jumped forward to grab the body of the bag. That was when the youth stabbed forward at her chest with the knife and she gave a kind of sigh, let go, and sank to the pavement. The youth was off in a flash, dodging down an alley, and was out of sight before anyone could give chase.

Stephen was among many people who tried to help the woman, and an ambulance was called, but by the time it reached the scene, she was dead.

Stephen's name was taken, and he was asked down to the police station. Could he describe the youth? He found the question incomprehensible. Of course he could, and did so in minute detail. Later, at an identification parade, he picked out the youth without pausing for an instant. As a witness in court, he was confident and not to be shaken by the defence attorney. Although he had to concentrate, so as not to be distracted by the faces of monsters and demons he could see in the pattern of the man's tie.

"Are you certain?" he was asked again and again. He was almost baffled by the question. How could anyone *not* remember a face?

The court case attracted considerable attention, due in part to the local newspaper's promotion of a law-and-order agenda at the time. Through that, Stephen's testimony drew attention, too.

A few days later, he was contacted by someone who said he was recruiting for a government agency, looking for someone with certain talents. Stephen, still uncertain as to his prospects after college, readily agreed to attend for an interview.

It wasn't much of an interview, really. Instead, they asked him to look quickly at a blurry photograph, apparently taken from a distance with a telephoto lens, with the man's face partly turned away from the camera. Then he was given a huge book containing thousands of photographs. It took him some time only because there were so many pages in the book. But the moment he turned the right page, he reached out and pointed to the man who had been in the blurry photograph.

The fact was, he never forgot a face. Once clearly seen, for however brief a moment, he could identify it again years later, even when under a disguise, even after cosmetic surgery. His memory for faces, it seemed, was vast.

He was recruited on the spot and he dropped out of college.

The next two years were good for Stephen, and it seemed that he had found his place in life. The pay was good, and the job endlessly interesting and, for someone with his talent, not hard to do.

But then something seemed to go wrong. At the age of 22, the voices started. The faces began to talk to him.

Almost every day, his job involved looking at hundreds of photographs of people. They began to speak. At first, it was just one or two, saying hateful, ugly things. Then he would turn a page of an identification book and a dozen faces would call out to him, telling him he was worthless, or urging him to carry out his own acts of terror. Then it was all of them. Voices with a hundred different accents, a babble of violent words, counselling despair or violence.

He tried to regain control, suppress the voices the way he had learned to control his reaction to the faces in the carpet or the bark of trees, but he struggled. He took leave from his job, to get away from the books of faces, but now every face he saw in the random patterns of the world called out to him in the same way. The faces in the clouds, in the ripples of water, in an arrangement of flowers; they had never gone away. And now they were no longer silent. It was like always being in the midst of a noisy crowd, a mob.

He should have sought help, he knew, but he remembered only too well the professional indifference of the child psychologist when he was young, remembered the laughter of his playmates when he tried to point out to them the faces he saw.

Everywhere he looked, there was a face, and now every face spat out the same message. He was worthless, and the only way to redeem himself was to carry out an act of bloody revenge against the world.

He had learned much about the methods of terror through his job.

With the cacophony of faces urging him on, he began his preparations.

September 2012

This story appeared in Story Shack (online magazine) in August 2013

A Song Before Sunset

It took him three weeks to find the sledgehammer.

He was hunting rats among the broken concrete and rusted metal of an ancient supermarket. The sun was beginning to descend over the jagged horizons of the city, casting shadows like giant gravestones onto the nearer buildings. An edge of blackness had begun to creep across the rubble that was all that remained of the store.

He picked his way carefully from one piece of concrete to another, skirting the twisted metal, looking for a hole or a cover that might make a suitable nest for a brood of rats, here and there using his stick to turn over a loose chunk in the vain hope of finding a can of food undiscovered after years of looting. At his waist hung three large rats, their heads squashed and bloody from his stick. Rats were still fat enough and slow enough these days to be caught by surprise with a blow on the head, which was fortunate, for his eye and his skill with the slingshot he carried were not as they had once been. He rested a while, sniffing at the cold wind. There would be a frost tonight, and his bones knew fear of the cold. He was getting old.

He was sixty-five, and the years had starved him. The flesh of his youth had loosened and sagged, leaving his frame thinly draped and his eyes starting from his bony head like some curious troll.

He was sixty-five, and his hair, grey many years ago, now raised a white halo about his leather-coloured face. That he had survived so long was a wonder to him, for his earlier years had not prepared him for this present world. But somehow he had learned to fight and kill and run and all else that had been necessary in the long years since the city had died.

The days now, however, were not so foul and desperate as they had once been. Now it was seldom that he feared he would starve to death. But in the bad days, like many others, he had eaten human flesh.

His name was Parnell and he had gone on living.

The sun was sinking fast, and he turned about to go back before the dark could overtake him. It was as he turned that he caught the dull shine of metal in the corner of his eye. He peered more closely, put out his hand and heaved a sledgehammer up from the rubble. He swung its mass experimentally, weighed it in his hands, and felt its movement. After a moment he was forced to put it down again, as his arms began to tremble with unaccustomed strain. But no matter: given enough time, he knew this was the tool to realise the hope he had been hugging to himself for three weeks. He tied the hammer awkwardly to his belt and began to hurry home, fleeing the shadow of the city.

It was almost dark when he reached his home, a weatherstained stone house hedged around with the tangled jungle of an overgrown garden. Inside, he carefully lit each of the smoky candles in the living room, calling up a cancerous light that spread relentlessly into the corners. His door was locked and barred, and at last he sat in peace before the woodwormed piano in the main room. He sighed a little as his fingers tapped at the yellowed and splitting keys, and felt an accustomed sorrow as the fractured notes ascended. This piano had perhaps been a good learner's instrument in its day, but time had not been kind to it. Even if he had not feared attracting the attention of the dwellers in the dark outside, the effort of playing was more agony than pleasure.

Music had once been his life. Now his greatest aim was only to quiet the rumbling of his belly. Then he remembered, his eyes drifted to the hammer he had found in the rubble that day, and his hope came alive again, as it had weeks ago.

But there was no time to daydream, no time for hoping. There was time before he slept only to clean and skin the rats he had caught. Tomorrow he was to go trading with the Tumbledown Woman.

The Tumbledown Woman and her mate lived in the midst of a hundred decrepit trams in an old depot. Why they chose to live there was a question none who traded with her had ever managed to solve. Here she stayed, and here she traded. Her store counter was a solitary tram left on the rails a few metres outside the depot, its paint peeling away but still bearing pathetic advertisements of a lost age. While the outside of the tram offered far-away holidays and better deodorants, the Tumbledown Woman inside traded garbage as the luxuries of a world which had died. Inside, arrayed along the wooden seats or hung from the ceiling were tin cans with makeshift hand-grips, greasy home-made candles, racks of suspect vegetables grown no one knew where, rows of dead rats, cats, rabbits and the occasional dog, plastic spoons, bottles, coats of ratskin and all sorts of items salvaged from the debris of oft-looted shops.

The Tumbledown Woman was old, and she was black, and she was ugly, and she cackled when she saw Parnell approaching slowly in the chill morning. She had survived better than many men through the crisis, by being more ruthless and more cruel than they had ever managed to be to her in the years before. She rubbed her hands together with a dry, dry sound, and greeted Parnell with a faded leer.

"Two rats, Tumbledown Woman, fresh killed yesterday," he opened without hesitation.

"I give you something good for them, Mr Piano Player," she sneered.

"Then that will be the first time ever. What?"

"A genuine diamond ring, twenty-four carat gold, see!" And she held the flashing gem to the sun.

Parnell didn't bother to smile at her taunt. "Give me food, and be done with your mocking."

She sneered again, and offered him a cabbage and two carrots. Nodding, he handed her the skinned corpses, lodged the food in his bag, and turned to go. But he was carrying the sledgehammer at his side, and she stopped him with a yell. "Hey, piano player man, that hammer! I give you good fur coat for it! Genuine rabbit!"

He turned and saw that she was not mocking him this time. "When I've finished with it, maybe. Then we'll see."

His reply seemed to make her pleased, for she grinned and yelled again: "Hey, piano man, you hear the news about Ol' Man Edmonds? Them Vandalmen come an' kill him, burn down that book place Ol' Man Edmonds live in!"

Parnell gasped in shock. "The Library? They burnt the Library down?"

"That's right!'"

"My God!" He stood, silent and bewildered for a long minute as the Tumbledown Woman grinned at him. Then, unable to speak further in his anger, he clamped his hands together in bitter frustration and walked off.

The sledgehammer was an awkward thing to carry. Slipped into his belt with the metal head at his waist, the wooden handle beat at his legs as he walked. If he carried it in his arms, his muscles protested after no more than a few minutes, and he was forced to rest. He was getting old, and he knew it. The slide to death was beginning to steepen and he was not, he thought, very far from its end.

In slow, weary stages he walked the distance into the heart of the corpse that was the city: long ago its pulse had stopped. He walked past the rusty hulks of cars and along the dust-filled tram-tracks, through streets of shattered buildings standing in rows like jagged reefs. Long ago the lungs of the city had expired their last breath; the tall chimneys were fallen, casting scattered bricks across the road before him.

He came at last to the centre and faced again the strongly barred and sealed doors of the old City Hall, half buried in the rubble of its long-crumbled entranceway. Even if he had been able to break open the bars of the door, he would have needed to clear away the rubble to allow the doors to open. Such was beyond him.

But at the side of the building, the skeleton of a truck lay crazily against the wall, mounted on the pavement and nuzzled face to face with a tree that now made a leafy wilderness of the cab.

Parnell climbed onto the truck and carefully ascended until he perched with little comfort on a branch of the tree, close to a barred window. Three weeks ago he had cleaned away the grime on the glass to see the dusty corridors inside. On the far wall of the corridor was a direction sign, faded and yellowed, but still bearing the words: CONCERT HALL.

Once again, looking at that dim sign, he was filled to overflowing with memories of concerts he had given. His hands followed a memory of their own on the keys, the music spiralled and, afterwards, the almost invisible audience in the darkened hall applauded again and again...

His memories vanished as he swung the sledgehammer from his shoulder, jarring it into the bars of the window. Dust showered and cement crumbled. The task looked easier than he had at first thought, which was fortunate, for the one stroke had weakened him terribly. He swung again, and the bars moved and bent. Somehow, he found the strength for another swing, and the bars buckled and came loose and smashed through the glass into the corridor beyond.

Triumph came to him in a cloud of weakness, leaving him gasping and his arms weak and trembling. He sat for a long moment on the branch, gaining strength and hope to venture within.

At last he swung his legs over the edge and dropped onto the corridor floor. Glass crackled. He reached into his bag and brought out a small candle and some precious matches. The box of usable matches had cost him ten ratskins at the Tumbledown Woman's tram two weeks ago. He lit the candle and yellow light flooded into the dusty corridor.

He walked along it, making footprints in the virgin dust. A memory floated back to him of telecasts of moon explorers, placing footprint after footprint in age-old lunar dust, and he smiled a grim smile.

Eventually he came to a set of double doors, barred and padlocked. Here he was forced to rest again before he could smash the lock with his hammer, and step into the space-like blackness beyond.

After his eyes had adjusted to the light of the candle, dimmed by the open space, he saw row upon row of once plush seats. Somewhere a rat scurried, and above he could hear the soft rustle and squeaks of what might be a brood of bats on the high ceiling.

The aisle stretched before him, sloping slightly downwards. Parnell walked forward slowly, kicking up dust. In the dark immensity of the hall, his candle was just a spark, illuminating only a tight circle around him and filtering through puffs of dust stirred by his passage.

On the stage, metal gleamed back images of the candle-flame from scattered corners. Around him were the music stands and music sheets of a full orchestra, filmed with years of dust. Here was a half-opened instrument case, and in it the still-shining brass of a french horn, abandoned by some long-gone performer in forgotten haste. And shrouded in white, topped by a tarnished candelabra, stood the grand piano.

Parnell's heart began a heavier, more rapid beat as he brushed dust from the sheet covering the piano. With an anxious hand he lit the candelabra with his own meagre candle, and lifted it high as the light swelled across the stage. He could see other instruments now, long lost by their players: here a violin, there an oboe, cast aside by a time that had made their possession unimportant.

Placing the light on the floor, he carefully eased the sheet from the piano. Yellow light danced on the black surface of polished wood and sparkled in the brass.

For a long, long time his aged hands could do no more than caress the instrument with a growing affection. Finally, he sat on the piano stool, realizing perhaps for the first time how tired he was. The key, he saw with relief, was still in the lock. No doubt he could have forced it, but it would have broken his heart to have damaged that perfect form.

Turning the key in the lock, he lifted the cover and ran his hand softly over the white and black of the piano keys. He sat back, and with a self-conciously wry gesture, flipped his ragged coat away from his seat and turned to face the hall.

A full house tonight, Mr Parnell. All of London queues to hear you. The radio stations are paying fortunes to broadcast your concert. The audience is quiet, expectant. Can you hear them breathe, out there? Not a cough, not a sneeze, not a mutter as they wait, hushed, to hear the first notes drop from your fingertips. The music trembles in your hands, waiting to begin — now!

Discords shattered the empty hall, and the bats, disturbed, flew in a twittering crowd above the deserted, rotting seats. Parnell let out his breath in a painful sigh.

The instrument would have to be painstakingly retuned, note by note. His goal had yet to be reached. But now, at last, he could reach out and touch it. Now, one by one, he began to realize the difficulties that remained. He felt his hunger and saw the candles burning fast. He could probably find pitch-pipes in the hall, but he would need some kind of tool to tighten the strings of the piano. And he would have to support himself somehow while he spent his time in here and was unable to hunt or forage. He would have to go back to the Tumbledown Woman, and see what she would offer him in trade for the sledgehammer. It was no fur coat he would be getting, he knew.

Outside again, he opened his bag and took out the food he had brought with him. He sat on the truck eating pieces of roasted rat and raw cabbage, pondering whether there was some way he could net and kill some of the brood of bats within the hall. No doubt they would make curious eating, but perhaps their leathery wings might have a use...? But all these schemes were impractical, and he dismissed them.

In the distance, over the broken buildings, a thin trail of black smoke was rising leisurely towards the sky. The day had become bright and cloudless, and the smoke was a smear against the blue. Puzzled, Parnell wondered what was burning. The trail was too contained to be a forest fire. Unless some building had spontaneously ignited, after all these years, it had to be the work of men. Unable to arrive at any more satisfactory a conclusion, he turned away, thrusting the question from his mind.

After bundling away the remnants of the food, he loosely replaced the bars of the window to make his entry less obvious to any passing wanderer. Heaving up the sledgehammer, he began the long walk away from his heart's desire.

The Tumbledown Woman had turned sour in the late afternoon, like a fat black toad basking in the last rays of the sun. She sat on the running-board of the tram; greeted Parnell with little enthusiasm. Her withered husband now sat atop the tram and glared menacingly at the horizon, an ancient shotgun beneath his arm, ignoring his wife and Parnell equally.

Parnell sat and bickered with the woman for nearly an hour.

She would still offer him the fur coat, but he wanted an adjustable spanner, candles, matches and food in exchange for the sledgehammer, and these were expensive items. In the end, Parnell gave in and accepted her final offer, which was everything he wanted except the food.

The Tumbledown Woman hung the sledgehammer in a prominent position within the tram and gave him the items he wanted. She turned and looked at him with a bitter eye. "You crazy, piano player man, you know that?"

Parnell, leaning wearily in the doorway of the tram, cradling his candles, was moved to agree with her. "I suppose you're right."

"Sure I'm right!" she answered, nodding her head vigorously. "You a crazy coot."

"Must be crazy to come and trade with you," he said, but the woman just glared at him. Then he remembered: "There was a lot of smoke in the south this morning. Do you know what it was?"

The Tumbledown Woman grinned and winked at him. "Sure I know. Didn" I tell you this morning about them Vandalmen? Them Vandalmen coming all over this town now. Last week burn down Ol" Man Edmonds and his books. Now it's that picture place. Sure crazy, them Vandalmen." And she pottered around the tram, arranging and rearranging her goods.

Parnell's heart sank a little more. "The Art Gallery?" "Yeah, that's what I hear. Limpin' Jack, he been south this morning, he told me. Them Vandalmen don't like them books or them pictures, no way."

Parnell's anger warmed within him, only to turn into bitter frustration for the lack of an object. Most of the things he treasured had been destroyed during the crisis. Now those that were left were going the same way, in senseless destruction.

"What do they do it for?" he protested, sitting down in an empty seat to stop himself shaking. "What point is there in what they do?"

"Who cares?" said the woman. "Can't eat them books, can't keep warm in them pictures. Them Vandalmen crazy to burn them, sure, but who cares?"

"All right," said Parnell, "all right." The answers he felt within him would mean nothing to the Tumbledown Woman. All he could do was smother his loss and sorrow, hide it away. He clenched his jaws and wearily picked up his trades, placed them in his bag and stepped out of the tram. The Tumbledown Woman watched him go with a tired disgust. Her husband sat above, glaring, glaring, at the darkening horizon, his gun beneath his arm.

Parnell spent the morning of the next day hunting rats again in the rows of time-shattered houses that still stood in uniform lines to the west of the city. After a few hours of vain search he was lucky and found a rabbit warren riddling the soft earth in an overgrown and enclosed back yard. He caught two surprised rabbits before the others ran for safety. He spent the rest of the morning cleaning and roasting the rabbits and salting their skins. In the afternoon he was again within the dark hall, beginning the long task of tuning each string of the piano to a perfect pitch. Had he been a professional tuner, he would have been able to proceed with greater speed, but he was forced to go at a frustrating creep, making trial-and-error decisions as he listened to each string, hearing it in relation to the others he had tuned, listening to the pitchpipes, then tightening the string again with his rusty spanner.

He measured time by the rate at which the smoky candles burned, and left again before darkness fell.

Days passed in this way, until he could hardly trust his hearing and had to leave off for hours at a time before he could resume.

Every time he emerged from the hall to eat or to let his eyes and ears repair, there was smoke somewhere on the horizon. There came a day when he was finished; when he had tested the piano with scales and simple exercises and was sure the tuning was perfect. He knew then that he was afraid to begin, afraid to sit down and play a real piece of music on the piano. His hands still remembered his favourite pieces but there was a hollow fear in his heart that he would fumble and distort the music in some way. He had kept his hands strong. and his fingers limber by fighting the aged monster of a piano in his house for all these years, but he could not tell whether or not he still retained his skill. It had been a long time.

Parnell made his way outside the hall and sat, despondent and trembling, on the rusty, overgrown truck. It was early afternoon and, for the first time in days, there was no smoke to be seen in the sky. He ate the last of the rabbit and realized he would have to go hunting the following day. He laughed at himself for an old fool, gulped water from his bottle, lit his candle and hurried back inside the hall, trailed by clouds of dust.

On the stage he had cleared the music stands to one side, leaving the grand piano alone and uncluttered. Now he dusted the polished surface one more time, buffed the brass lettering, raised the lid, lit the candelabra, and sat before the keyboard. The bats twittered tumultuous applause. He bowed his head slightly towards the moth-eaten velvet of the empty seats, and began to play.

He began with a Beethoven Piano Sonata, Opus 109. It flowed; it swelled; it poured from the strings of that magnificent piano as his hands moved and fell, remembering what his brain was unsure of. And he knew, listening, that he had not lost his skill, that somehow it had been kept somewhere safe within him, sleeping through the years of torment. He wove a web of music, cast motion and light and harmony into the darkness, wrapped himself within its sound, and played on. And as he played, he wept.

The piece ended; he began another. And another. Beethoven, Mozart and Chopin were resurrected. The music expanded through the hours, a torrent of joy, of sorrow, and of yearning. He was blind and insensate and deaf to all but his music, insulated from the outside world by the castle of sound he was building around himself.

At last Parnell stopped, his hands throbbing and aching, and raised his eyes above the level of the piano.

Standing before him was a Vandal. A sneer was on his face, and in his arms he cradled the sledgehammer Parnell had traded to the Tumbledown Woman. There was blood on its head.

The Vandal stood and regarded him contemptuously, all the time stroking, stroking, the shaft of the hammer he carried. He was dressed in roughly cured leather and rusted metal. Around his neck he wore a dozen metal necklaces and chains that dangled on his bare and hairy chest; crosses and swastikas, peace symbols and fishes clinking gently against each other. He was dirty, his hair was greasy and awry, and on his forehead was burned a V-shaped scar. He smelled foul.

Parnell was unable to speak. Fear had made stone of him and his heart flopped around inside him like a grounded fish.

The Vandal uttered a hoarse giggle, enjoying the shock on Parnell's face. "Hey, old man, you play real pretty! Tell me now, Music Man, how well do you sing?"

Parnell's voice was a rustle in his throat: "I can't."

The Vandal shook his head in mock sorrow. "That's too bad, Mister Music Man. But I tell you, you're gonna sing real good when I'm finished with you. Real good and loud." He shifted the sledgehammer to bring out a long knife. It cast fiery gleams about the stage as its edge caught the candlelight.

Parnell felt as though he was about to be sick but, insanely, his old anger grew in him even in the face of his fear. "Why?" he asked, his voice trembling, "why do you want to kill me? What harm am I doing you?"

The eyes of the Vandal narrowed in concentration and fierce humour. "Why? Why not?" And the knife flashed yellow at Parnell's eyes.

"All that you do... destroying all the beautiful things, the books, the pictures..." Parnell was becoming excited in spite of his fear: "Those things are all we have left of our heritage, our culture; of civilization, of Man's greatness, don't you see? You're no more than barbarians, killing and burning..." He stopped as the Vandal waved the knife towards him, his face losing its mirth.

"Listen, pretty music man, you're pretty with your music and pretty with your words, but you talk a lot of shit. You know what your pretty culture gave us? Gave us dirt and fighting and eating each other, man. You're nice and old, pretty man; you were old when the murdering and the hunger started. Me and mine, we were just kids then. You know how it was for us? We had to run and hide so as not to be food for grown-ups; we had to eat dirt and scum to live, man. That's what your pretty heritage was for us, pretty man, so don't bullshit me about how great Man was, cause he ain't."

The Vandal was leaning over Parnell, breathing his foul breath hard into the old man's face. Parnell grew silent as the Vandal drew back and glared. "And you sitting here in the dark playing that nice music — all you wish is that it was back the way it was! Well, me and mine are making sure that it ain't never back that way again. Now you tell me, man, what good did that music, that culture, ever do, hey?"

Parnell's thoughts were tumbling. At last he said simply: "It gave people pleasure, that's all."

The Vandal regained his sneer. "Okay, Mister Music Man, killing you is gonna give me lots of pleasure. But first, man, it's gonna give me real kicks to smash up this pretty music thing in front of you just so you can enjoy it too. How about that?" And, turning, the Vandal hefted the sledgehammer and raised it high above the strings of the grand piano.

Something snapped within Parnell.

He leapt up and grasped at the Vandal's arms. Surprised, the man let the hammer drop. Parnell clawed at his face. The

Vandal swung out a hairy fist, catching Parnell a jarring blow on the jaw and almost striking him to the ground, but Parnell's hands were about the Vandal's throat. Parnell's hands were the only part of him that was not weak and trembling - hands made iron-firm by decades of exercise on the keyboard-and his thumbs were digging into the Vandal's windpipe. The youth began to choke, and tried vainly to tear Parnell's hands away, but the gnarled fingers were locked in a murderous grip; they tightened with hysterical energy. For a seemingly endless moment the two hung together in a bizarre embrace. Then the Vandal crumpled to the stage, with Parnell on top of him, throttling the life from him. The Vandal was dead.

Parnell let out a choking cry and retched violently over the edge of the stage. He crouched on his knees for some time, transformed by reaction and horror into a mindless animal. Eventually he turned around and stared with strange emotion at the body of the Vandal. Outside the hall, very faintly, he could hear the yells and shouts of the rest of the pack of new barbarians as they burned and looted. Inside, there was only the quiet of death and the soft twittering of the bats.

He crawled towards the piano where the sledgehammer lay. He stood, using the hammer as a prop for his trembling legs, then took it into his arms.

With one anguished swing, he brought the sledgehammer crashing down into the piano strings.

The shock jarred his whole body. The strings snapped with violent twangs and wood splintered, filling the air with jagged sound. The candelabra, toppling, plunged to the floor and went out, spilling darkness throughout the hall.

The sound faded into long silence.

July 1974

This story was first published in the anthology *Beyond Tomorrow* edited by Lee Harding in 1975. It was reprinted in the anthology *Wastelands* edited by John Joseph Adams in 2011.

The Wall

THE DAY HAD STARTED WELL, as Jack and Cathy worked their way up along the woodland track toward the high plains.

The sun had been shining brightly down there, and Jack had felt that they were making good progress on their hike, even though he was slightly annoyed at how often Cathy kept stopping to take photographs. She got a beautiful shot of a spider's web strung between two trees, nested with dew, and lit up by the morning sun. Jack had had to keep reminding her of the need to get on.

"We've got to get across the moorland and down to the village on the other side before it gets dark," he'd kept saying.

"Yes, yes, I'm coming!"was her inevitable refrain.

Once the slope had levelled out into moorland, though, there was much less to see or photograph, though the bleak sweep of the moor was interesting in itself.

Now, a couple of hours later, they were well across the moor. They were no longer following a well-trodden path, but were making their way through short grass and low bushes of heather. Jack was carrying his latest toy, a new smartphone with inbuilt GPS, and was confident about using it to find their way to the village they had picked out for the night's accommodation.

The weather took a turn for the worse, however, and a light drizzle began to fall. They both turned up their hoods and plodded on with their heavy packs. The worst part about it was that the visibility started to close in, so that they could only see a few hundred metres ahead.

That's when they came upon the wall.

It crossed their planned path at a slight angle to the left, and seemed to run straight as a ruler away into the distance in both directions.

"Damn,"said Jack. This wasn't marked on his phone's GPS map, but then not everything was.

"It's a funny kind of wall," Cathy said. "So neat."

It was true – the wall was beautifully built with regular flat stones and some kind of tile capping it. It seemed very different from the kind of dry stone wall that Jack knew from around where he lived. Those walls were much rougher, constructed out of all the different chunks of rock that the weary farmers had dug up over the years as they tried to plough their fields.

This wall, on the other hand, looked as though it had been made from even-sized brick-like stones.

It was only about a metre high, and Jack looked over it.

"Must be an old church-yard," he said.

"Up here?" said Cathy. "What makes you say that?"

Jack pointed. On the other side of the wall the ground was fairly level, but there were occasional depressions, and in one they could see part of what looked like an old moss-covered skull and, nearby, an arm-bone.

"Yuk!" Cathy said.

"Over there, you can just see through the mist, there's some kind of building, must be the church. It must have been abandoned years ago. Centuries, I suppose. I think I read somewhere that there were some villages up here on the moors that got abandoned when the Industrial Revolution happened. A lot of craft-workers were put out of business then."

"Oh. Well, what do we do? Should we climb over and keep to the line?"

"No," Jack said. It can't be all that big, we'll just walk around it. It's not far off our path."

So they kept walking for another ten minutes, following the direction of the wall. It seemed to be a very big churchyard. The ground must be sloping down slightly as they walked, too, because the wall seemed to be built up higher to keep the level the further they went.

"Jack?"

He looked up from the GPS display. He'd tried flicking the map to the satellite view, but that didn't show the church either. "What is it?"

"There's another wall over there on our left."

The mist was pretty heavy now, but he squinted and could see that she was right. There was another wall about twenty metres away on the left. "That?s funny," he said. "Can't be another church, surely? Maybe it's the wall of a manor or something."

They walked for another few minutes before they came upon another wall directly across their path, emerging from the drizzle. At the same time, the church-yard wall which they had been following bent away to their right in a corner to match the new wall. It was as though they had come to a T-intersection in a road.

"Hmmm," said Jack. "What a nuisance. We can turn right here, I guess, but it takes us well off our path." He showed her the GPS display, with their planned track and their actual path.

"Perhaps we could climb over this wall, then?" Cathy said, with a slight tremor to her voice.

Jack took off his pack and tried to climb the wall, but it was about two metres high here, and for some reason he found it impossible to get a foothold. The stones were too evenly packed and slippy with the drizzling rain. He put his pack back on reluctantly.

"Well," he said slowly, "let's follow this lane, or whatever it is. Surely there'll be a bit where the wall has crumbled down and we can get over."

So they set off down the lane. After a while, though, the lane made a shallow right-hand turn, and then another and another. The track on the GPS was beginning to look like a shallow spiral. Nowhere was the wall broken down or low enough to climb. Finally it seemed as though they had been turned back and had entered the church-yard itself. Everywhere around them, at random spots, they could see the shallow depressions Jack had seen when they first encountered the wall, and in some of them, whitened bones.

"This is hopeless," Jack said savagely. "We're completely off the track. I suppose we're going to have to turn back and retrace our steps."

They turned about.

"That's strange," Jack began. "I don't remember walking past the church."

Half-unseen in the mist, they could see the outlines of a tall church, flying buttresses supporting its walls on either side, mossy tiles covering its roof.

Then one of the butresses *moved*, moved like a huge arched leg. Then the one on the other side swung too, and the bulk between slouched forward towards them. It was covered not with moss and grass but with fine green hair, and what Jack had taken for the arched doorway was, in fact, a gaping mouth.

Cathy was screaming. Jack barely heard her, screaming himself and turning to run. He ran with terrified desperation, stumbling and half-toppling as he put his foot down into one of the shallow depressions, feeling the dry bones crack under his boot. He regained his balance and ran, ran fast enough to burst his heart.

Until he reached the wall. Scrambling, slipping, clawing for a hold, breaking his fingernails unheeded; it was impossible to climb. Jack gave it up and turned, his back to the wall.

Somewhere near the looming mist-shrouded shape, Cathy's voice shrieked in an even higher note, and then stopped. The sudden silence was like a knife in his gut.

The thing lumbered onwards, towards Jack. Trapped in its stone net, he could only wait for the end.

November 2011 and June 2014

Uplift

THE KING WAS DEAD.

Standing with the assembled ranks of nobles in the magnificent cathedral as the glittering funeral procession passed down the central aisle, François Léonard, *Comte de Courgeron*, considered the king's death to be his greatest accomplishment.

He would have to move on now, of course, and take with him as much of his wealth as he could. There would be no place for him at court with the vigorous young Dauphin now installed as the new king. Still, Léonard couldn't complain. He had achieved everything which he set out to do, and the rewards had been almost beyond measure. He was wealthy beyond all his dreams.

It had taken a long time to work his way upwards after his arrival, although he had thought himself well prepared. The language had been the biggest struggle, despite how hard he had worked to learn it. Almost no one he spoke to could understand his atrocious accent, and there were countless customs and turns of phrase which he hadn't anticipated from his reading. He got by only by posing as a foreigner recently arrived in the country. Which, of course, was true, in its way.

He told those he met that he was from Estonia. He knew enough Swedish to pass that off, though he still dreaded meeting a real Estonian; there had been a couple of close calls. He could have said he was English, or from one of the English colonies; but England and France were in the middle of one of their interminable wars, and he would have been suspected immediately as a spy. As it was, there had been some suspicious looks from the courtiers to whom he had been introduced. He would never have been able to succeed if the value of the services he offered hadn't been so much in demand.

Inside the cathedral, the music soared and the choir sang the praises of the departed king. By all accounts, the king must now be seated, if not at the right or left hand of God, then at least at His feet. Léonard was appropriately sceptical.

The long ceremony came to an end, and the coffin was carried out of the cathedral. Léonard joined the procession of nobles following. As they emerged into the bright, cold morning outside, a gorgeously attired man came up to Léonard and whispered: "My lord, I have had a letter from my cousin. He is, you understand, a Gentleman of the Bedchamber for the King of Bohemia. The King has made an enquiry as to your availability. Would you favour him with a reply?"

Léonard smiled. Bohemia was something of a come-down from France, but it would keep him employed and very well rewarded. "I will certainly do so," he murmured.

He walked on and looked up into the chill blue sky with a grin. Alone for a moment as the crowd followed the procession, he laughed out loud. Not a bad result for someone born in a slum as plain Frank Lennard. Or rather, someone who *would* be born, some three-hundred years or so from now.

As a history professor, he hadn't had much to do with the Physics department at the University. But he knew one of the researchers there slightly; he was a second cousin twice removed, or something. Lennard had met him once at an extended family gathering, and they had talked for some time.

So perhaps it wasn't strange that Bill Jackson sought him out with an unusual request.

"We're looking for an area around here that we can guarantee has never been built on, or disturbed in any way, for the last two hundred years. You've studied the history of this town, Frank, so I thought you could help. It's a bit out of our line in neo-relativistic physics."

Lennard had been able to quickly identify several nearby places, but he was naturally curious as to why Jackson needed them.

Jackson had given a laugh. "Well, the truth is, we're having some success in temporal interference. In a crude way, you could call it time travel, but it doesn't work the way it does in the sci-fi books. We've found that we can project objects into the past."

"My God! Then you could go back and..."

Jackson had laughed again. "Kill Hitler? Or your grandmother? No, I don't think so. Well, you might, but it would have already have happened. Hitler would always have had to be killed by some stranger. Thing is, we can push things into the past, but we can't ever get them back. It's strictly one-way."

Lennard had frowned. "Then how do you know you've done it?"

"Well, we can dig stuff up that we've sent back. There's a fair bit of spatial uncertainty, things don't end up in exactly the same location they left from, and we can only target a date to within a few years. But if we send back a 21st century coin and then it's found in an archaeological dig under some provably older material, that's proof. That's why I am looking for undisturbed spots. We're trying to extend our temporal reach and prove that there's no trickery involved."

That conversation had been a few years ago now. Jackson and his colleagues had developed their techniques and extended the size of their machine. When they started looking for a human volunteer, Lennard had been on the spot.

It was a big ask. It would be a one-way trip. Whoever went into the past could never return. But Lennard had no close family, and his life as a poorly paid un-tenured lecturer wasn't all that attractive. He had promised to write extensive reports on his experiences and hide them in an agreed spot they would survive until Jackson's people could uncover them in the modern day. His only stipulation had been that he could choose the approximate time and location of the drop, and that he could take along with him whatever he chose to help him survive. The physics bods had agreed readily.

He'd never written the reports, had never intended to.

Now, in his new persona as François Léonard, he made his way back from the cathedral to his apartments in the Louvre. His title as *Comte de Courgeron* was a recent gift from the grateful King, now sadly departed. The old King, it was said by his courtiers, had died with a smile on his face, in his bed with the two young maid-servants.

In his own rooms at last, Léonard went to the large ornate chest in the corner. Unlocking it with a brass key he opened it up and started to count the contents. There were plenty still remaining. The King of Bohemia would be appreciative.

In the chest lay box after box marked *Viagra*.

July 2012

Down Deep

Deep in the dark earth
Dwelling in hot rock below
Microbes rule the world.

Ancient beyond words
Is the conscious biomass
Speaking without speech.

Never in an age
Ruling in its dark domain
Does it dream of men.

February 2013

The Bronze King

PRESSED UP AGAINST A STONE WALL IN THE PITCH DARK, Marguerite tried to control her breathing so as not to let out the smallest sound. She could hear her husband moving about the bedroom, muttering curses. No doubt he thought she was still asleep, had entered the room without a light so as not to awaken her. She was sure that he was drunk and had lost his sense of direction in the dark. Hence the cursing.

Her husband. The King. Driven mad by his superstition.

Inside her belly, the baby kicked again, hard, and she winced, stifling an exclamation. Slowly, slowly, on bare and quiet feet she edged along the wall towards where she knew the door must be, feeling for it with her left hand.

Her attendant ladies, her maid, where were they? Had the King already killed *them* ? No, more likely he had simply ordered them away. She had told the women not to admit him on any account, to use her advanced pregnancy as an excuse. She hadn't slept with the King in weeks, not since... not since he had become so strange. But he was, after all, the King. He could order them to admit him and they must obey. He held the power of life and death over all of his subjects. And death, it seemed, was what he was here to deliver this night.

He could, of course, have just ordered her death, ordered one of his soldiers to kill her. But that would not have done. She was a popular Queen, her pregnancy a source of joy and rejoicing amongst the people. If she were to die, it would need to seem like a terrible accident or a sudden illness. To have a third party involved would risk exposure. No, she thought, he had to do the deed himself. She had been expecting it, fearing it, for months now. All because of that damned book.

She had been so happy before that, only just over a year ago. Princess Marguerite, married in a beautiful ceremony in the cathedral to the man she loved, Prince Mark. The one they called the Scholar Prince.

The youngest son, he had had no thought of ever becoming King of Illyria. A gentle, studious young man, he had loved his books and his music far more than the exercise of weapons. In that he was very unlike both his father and his older brother Robert, the Crown Prince. They loved nothing more than going out to battle in the endless wars with the neighbouring countries.

Marguerite had loved Mark for his gentle nature and his interest in books. She, too, loved reading the old romances, and had admired the ancient volumes ranked in row upon row in her new husband's library. He was always looking for more. Together, they had investigated the remotest corners of the huge and ancient castle. Much of it had fallen into ruin over the years, but in the less crumbling parts there were storerooms which hadn't been opened for centuries. Mark and Marguerite had delighted in breaking open dusty chests and worm-eaten cupboards to discover what might be within.

She had been so happy, already suspecting that she was carrying a child, the day they had come across a half-burned old volume filled with barely-decipherable handwriting.

Taking it to a window and holding the book open in the bright sunlight, Mark had leafed through the remaining pages in fascination.

"Seems like a book of prophecies," he had said, smiling. "What fun! What do you think it will say about what our future holds?"

She had smiled too, and shaken her head as Mark had squinted at the crabbed script.

"Here's an interesting bit," he had said. "'In the fifth century...' The fifth century after *what*, I wonder? '...the golden king of Illyria will destroy the Southrons.' Could easily be talking about my grandfather. He conquered Surdia when he was a young man, and burned their capital to the ground. He had blond hair, that could be described as golden, I suppose." He laughed. "Pity he went crazy once he was old. Maybe that explains the next bit. '...and his line shall be cursed unto the third generation'. The fellow who wrote this must have been a Surdian, I suppose."

"What else does it say?" she had asked, playing along, amused. "What next?"

"Hmmm.... it's very hard to make out. 'The golden king shall yield to a silver'. There you go, that could be father, he was already grey-haired by the time he got to be King. Now... I think it reads 'The silver king shall die in battle, cursing the gods, and yield to the bronze king.' Oh dear, how predictable. We'll have a leaden king next. Anyway, better tell father to watch out." Mark had leaned easily against the stone windowsill, his face full of delight.

"Nearly at the end of it now. What? Ugh! I think it says 'The bronze king shall have a son, and it shall be the burden of the son to destroy his father.' A bit grim, that. It's lucky Richard hasn't married yet, we'd better warn him too, hey?"

A cloud had passed over the sun just at that moment, and as the light darkened Marguerite had started to become uneasy. These threats of curses and slaughter had suddenly seemed a lot less amusing. "Come on," she said, "throw that ugly old thing away, it's not worth keeping. Let's go back for dinner." He had shrugged, and came with her. But she noticed that he didn't throw away the old volume, but kept it tucked under his arm.

Four months later there had come terrible news. An armoured courier had come galloping in through the castle gates, blood streaming from a wound to his head. The King and the Crown Prince had been leading their troops against the Carpathians in the west, and had been expected to defeat them easily. But there had been a treacherous ambush. Carpathian archers, hidden on the wooded slope of a narrow gorge, had sent down a dense storm of arrows. Prince Robert had been struck by an arrow which passed through an eye-hole in his visor and had died instantly. The King had also been struck several times and grievously wounded as he had cursed and tried to rally his troops. He was being brought back to the castle as quickly as could be managed.

But when the party of knights had reached the castle and lain down the stretcher, it was clear that the old King was already dead. Duke Matthew, the leader of the knights, knelt down and closed the old man's eyes. Standing, he had called out in a rough voice to the crowd gathered around, "The King is dead! Long live the King!" All eyes had turned to Mark, standing watching from a balcony with Marguerite swollen-bellied by his side.

"'The silver king shall die in battle,'" Mark had murmured, stricken. "I must be the bronze king."

"Don't be foolish, my love," she had said. "Forget that stupid old book. You are King now, you must do your best to be a good king."

He had nodded then. "Yes, yes, of course. And I shall. I shall."

He *had* been a good king. He had sent a strong force to crush the Carpathians and demand the heads of the leaders of the rogue band of archers who had killed his father and brother. But, that done, he had then made peace with Carpathia and his other neighbours.

In public, he seemed calm and determined. But in private, to Marguerite's dismay, he became increasingly erratic and distracted. One awful night, she had found him poring over the half-burned book of prophecy by the light of a lantern. "'The burden of the son shall be to destroy his father'" he quoted. And he had looked at Marguerite's swelling body.

"No," she had said. "No, Mark. That is just foolish nonsense. You must put it out of your mind. Promise me!"

He had made a lop-sided smile then. "Yes, yes. You're right, of course. Just a stupid old man writing centuries ago. Nonsense." But he had still refused to get rid of the book.

As the days passed, he grew worse. The constant side-long looks at her belly, the muttering when they were in private together, the obsessive reading of the ancient volume. "But what if the book tells true?" he demanded one morning, his eyes shadowed by dark patches which betrayed his lack of sleep. "It told true about the golden king and the silver king. And I am the bronze king."

"Mark! Listen to me! Those words could have applied to any number of the kings of Illyria. That book was telling of a time long past. I am carrying *your child*, your heir. The child will love you just as I do, and..."

He had looked up and said bleakly, "And he will grow up and might kill me one day. *Destroy* me, that's what the book said. I fear it, I fear it. Perhaps... perhaps we can send him away before he is fully grown, or... or... perhaps..."

She had flared up in anger. "I won't have my child harmed, do you hear me? I won't. If you harm it in any way, I shall tell the world of your crime. The people will rise up and tear you down."

He had flushed, his nostrils flaring. "You misunderstand me. Of course I won't harm our son. Don't think it." But his words had sounded hollow, and he glanced away from her before he had finished speaking.

That conversation had been weeks ago now. After that, she had tried to stay away from him, pleading for rest as the baby's time grew near. But Mark's face had grown more and more haggard, his eyes darting from side to side. Each time he looked at her, she could tell that he was thinking: *It might be best if the child is never born.* He had begun to drink himself into a stupor every night. Even his councillors had noted the change in him and started murmuring amongst themselves. Mark had told no-one about the book, forced Marguerite to swear to keep it secret.

Fearing the worst, she had lain awake many nights trying to decide what to do. The best thing would have been to flee the castle entirely, but it was not easy for someone in her physical condition and exalted role. Where could she go that would not be quickly discovered? So she sat with her ladies, busy with them over embroidery and tapestry work, thinking, thinking, trying to consider what resources she had, what preparations and defences she could make.

And now here she was, in the dark bedroom, her back pressed against the cold wall, listening to him rant under his breath as he sought her. She edged along the wall a little further, found the door frame with her hand, and edged more toward it.

There was a sudden loud crash from the direction of the dresser. A musical crash and the tinkle of chimes. He had knocked her music box off its stand. He swore loudly then. Marguerite knew there was no time left. She pushed open the door and ran out.

It was brighter out here in the ante-room. A lantern sat glowing on a small table where Mark must have set it down. There was no sign of her handmaiden or the ladies of the bedchamber, their beds empty. Behind her she heard Mark reach the bedroom door and call out "Marguerite!" Then "Damn it!" as he stumbled over something. She seized the lantern and overturned the table, and then ran out into the corridor, slamming the outer door behind her, leaving the ante-room in darkness. It might gain her a few more seconds.

She was dressed only in her night-shift, but she was not aware of the cold night air. She knew that she could not run for more than a few steps at a time with the child grown so large within her. Without hesitation, she turned to her left and went around a corner. Realising that the lantern light would give her away, she threw it out of the nearest opening and heard it clatter briefly on the cobbles below.

Heavy curtains had kept her rooms dark, but out here there was a weak moonlight, just enough to see by. Suppressing panic, she walked on as swiftly as she was able, along the route she had planned out days before. When Mark reached the corridor, he would automatically turn to the right, the way to the Great Hall. That would only delay him for a short while, but she prayed that it would be enough.

She already knew the labyrinthine layout of the ancient castle quite well, from those happy times when she and Mark had explored it together, hunting out books and manuscripts. But in recent weeks, sneaking away at night while her ladies were asleep, she had paced out the passages near her room, and now she knew them intimately. She turned left, then right, then left again. The child kicked again within her and she let out a small gasp.

Along the corridors she could hear Mark raging in fury, and knew that he had now turned back towards her. But there might still be time. There *must* be time. She tried to run.

Her breath coming hard now, she reached the door she had been looking for. She grasped the latch and tried to lift it. It was stiff, little used, as it had been when she had first discovered it days ago. It took time to work it open. Now she had so little time, so little. She sobbed in panic, her hands beginning to bleed. Finally, it worked loose, and the door swung open. Dimly she could see the spiral staircase behind it.

At that moment, she heard Mark only a few paces behind her. The King, his voice slurred with drink. "You bitch! I'll kill you, kill you and that whelp!"

She dodged through the door and tried to slam it behind her, but his booted foot jammed in. She leant with all of her strength against the door, crushing his foot. He cried out in fury, but he kept pushing on the door and it started to swing open again. She left it, and started up the stairs. Hysteria gave her strength and speed, and she managed two turns before she heard Mark begin to follow, limping and cursing.

There was another door, faintly outlined by the moonlight. The latch of this one was almost rusted away and it opened easily. Marguerite however only opened it a fraction and then on tiptoe ran up another turn of the spiral stair, over broken steps, until she was almost out of sight of the door. She stopped then, making a superhuman effort to control her gasping breath.

Here came the King. As she peered around the stone staircase, he ran up to the door she had left ajar. Ranting, raging, he threw it open and surged through. Only to fall forward, screaming.

Marguerite, her heart battering inside her, listened. To her horror, his curses and rants continued unabated, though now there was a note of awful desperation to them. Slowly, step by step, she went down to the open door.

Stepping carefully over the plaited cord of black embroidery wool she had tied across it days before, she stood at the edge of an abyss. There were only ruins beyond. The tower here had long ago broken away and the door looked out into empty space.

In his madness and drunkenness, Mark had tripped over the cord, as she had hoped he would, and fallen. But not all the way to the distant ground. She stood holding on to the door frame and looked down into his face as he swung there above the awful descent, clinging with one hand to a remnant of the old stone floor.

"Help! Help me! I command you, help me!"

She looked down at him, pitiless, her love long since gone. "No," she said coldly.

"But I... I can't die this way. The book... the book said..."

"The book said that your son would destroy you," she said calmly, as she placed her heel onto his clasping fingers and then threw all of the weight of her pregnant body onto it. "It didn't say that your son *had to be born first!*"

He screamed once, piercingly, as his hand was crushed, and then again as she released it and he fell into the darkness.

October 2012

This story was published in the December 2012 issue of *eFantasy Magazine.*

Islands

THEY CAME TOGETHER HIGH ABOVE THE ECLIPTIC, twin moving stars in an empty universe.

As soon as Mikhail saw the other asteroid – a tiny flickering point amongst the constellations – he went in through the airlock and turned on the communicator, hoping to pick up the sound of another human voice. It had been a long time.

So when a voice came crackling out of the speaker, and the first static-filled image swam onto the screen, his feelings were of great joy.

They were still light-minutes distant, of course, and would be so for some time yet, but Mikhail began speaking as soon as he picked up the other's signal.

"Hello," he said, "I'm Mikhail Brinski. My asteroid's *Elaine*. Who's there?" Then he sat back and waited. Feelings that had been dormant within him through a long winter had stirred at the first sound of a human voice.

"Janys here. My rock's the *Isolde*. Who's out there? Are you a miner? That's what I am, after tin".

Mikhail pushed himself away from the console, and stared at the distorted image on the screen. His own words, he knew, had not reached her yet. "*Janys?*" he said, for his own ears, not for hers. Janys?

Was it possible? Out here? An old, old pain throbbed again within him: Janys? *That* Janys?

Her voice came again, startled, urgent: "Mikhail Brinski? From Vostok? Do I know you from Vostok? Vostok and London?"

"Yes," he said, again to himself. "Yes, from Vostok." He almost turned off the screen and speaker. *That* Janys. It was. And of everything, it was the anger he remembered, the hurt from those days.

Vostok and London. It had been London where she'd left him. London where they had met, Vostok where they had loved. And London again. London in the quiet green park, and her walking away along an endless sun-striped lane of trees. London.

At last, he said out loud to the wavering face on the screen: "Yes, Janys, it's the Mikhail you knew." He forced a smile to his face. "How long is it now? And what are you doing chasing rocks up here? Weren't there enough on Earth for you?" He could not keep the sadness out of his voice. Perhaps it wouldn't show. Perhaps she might ignore it. She had been good at that sort of thing, had Janys.

To keep his mind still, he looked at the instrument readings and forced his mind to absorb what they said. The faltering pinprick of light indicating the other asteroid still trembled in the centre of the viewscreen.

Mikhail hung in the centre of a floating chaos. Since moving out into the Belt, he had become a sloppy hermit. His untidiness on Earth had always been a failing; out here it was worse. Broken pencils, papers, microfilms, cannisters of food and all the other kinds of kipple that made up Mikhail's monastic life wandered like a miniature asteroid swarm of their own around his room. Now Mikhail himself drifted there, feeling very lost, very much alone, watching the woman on the screen.

The image was slowly improving: the two planetoids were getting closer in their orbits. The time lag would get shorter, too.

"Hello, Mikhail," came her voice. There was an expression on her face that he found hard to interpret. Was it pity? "It's been six years, I think. I've been working hard. What am I doing up here? What are you doing? I thought you were going to go back to Moscow to work on your maths? Well, you know, I got sick of trying to sniff out new ores on Earth. There weren't any!"

"Do you remember..." he said before he could stop himself. For a brief instant, he wished he could chase after his words and fetch them back. Do you remember... how it was?

—

It had been in London's dirty winter. The pure snow that had fallen days before had become the filthy slush that now lay in the streets. They'd met at the Technic, shared a few classes, though their majors were different, and he had started walking her home to her flat in one of the dingy, endless terraces that still existed then. And that day, walking with soaked boots through the slush, she'd suddenly stopped and looked up at him.

"I like you, you mathematical mastermind," she'd said, "I do. Come up to my room." And he, startled into new emotions, had gone up.

—

"Yes," said Janys, from the clearing screen, "Yes, I remember, Mikhail. It is a long time, but I do. Yes." She smiled and looked away from the camera for a moment, away from his eyes. "How do you find it up here? Gets lonely, a bit. But the view's the best for miles. When I first went mining, I became a regular tourist. You know, kept taking photos of all the stars, pictures of my very own asteroid at a distance, and all that. Then I realised I was crazy: if I stayed where I was I wouldn't need to remind myself with pictures, would I?"

He smiled a polite smile for her. "No", he said, "no, you wouldn't." The time delay was down to about twenty seconds, now. It would get less. "As for why I'm here ... Well, I'm still working on my maths. It needs a lot of quiet, a lot of thought. I'm being a bit of a hermit, living in a kind of ivory tower to end all ivory towers." The picture of her face was clearer: he could see new wrinkles. But he could still not see through her face to see what she thought.

He wished for an instant he could go outside and just watch the asteroid that she had called *Isolde* getting closer, to use his eyes directly, to remove the barriers, somehow. In the viewscreen at least, the rock was now a tiny slowly turning pebble.

—

They had gone fossicking up in the hills in the spring, she looking for samples of rock, and he just for the peace, to think. She'd captured a photo of him sitting just like the statue of Rodin, chin in hand, and shown it to all their friends. At the top of a crag, he'd pulled up a flower and solemnly proffered it to her. She'd made him replant it, scolding him all the way.

It was strange. They had first talked of spacing one day on the moors amongst all the harsh glory of the Earth. Somehow the thought of space had seemed more glamorous then, more romantic. The scenes that the Brontes had described seemed of another age, past, forgotten. So, sitting on the heather, they had talked of the planets, the new expeditions out past Mars. He had been the more interested, and she had teased him about his fascination:"Two plus two is four wherever you are, isn't it? Or will we have to learn our sums again on Jupiter?"

"Maths is the same," he'd said,"but people aren't".

—

Isolde and Elaine, rocky sisters, were at opposition. The time delay on the radio was as short as it would be: five seconds.

"I'm doing some work on the Kroeger functions," he said, seeking any trace of old affection in her face on the screen. "In another six months, I should have a paper for the Journal. I'm getting quite well known . . .."

"Well known to all your stuffy professors, Mikhail, but I'll bet there's hardly a Belter knows you're out here. But I'm glad for you. Did I tell you I'm thinking of leaving the System?"

"The solar system?"

"I've applied to go out on the *Transstar*: they'll need good geologists." Her smile now was more honest, more open.

Mikhail stirred amongst his floating rubbish, realising for the first time she could see his littered surroundings. What he could see of the cabin she was in was very neat, everything clipped into place. He felt drained: his hands had at last stopped trembling; they seemed to have absorbed a kind of numbness.

"How have you been, Janys?" he said.

"Pretty well," she said after a pause. "Jason went out to Callisto, did you know? I was . . well, pretty lonely after that, but, well, it's gone."

"Being on your own in space is rather strange," he said, "but somehow it seems, I don't know, more acceptable out here..." He looked around him for a second, looking at the slowly shifting debris, looked back with a small, embarrassed laugh: "Sorry for the mess."

"You always said that! You never got neater, though. Your mother trained you very badly." There seemed a softness in her eyes, a look, perhaps, of understanding.

He smiled at her gentle scolding, and shrugged.

—

Summer had been in Vostok: Mikhail's home town. With the new government, everything was changing very rapidly. Everything had seemed bustling, busy, uncertain. They had lived together there for the season.

She would drag him along to the market each week to buy their vegetables and meat, against his protests. He had tagged behind her like a tall, shy puppy, threading his way through the crowds, trying to keep up. Then she would load him up with parcels, one on top of the other until he nearly dropped them, and he would smile at her over the top of his burdens.

Perhaps it was in Vostok, though that here had come harsher notes into their mutual symphony. It could have been their closer proximity. It could have been the city. She had talked of going to Australia in search of the rarer minerals. He had wanted to go to Moscow to meet some of the mathematicians there. There had been arguments, and tears, in Vostok.

—

The delay was increasing again: the worldlets were drawing apart. He seemed to look as often at the diminishing asteroid as he did at Janys' face.

Mikhail tugged at his chin with his hand, drifted away a little from the screen. "It's good to see you, Janys."

There was a pause as the radio waves traversed the space between them. A little longer, perhaps. She made a small frown, scolding him a little again, and said: "It's been nice to see you, too, Mikhail. It's fun to remember old times." A brief burst of static obscured her face, and when he could see her again, the frown was gone.

"You remember that time in Vostok," she said, "the day we bought that doll? You know the kind that fit inside one another, right down to the smallest little doll? I've still got that, here in my rock." She went off the screen for a moment, returned with the doll. The picture was getting worse: Janys seemed to have a soft ghost beside her. The speaker was beginning to crackle.

"I've still got the photo you took of me as the Thinker," he said. "Somewhere in here. . ."

He watched her silent, attentive face for the long, long seconds to pass before she responded with a smile: fresh, even teeth.

—

In the end they had decided to go back to London. The trees in Hyde Park had turned to gold. They went walking there, very often. But there seemed to be something that had distanced them: they touched, and it was as if they touched only a pane of glass that stood between them.

He talked more of his work to her, she more of hers to him. She needed to travel, to dig, to pick up rocks, to test sites. His need was to be still, quiet, thinking within himself.

And at last, in late autumn, he had sat still on the park bench, watching her walk away, knowing she would not turn back.

—

Static patterned the screen: he could hardly glimpse her face any more. It was hard to pick up what she said. He spent long minutes waiting for her replies.

"It was good," she said, "good to talk."

"Yes," he said, "very good..." The minutes passed. The picture was all static now, as the asteroids moved on in their inevitable orbits. But at last, half obscured by hiss and noise, her voice came back: "Farewell, my love."

He nodded, smiled softly. "Farewell."

August 1975

This story was developed as part of a writer's workshop in 1975, and published in the workshop anthology *The Altered Eye* in 1976.

Blackfall

As HE STEPPED OUT OF THE AIR-CONDITIONED COURT BUILDING into the warm outside air, Jamieson looked up and frowned. The sky was dark, with a funny mottled look to it. Rain coming then, perhaps a thunderstorm. A bad one, by the look of it. He couldn't recall seeing a darker sky in the middle of the day.

Long ago, when he had been a boy, he would of course have thought it was going to snow. It was February, after all. But there hadn't been a snowfall here now for – what? Thirty years, perhaps. No, it would be rain, maybe one of those torrential downpours that were happening more and more often now. Some people were saying they should be called monsoons – here in Edinburgh!

As he made his way down the street, the first drops began to fall, and he cursed himself for having forgotten his umbrella.

Except that the drops weren't wet. He stopped, as many others were doing, and looked up. Black flakes were drifting down gently from above. Snow, then, after all. But... snow was white, wasn't it? He couldn't have forgotten that, could he? But these flakes were pitch black. Was there a fire somewhere?

He held out his palm and several of the flakes fell on it, each about a half-centimetre across. He rubbed one between his fingers and it crumbled into a very fine, black dust. Like black talcum powder, he thought. Irritatedly, he noticed that his fingers were now black, and rubbing them with his handkerchief didn't clean them much.

He pulled out his phone and asked for the news. The first item sounded like some kind of international incident, typical stuff:

The United Nations Security Council has unanimously condemned India for its unilateral geoengineering action in the possible strongest terms....

He flipped past that story to the local news. Nothing about a fire there, but reports coming in about strange weather conditions.

The black flakes were falling fast now. His white shirt was going to be ruined. The flakes were so fine that they came apart on the slightest movement, and were powdering all over it. Damn, that was a £200 shirt!

The stuff was starting to build up on the pavement, too, and people were making tracks in it, their footprints looking remarkably like the prints that the original Apollo astronauts had made on the Moon before he was born. What a nuisance! Someone should be doing something about it.

Unwilling to get more of the stuff on him, Jamieson ducked into an arcade and lifted up his phone again. Surely there was some explanation?

But the front page was still stuck on that international story:

In Breaking News, the Indian Foreign Ministry has just released this statement....

Jamieson flipped directly to the statement. He fast-forwarded through the first few paragraphs.

...millions of Indians have died and are dying this minute due to the excessive heat, which has rendered many parts of India a desert. The intransigence of the major polluters in refusing to

make the same drastic cuts in emissions that India herself made a decade ago...

More of that climate change claptrap, then. Jamieson looked out into the street. The black fall seemed, if anything, to be getting worse. The stuff was starting to form into drifts, and cars were starting to skid in it. There would be an accident any minute.

He looked back at the phone. It was saying:

...for this reason our scientists have developed a radical solution based on advanced nanotechnology. We have been working on this technique for the last twenty years in secret due to its possible military applications. However, today we have applied it to solving the world's greatest problem...

Buckets-full of the black stuff now. It was starting to pile up, and for the first time he started to feel real unease. Would he be able to get home?

...powered by solar radiation, the nanomachines we released today are already converting carbon dioxide and other greenhouse gases like methane into their elemental components...

A car skidded in the slippy, sooty material, and came sliding, swerving, directly towards Jamieson, not fast, but too fast for him to dodge. He dropped the phone and tried vainly to stop the vehicle from squashing him into the brick wall behind him. As a horrid internal blackness fell down upon him, the last words he heard were:

...further, the intelligent agents in these nanomachines have been directed to concentrate their efforts over the cities in the world in those nations which have been most responsible for our current situation, as a punishment for the refusal of the major powers...

Two hundred and fifty years of the Industrial Revolution, triggered off by the Scotsman James Watt, two hundred and fifty years of belching chimneys, of steam trains, of cars and ships and planes powered by fossil fuels, by coal and gas and oil.

Two hundred and fifty years later, the carbon was coming home.

November 2011

Intelligent Design

As Miles Beckermann watched, yet another huge chunk of pale-blue ice split off the glacier and plummeted into the ocean. The research vessel that he was on was far enough away to be safe, but still it heaved up and down when the ripple passed by.

Beckermann consulted the system which he was monitoring. Applying very clever video processing, it was able to closely estimate the volume of each chunk and shard it saw falling, and feed the results into the progressive log. It all went into giving accurate assessments of how quickly glacier movement was speeding up in Antarctica as global temperatures rose.

He glanced upwards. The sun would not set for another couple of months down here, but even in the daylight, he could see flickers of the vivid *aurora australis* dancing in the sky.

Pretty as the aurora was, Beckermann clucked his tongue as he looked at it. It had been playing merry hell with their communications for the last three weeks. There had been a huge solar storm, a torrent of charged particles belched out by the Sun, knocking out several key relay satellites and filling the Earth's ionosphere with static.

He headed back to the mess room for a much-needed cup of coffee.

Bob Peters, their team leader, was sitting at the table, a steaming mug already before him. He was surrounded by several tablets, the screen of each showing a different data display. Though any one of the tablets could have shown him all of the data, Peters found it much easier to have several of the cheap tablets around him so he could easily compare several readings at once.

Peters looked up. "Ah, Miles! I think our CO_2 sensor must be broken, or maybe the inlet has frozen up. Could you have a look at it?"

"Sure," Beckermann said. "Why do you think it's broken?"

"Oh, simple! The readings have been dropping all week, slowly at first, but now it's just plain silly, dropping off a cliff. You can practically sit there and watch them go down. The inlet must be blocked."

Beckermann started to reply, but before he could answer, Anne Sanders came in carrying one of the ubiquitous tablets. Its speaker volume was turned up, and they could hear some kind of news bulletin. She muted it quickly with a touch.

"You've got to listen to this," she said in her clipped New Zealand accent, clearly excited. "You know how bad our comms have been lately?" Among Anne's many responsibilities were those of their Comms Officer.

"Well, I've been trying a new filtering technique this week, and I've been able to get snatches of news from time to time. There's been some big international hoo-ha going on. The Security Council is imposing some really tough sanctions on India for something they've done. But I wasn't sure what that was, thought it must be some new nuke they'd developed, though why they'd need one now, I don't know."

"So what is it that they've done?" asked Beckermann distractedly, not much interested in politics. His mind was still thinking over what could be causing the problem with the CO_2 indicator.

Anne grinned in a kind of triumph. "Unilaterally done something about global warming, that's what! Everybody else is totally pissed, but you know how much India has been suffering. Millions have been dying. That's what they said in their statement."

Peters looked up, his mouth slightly agape. "What? What do you mean? What have they done?"

"Seems they've been working on nanotechnology in secret," she said. "They've released a cloud of nanobots which are using solar energy to crack carbon dioxide and methane back into their elements. The carbon is precipitating out."

"Jesus Christ!" exclaimed Peters, "But..." He stopped suddenly. All three of them sat there, thinking through the consequences in silence.

Finally, Beckermann said slowly: "Those CO_2 readings..."

Peters looked across at him in astonishment. "My God, you don't think the sensor could be *accurate*, do you? That's impossible, surely? How long would it..." He glanced sharply at Anne. "When did they do it, do you know?"

"Not sure, I'm only getting snippets of data from the net. But from what I can gather it's been a few weeks now."

"Nanobots," said Beckermann, in a kind of daze. "They would have to be self-replicating, wouldn't they? You couldn't manufacture enough of the things otherwise. Self-replication would be the key, the first thing you'd need to crack."

Anne smiled. "Don't you see, though? This means our research project is out of date. We might as well head back home. This will put a stop to the warming. In a few decades..." Anne was a biologist by trade, her face was lighting up with relief that the species extinctions would be coming to an end.

Beckermann was an engineer, though, and he was starting to get a bad feeling. "What limits the action of the bots? What stops them?"

Anne was puzzled. "Stops them? Oh... Well, I got the whole statement put out by the Indian Foreign Ministry." She touched her tablet a couple of times and they listened through the slightly bombastic statement, the threats against the main polluting nations, the targeting of the carbon precipitation over major Western cities. Then came the statement Beckermann was looking for:

These nanomachines will cease their operation once carbon dioxide levels reach pre-industrial levels, and will then auto-destruct...

"Bob," he said to Peters with a sudden calm and steely tone, "what's the ambient temperature?"

Peters laughed. "Come on, Miles, it can't possibly..."

"What's the temperature, and the trend?" Beckermann insisted.

Peters picked up one of his tablets. "Minus 25 right now, which is pretty cold for this time of year. And the trend... It's been falling steadily all week, getting steeper. But that can't..."

"It's not the reduction in the greenhouse effect that's doing it, not yet. That will take decades. It's the solar energy these damn things are sucking up. Self-replication, remember. Their population is probably exploding exponentially."

Anne said, a little hesitantly, "But that's good, isn't it? It means it will all happen quickly."

"And then?" asked Beckermann savagely. "Anne, you're the biologist, think it through!"

"Biologist..." she said in confusion. "What does...?"

Beckermann stood up angrily. "You're thinking about these things as if they were just machines. But they *replicate*, Anne! Think of them as bacteria or as viruses. Replication with the occasional error, bound to be. What does that suggest to you?"

"Na... natural selection," she stammered.

"Damn right. Out of those billions of bots, some of them are going to get replicated with errors. Maybe a different CO_2 level to stop at, or none at all. The *good* little bots will self-destruct. But the *bad* bots... Which bots will be better at replicating themselves, do you think? Christ, it's basic Darwin 101! The entities which are best at surviving and replication *make the most copies of themselves!*"

"You mean... they won't stop."

He nodded, and looked out the window. "They won't stop."

Outside, the ocean was beginning to film over with floating ice.

November 2011

Brave Companions

"MORE SNOW COMING," SAID JOSEPH WEARILY. The flat, dense grey clouds ahead were ominous and full of threat.

He stopped and turned to look back at his companion, plodding steadily upwards towards him. He was worried about Felix. The big man was usually so strong. But he had been wounded in the left shoulder during that last battle, and it seemed to have weakened him and shattered his confidence.

It had been a bloodbath. All because of the stupidity of their commander, and probably the stupidity of the Emperor too, for starting the war. All Joseph knew was the terror and the misery of the campaign, and he had had enough of it. When their commander tried to round up the remaining troops, he and Felix had hidden themselves and decided to make their own way back home.

Maybe that was when they had made their big mistake. They had decided to avoid the main pass through the mountains — the army would be taking that route, the same way they had come. Instead, he and Felix had decided to try one of the more obscure, smaller passes. But they had no map, and now Joseph thought that they might be lost.

Felix drew up alongside him, silent. His face, like Joseph's, was hidden behind the wrappings of cloth they had wound around their heads to try to protect themselves against the bitter cold.

"All you all right, old friend?" asked Joseph. Felix simply nodded slowly.

"It's not far now to the top of the pass," Joseph said. "All downhill from there!" That probably wouldn't be quite true; there would be plenty of hills still to cross, but the trend would be downwards. And at least they would be back in their own country. Here they were enemy soldiers, and couldn't trust anyone.

Felix just continued to nod. Felix never said much, but now he seemed almost to have lost the power of speech. Joseph turned and started the weary trek again, one foot after another, sinking into the soft snow.

Those clouds bothered him. If it started to snow heavily again, they would die out here. Still, he thought glumly, it would be a better death than lying on a battlefield with a lance through your guts, screaming for your mother.

They plodded on for another half-hour or so. Snow started to drift down, at first slowly and then heavily. It became hard to see more than a few feet ahead, so Joseph slowed and fell into step beside Felix, to ensure that they were not separated.

Felix was Joseph's oldest friend. They had been through a lot together. Some ugly battles. There had been many times when Joseph had been terrified out of his wits, but Felix had saved him, always finding the courage to press on against the odds, or finding the safest place to crouch as a troop of cavalry raced past.

Now they plodded on side by side, facing their toughest enemy yet. It was starting to get dark, but Joseph knew they couldn't afford to stop. Fortunately, after about half an hour, the snow eased off and then ceased. But as the clouds cleared, he could see the stars coming out one by one.

A great weariness began to overcome him, and he realised that he could hardly feel his feet any more. Beside him, Felix was slowing, and starting to stumble. Joseph, too, was weaving from side to side.

It was then that there was a kind of miracle. In the faint remaining light, Joseph saw a small building up ahead. Some kind of hut. A shepherd's hut, perhaps? Shelter, anyway. If the shepherd was there and made any objections, well, Joseph still had his knife.

He pointed out the hut to Felix and they changed direction towards it. It seemed a long, long time before they reached the door. There was a dim yellow glow from inside glimmering through the cracks. Joseph, astonished at how weak his arms felt, thumped feebly on the door. In a few moments it was opened, pushing outward through the drift of snow at its foot.

"Marone e mia!" exclaimed the lean figure who stood there. *"Prego, entra, subito!"* Joseph didn't speak much Italian, but the gesture was obvious. He and Felix stumbled into the little hut and their host quickly closed the door behind them on the whirling snow.

It was warm and close in there. At the far end of the room, next to a small stone fireplace, was a tethered goat, looking at them incuriously and chewing contentedly on some hay. There was a single, narrow bed, a wooden table, a small desk with a crucifix mounted behind it, and some cupboards. The occupant of the hut had a tonsured head, and was wearing a coarse brown robe. A monk then, not a shepherd.

All of this Joseph saw in an instant or two. Then, suddenly, he found his legs giving way and his vision blurring. He fell forward and blackness claimed him.

Over the next few hours, consciousness came and went. Flashes after that; awakening with a terrible thirst and the monk gently tipping sips of warm milk between his lips. The monk, leaning over him, unwrapping his clothing, doing something painful to his shoulder, Felix's muffled face looking on in concern.

Terribly hot; terribly cold. And then true sleep at last.

When he woke, it was to bright sunlight in his eyes: the monk had opened a shutter and a cold breeze swept in along with the light. Outside, snow lay everywhere.

Joseph found that he was on the monk's narrow bed. The monk came across and put a hand on his forehead, and said something in Italian. Joseph tried to respond, and the monk switched to good German.

"Your fever is gone, that is good. That wound in your shoulder is a problem, but with rest and food you should recover."

"Where's Felix?" Joseph croaked out. "He's wounded, too, you must look after him."

"Felix?" asked the monk. He was lean and wiry, with a grey stubble beard and eyes nested in wrinkles.

"My friend. He's called Felix. Is he outside?"

"Oh, of course. Felix." said the monk. "And what is your name? I am Brother Marco, and you are safe here, do not concern yourself."

"Joseph, I'm Joseph. But Felix..."

"Yes, yes, I will attend to Felix soon. Just rest for now. You had a bad night of it."

Joseph slept again for a while. When he woke again, he felt much stronger, and the sun outside was high in the sky.

He needed to piss, and Brother Marco helped him up so he could use a pot. After that, he felt able to swallow some bread soaked in milk.

"But Felix... don't tell me Felix has gone on without me? Where is he?"

Marco looked steadily at Joseph. "Come with me," he said. "I will help you to the door."

Together, they stood at the open door, with a cold wind whistling by them. There had been no more snow since last night, and Joseph could still see the tracks that had been left in the snow.

"My son," said the monk gently, "I have not seen anyone called Felix. You were alone when you came to my door."

In the snow was one set of tracks. One set of footprints.

August 2012

Into the Night

A SOFT DRIZZLE OF RAIN WAS FALLING IN THE LONDON NIGHT as Phillip Henderson stood waiting outside the dance hall. A motor-carriage trundled past, puffing small clouds of steam. All along the street, the gas lights glimmered off the newly wet surface of the road. No blackout required tonight.

Phillip tipped down the peak of his cap to ward off the drips from his face, and pulled his great-coat tighter over his uniform jacket. He hoped to hell the weather would clear up by the following night.

From inside the hall, he could hear the welcoming sounds of music and laughter. He could go inside to wait, but he didn't want to miss his girl, or take the chance that someone else would try and chat her up before she found him.

As he stood there, another man approached along the pavement, dressed in the same Aeronautical Corps uniform as his own, the great-coat flapping wide. A moment later, Phillip heard a familiar Scots voice: "Phillip, y'old bugger. What're you doing here? Waiting for that wee bit of a girl of yours?" It was Jim MacDonnell, his navigator and his best friend for many years.

Phillip laughed. "Yes. Are you here for the dance, too?"

"Me? Not likely, I canna dance a step. No, I'm off down to the Dragon. I reckon I've got a look in with that big barmaid of theirs." He shoved his hands into his coat pockets. "It's a braw night to be standing in the rain. Is she late?"

Phillip smiled. "Yes. She often is, I'm afraid."

"That skinny chit from the typing pool, is it?"

"Yes. Mary, her name is. I..." Phillip hesitated. It was all too easy to be embarrassed by your male friends if you dared reveal your true emotions. And how he felt for Mary was hard to put into words. You couldn't say to someone like Jim that your girl made your heart want to sing, now could you? No.

"Aye, well," said Jim, "I'll be off, then. Tomorrow night, it's still on?"

"If the weather's good and the wind's in the right direction." Then Phillip dropped his voice to a whisper, "And if they have that new bomb ready to go."

Jim nodded soberly. They had been to a demonstration of the new secret weapon just last week at Finchley and had attended a lecture on how to drop and trigger it without danger to the airship. A new type of bomb. It was all timed by clever clockwork. First a container of highly compressed, volatile fuel broke open, creating a huge cloud of vapour. Then a few moments later, the conventional explosive went off, igniting the fuel and adding its own force. The result was a tremendously wide-spread and powerful explosion, and one guaranteed to set fire to everything within range. Watching its destructive power had shaken them both.

"Bloody boffins, always something new," Jim said quietly. "And usually useless. That bomb, though... Still, if it works it'll be a good kick in the trousers for old Boney, eh?" He laughed, saluted Phillip mockingly, and walked on down the road. He stopped and turned after a few steps. "Oh, and good luck with the wee lassie, eh?" He waved, and went on.

Only a few minutes passed after that before Phillip saw a slight figure hurrying down the street, wearing a belted raincoat and carrying an umbrella. Golden hair reflected back the street lights. It was Mary. She came up to him and kissed him lightly on the cheek. "Brrr.... let's go inside!" she said, and so they did, arm in arm.

The hall was crowded with servicemen and their girls. Men from all of the different arms of the military. Royal Navy men, of course, many of them. They were still the frontline defence against a French invasion. Several Army officers, too, in their bright red dress-uniforms. Phillip had heard that in the field the infantrymen were now wearing darker colours, a funny muddy mixture of green and brown, the better to hide from Frenchie snipers. But no Army officer worth his salt would dream of turning up to a social occasion in such a drab outfit.

Together with the Army and Navy men, there were just a handful of officers like Phillip from the Royal Aeronautical Corps, the newest branch of the armed services.

Mary was a wonderful dancer, and Phillip always felt clumsy with her on the dance floor, though he had taken a few lessons. Still, she didn't seem to mind his straying feet.

A couple of hours later, exhausted at last from dancing, and just a little tipsy from the spiked punch that the Ladies' Auxiliary served up, Mary and Phillip decided to leave. There was a bright, speculative sparkle in Mary's eyes as she said to him, "How about coming back to my flat? My room-mate's out tonight, staying with her sick mother."

"I'd love to," Phillip said, a warm eagerness growing in him. Could this be the night? "There's something I'd like to talk to you about, anyway."

She smiled, her bright red lipstick so attractive on her pale face that he could almost cry. "Let's go then," she said, and they left.

In her flat, Phillip sat down on the edge of the room-mate's bed as Mary sat on her own. He found that he was trembling. How stupid! He had faced dozens of missions over enemy territory, every moment risking being shot down by one of the deadly French rocket guns. There had been many times when he had been afraid, but never paralysed by terror. Now, though, he found himself almost unable to speak as he looked longingly across at the lovely girl opposite.

"Mary, I..." He stopped, and she smiled, encouraging him to go on.

"Well, tomorrow night, there's a mission. I think it's going to be very dangerous. I don't know the details yet, of course, but the rumour is that it's audacious, something the French aren't going to expect. If we're lucky, it might even bring this damned endless war to a close." Endless was the right word. The English had been at war on and off with the French Empire ever since the first Napoleon Bonaparte had come to power, three generations ago. Now they were fighting his great-grandson, Napoleon IV, newly ambitious to attack England's interests.

"Oh, Phillip," Mary said. "I hope you'll be safe, darling. Can you tell me any more about it? Are you flying one of those new stealthy airships?"

He frowned and looked at her a little sharply. "How do you know about those?"

She laughed. "Darling, I *do* work at the base, and I do have eyes. I type most of the Commander's memorandums and orders. It's only the most secret ones which he tries to thump out himself, poor old dear."

"Oh, I see. Well, look.... Oh hell, I'm making a mess of this. The fact is, Mary, that I might not come back. And I wanted... I wanted to ask you to marry me."

She came across to him then, put her arms around him and kissed him. "Of course I will, Phillip, of course I will. I love you, darling." Then she paused, and looked down. "Only... well, I need to tell you something about myself first. You might change your mind after I tell you." There was a little catch in her voice, and then she buried her face in her hands and began to sob loudly.

Phillip was astonished and concerned. He held her tightly. "It doesn't matter," he said, "whatever it is, it doesn't matter."

Her face still in her hands, she said in a muffled voice, "The fact is... the fact is, Phillip, that I'm not a virgin. There was a man when I was quite young, who, who... I struggled, but I couldn't stop him."

"Oh. Oh, I see." He was silent for a long moment and then made up his mind. "That doesn't matter. It wasn't your fault. Let's not talk of it again."

Sniffing, she looked up. "You are so good to me, Phillip. I'm so relieved."

They sat silently for a long while, before she said, "Let's get married just as soon as you get back. Tell me a little more about your ship. I want to know how well you will be protected. Will you really be hidden from the spotters? I just want to know so that I can keep calm about your mission."

Phillip found himself telling her about his pride in the new airship and its special features. It was a little against the rules, of course. Well, a lot against the rules. But after all, Mary worked at the airbase herself, and she must have been screened by the security people, particularly if she was regularly typing the Commander's work as she said. The only thing he didn't mention to her was the new bomb which he and Jim had seen demonstrated. That was too fearful a weapon for him to want to dwell on, even in his own mind, and he knew it would just make Mary more afraid for him.

There came a moment when she snuggled close to him and he cautiously placed a hand on her warm breast. Not long after that, they were together in her narrow bed, their clothes scattered on the floor.

The next day, feeling a warm glow of happiness, Phillip was at the airbase, staring up proudly at the black bulk of his new airship, the HMA *Agincourt*, named for England's most memorable defeat of their ancient enemy, the French. The ship swayed a little in the freshening wind, but it was firmly attached to the mooring mast and securely tethered to points on the ground at three other places.

It was late afternoon. Darkness would be falling soon, and he had better get ready for the mission. The rain clouds had thankfully moved on, and the wind was from the north-west. Perfect conditions for the trip out, though coming back would be much slower.

Here across the field came Jim MacDonnell and their rear gunner, Brad Palmer.

Jim slapped Phillip on the back. "Ready then, my old mate?" Phillip nodded. Brad, a rather glum, solitary man, just nodded to them both and climbed up into the airship.

"Do you ken where we're going tonight?" Jim asked.

Phillip held up a sealed envelope. "Not to be opened until we're on the way. But I've got a pretty shrewd idea."

"Aye, well, let's get on with it, then." Jim started to climb up the narrow steps.

Phillip looked back at the administration building. Somewhere in there Mary would be working. Maybe she was looking out now. He gave a half-wave, just in case, and then followed Jim up into the cockpit. Brad was out of sight, already installed in the rear turret, no doubt.

The sun finally set, and the dusk was brief. As soon as it became fully dark, Phillip gave a sign to the ground staff to release the tethers. The ship started to rise, and he engaged the engines. They set off towards the coast, headed toward France.

Only once they were over the Channel did Phillip break the seals on their orders.

Paris. The very heart of Boney's empire. And the frightening new bomb was already aboard and armed. Phillip prayed that it didn't go off prematurely due to some miscalculation by the boffins.

They moved swiftly on, the engines working with the direction of the wind. Outside the cockpit window the night was dark, dark; as dark as they could have hoped for, and more. Phillip could barely make out the division between land and sky. It was so faint that there were times when he felt that he was only imagining it. He looked down at the reassuring gleam of his instruments, the only illumination in the cockpit. Not long, now, surely, before they passed over the coast of France and into enemy territory.

Even as he had that thought, Jim confirmed it. "Just passing Dieppe," he said. "Three hours should see us over Paris with our little present for young Boney. If we get that far, o'course."

"Jesus, Jim, cheer me up, why don't you?" said Phillip, but Jim just laughed. That was always Jim's way.

"Turning on the noise suppressor," Phillip said, and flipped a switch. Immediately, the already moderate sound of the airship's engines dropped to no more than a hum. Their forward speed also slowed a little. The suppressor worked well, but it also reduced the engine efficiency. Still, it was better than being picked up by the giant 'ears' of the enemy's AUDAR installations. And the boffins assured them that their new, top-secret, matt black, sound-absorbent coating would make them essentially invisible and inaudible. Phillip hoped to God that it worked.

Not much to do now for a couple of hours until they reached Paris, at which point it would start to get really hairy. Though of course they always needed to keep a watch along the way for enemy spotter balloons and the tethered blimps the French used as gun platforms.

Jim leaned back. "Did your girl turn up last night?" he asked. "I was rogering that barmaid from the Dragon. Told her it might be my last chance, she ought to be kind to me."

Phillip laughed. It was better than thinking about the dangers of this mission. "You tell every girl the same thing, a different girl every week."

"Aye, well, it'll be true one day," Jim said, sounding mock-offended. "But how about you? Did your lassie turn up for the dance?"

"Yes. Yes, she did," Phillip said, then stopped abruptly, not wanting to say much more, his heart swelling as he thought of Mary, her gentle nature, her soft dark eyes, the smooth curves of her pale body lying on the bed last night.

"In fact," he said after a pause. "In fact, I proposed to her last night. And she said 'yes'. We're going to be married as soon as we can manage it, in case, you know..."

"Aye, I know well enough. Well man, congratulations! Though I don't know what she sees in an ugly lump like you."

Phillip gave him an affectionate but solid thump on the arm.

Jim flipped on the intercom so that he could talk to Brad, in his lonely bubble at the rear of the airship. "Brad, man, did you hear? Old Phillip here is going to get hitched!"

Only silence came back, and a little static. "Brad?" Jim called again. "Are you asleep back there, you old bugger?" Nothing.

"That's funny," said Jim. "Intercom out, do you think? I reckon I'd better go back and check he's OK." He began to stand up.

"You don't need to move," came a soft voice from behind. "Brad's having a little lie down. He was quite surprised to see me. And my knife."

Phillip whirled around at the sound of that voice. A voice he knew well. Barely visible, outlined only by the faint orange light from the instruments, stood a woman, her arm outstretched towards them.

"My God! Mary!" he said. "What on earth are you doing here? How...?"

Jim came to his senses much more quickly than Phillip, and surged to his feet. "She's a fucking *spy*, you idiot!" But before he could make a step forward, there was a bright flash and a deafening bang. Jim screamed, and fell back to the floor. He lay squirming and cursing with pain.

Phillip was stunned. "Mary, what...?"

She stepped forward, closer to the dashboard lights. She was holding a gun, and her face was calm but unsmiling.

"It's *Marie*, actually. Marie Girard. Of the *Direction de la Sécurité Impériale*. Your friend was quite right, you see."

Phillip's mind lurched. He felt as though his world had been shattered and put together again in a new, crazy pattern. Bewildered, he looked down at Jim, still writhing on the floor, but now becoming quiet. Even in the dim light, Phillip could see the dark patch of blood spreading on the front of Jim's uniform. "You... you've killed him," he said, with a stab of awful grief.

"My, my, we are sharp tonight, aren't we?" said Mary. Said *Marie*. Marie. He couldn't believe it. Only last night...

"Now," she said. "We are going to take this ingenious craft as a gift for the Emperor. So good of you to tell me all about it while we were in bed. The stealth technology will prove very useful for our own airships when we return to bomb London. You may think the war has turned in your favour. But you are wrong. His Imperial Majesty has many tools at his disposal. I, for example, am one of them."

"Mary," he said hopelessly as he stared at her lovely face, her blonde hair a faint halo in the dim light. "I thought that you loved me... Oh God! I've been such a fool!"

"Yes," she said. "You have. Now, no more delay. I cannot allow you to bring the airship and its bombs any closer to Paris. Instead, we will divert to the airfield at Rouen."

Phillip finally gathered his wits and looked up at Marie, this stranger, this enemy. "I don't know how to find my way there," he said grimly. "And you've killed my navigator." *My friend*, he thought, mourning silently but painfully.

"It is not a problem. It has been arranged. Each night this week my compatriots will turn on the lights at Rouen, for one hour only, starting at midnight. We only need to be within range of the airfield to see the lights. Give me a moment."

Still pointing the gun at him, she bent and picked up Jim's map, on which he had been marking their position by dead reckoning. She made a quick calculation by eye.

"Turn the ship now, Phillip, to a bearing of... let me see, allowing for the wind, 192 degrees." She stood over him with the gun to make sure that he followed her instructions. His hands shook terribly, as he tried to stop remembering how he had felt about this woman. *Mary...* It was as though he had to mourn two dead people. Jim, lying on the floor at his feet, and the woman that he loved. Had thought that he loved.

Once the ship was turned in the right direction, there was little for Phillip to do. He tried to come up with a plan to overcome Marie, but with her gun pointed unwaveringly at him, he couldn't see any hope. He had no doubt that if forced to shoot him, she could still pilot the ship alone to her destination.

It was, in truth, not very hard to control these ships. Their huge flotation tanks full of hydrogen meant that there was no danger of crashing even if they ran out of fuel or the engines failed. It was just a matter of settling it down onto the ground. He had sometimes dreamed of flying in a more natural way, like the birds. A pity the boffins had long ago proved that heavier-than-air flight was impossible for any craft big enough to carry a person.

Phillip's mind was flooded with regrets. Losing the stealth technology to the Frenchies was bad enough, but there was another secret on board, far more valuable still. The bomb. The special bomb.

Their written orders had been to give the new and complex device its first operational test. The plan had been to drop it over the palace of the Emperor, hoping not just to kill the young tyrant and his court, but to create awe and confusion among his followers. Perhaps put an end for good to the long struggle between the two nations facing each other across the English Channel.

But that was all lost now, at least for Phillip and his crew.

Up ahead on the horizon, he could see a rectangle of bright lights in the otherwise dark landscape. Rouen airfield. Marie pushed the gun firmly into his back. "No silly moves, now, Phillip. I promise that you will be taken good care of. You'll be given the best treatment we can manage in one of the camps. And when this war is finally over, when France has won its birthright, well then, you will be released. Perhaps," she said in a gentler tone, "perhaps you can even get married then. But not, *hélas*, to me."

"Did you feel nothing for me, then?" he asked bitterly. "All those times we kissed, those times we talked. Last night, in bed. Was it all a sham?"

"All? Perhaps not all. You were not a bad lover, you know. Which is saying something, coming from a Frenchwoman to an Englishman, let me tell you. I would rather not, really rather not, have to shoot you. But do not make a mistake. I *shall* do so if you do anything stupid."

They approached the lights. With their benefit, Phillip could see ranks of motor-carriages drawn up around the airfield. No doubt there were a lot of French officials with their own Frenchie boffins, eager to examine the stolen technology of his airship.

Resignedly, he throttled down the engines, then gave them a little reverse thrust so that the airship would stay on station as it descended.

As he manoeuvred with half his attention, Phillip found himself thinking about how strange love was. The love he thought that he had had for Mary. For *Mary* but not for *Marie*. A false love, based on what? An attractive face? A gentle voice? A soft body? He hadn't known this woman at all, that was the truth of it.

He glanced down at poor Jim MacDonnell, now unmoving on the floor. As still as death. He had been a good friend, Jim, over many years. Phillip realised that he had loved Jim, in a way. That was a true love, based on mutual support and long familiarity. That kind of love demanded something of you, demanded that you be prepared to sacrifice something for it. And then there was love of country. That was something to be reckoned with, as well.

Marie was looking out of the cockpit window as Phillip descended to be level with the mooring mast, and nudged the airship towards it. It was always a delicate and nerve-racking operation. There had been that German airship a few years ago...

Marie's eyes were fixed on the metal framework outside, edging slowly closer. Phillip smiled a little, sadly, as he saw her momentary distraction.

He reached out and threw the switch to drop the new bomb.

Seeing his movement, Marie cried out and raised the gun. Phillip barely had time to register the searing pain through his chest before the terrible blast from outside. The cockpit lurched, and the world filled up with flame, engulfing them both in a last fiery embrace.

As he fell into eternity, Phillip felt only a triumphant joy.

November 2012

This story was published in the April 2013 issue of eSteampunk Magazine.

Mindclasm

THEY HAD TOLD ALICE LITTLEHALES that it was the only way for her to survive. Her 120-year-old body had reached the end of its limits, despite everything that a trillion-dollar fortune could buy her.

"You could potentially live forever", they had said. "Inside the computer."

This was how it worked: using the latest hardware and software developed by her own company, her brain would be instantly scanned in 3D to a resolution down to the molecular level. Every synapse, every receptor, every electronic impulse, would be captured instantly. A snapshot of her brain. Then the software would map every connection and impulse into a simulation of her mind, all running on an incredibly powerful computer. They would start up the simulation, and it would be the same, to her, as it had been before. She could think, observe, consume media, keep in touch. In her decrepit body, that was the most she had been able to do anyway.

It wouldn't exactly be the same as being alive. But it would be better than being dead, she thought. Anything would.

She'd had the money to set it up in the most secure facility that could be built, and provide for its on-going maintenance. She herself, once her mind had been transferred, could arrange matters if any changes turned out to be needed to the set-up. Her fortune, already massive, was well-invested, and would grow in time beyond any need she could conceivably have.

And so it was done.

When she awoke – for it was like waking up – she could think as clearly as before. Better, probably, because although dementia had long been cured for those as rich as her, the aged brain cells themselves must have been getting weary.

What it was like, more than anything, was like being in a room by herself, with huge media screens all around her, on which she could call up anything she wanted to see. Breaking news, business data, the latest novel, the latest movie, all were instantly available. And for that matter, any book written in the last several hundred years. She could take her time to work through the world's greatest literature, something she had always promised herself.

What it wasn't like, was being alive. She could feel her arms and legs, move them about in the same way, she thought, that an amputee could feel a phantom limb. Except she had a complete phantom body. She had retained her body image, could indeed call up a virtual mirror to view herself. But not as she had been at 120. No, as she had been at 18. She'd never really thought of herself as any older.

But she could not physically interact with the world, could not drink, taste, feel the touch of clothing on skin, take a plunge in a pool, or have sex. Eventually, they had said, advances in the simulation software might allow even that to be possible. But not for now.

Years went by – years experienced at the same rate as when she was alive, because if she wanted to stay in touch with normal people, with the pace of international events, she had to experience them at the same rate.

And then came the nuclear war. And the mindclasm.

It was the electromagnetic pulse which did the damage. Or rather, the third or fourth such blast in space, breaking down, one after another, the shields around her secure computer facility, destroying the careful arrangements for emergency power, finally zapping large parts of the computer's memory and circuits.

Alice had followed the lead-up to the war, of course, but when the blasts came she was left unprepared.

Her vision skewed into a myriad of bizarre blocks of colour, continually shifting. Great slabs of text appeared at random in her visual field. Her body image was shattered and for a long crazy time her limbs moved around, her legs protruding from her head, her hand replacing her nose.

She was not helpless. She had retained the ability to run diagnostic and repair programs, and gradually some kind of sense returned, and her normal body image reasserted itself. But her vision was still a mess. Toward the right-hand side of her visual field there was a gaping black hole. In other areas, random clips from movies came and went. Random words drifted across her sight.

It could not last forever. Her computer was now running on its last reserves of battery power, and when that was gone it would be all over.

When the white rabbit finally hopped into her view, she greeted it with relief, and with gratitude followed it down the hole.

November 2011

The Great Circus Robbery

LOOKING BACK, it's easy to see that Pa's plan to rob the circus was a really bad idea.

At the time, though, it seemed to make as much sense as any of his crazy ideas. And I was only twelve then, so what did I know?

There was just Pa and me, living in the draughty rooms above the scrapyard. Ma had left us two years ago, ran off with a door-to-door brush salesman, Pa said, and good riddance. I wasn't so sure about the 'good riddance'. I missed Ma.

Anyway, we were in the front room when we heard the hullabaloo out in the street. Pa poked his head out the window. "Lizzie," he said in that gruff voice of his, "get down there and see what's going on."

So I ran down into the yard, past all the piles of junk and scrap metal, and out into the road. It's the main road that runs through the town. Seeing as how we lived in the scrapyard, you'd be right in guessing this was the poor side of the town.

A bunch of kids was out there, all yelling and cheering, and some grown-ups, too, waving their hats. And along down the road comes the circus.

It was a big outfit, trundling into town on twenty outsized wagons, all pulled along in a line by the biggest steam tractor I'd ever seen. As it came into town, it started to sound its whistle, high and piercing and all full of mystery and promise.

All of the wagons were covered in huge pictures showing the delights of the circus: the trapeze artists, the steam-horse riders, the jugglers, the mechanical elephants, the clowns, the sleek steel lions and tigers. A crowd of kids surged along the road, following the train. My heart skipped a beat and I found myself clapping my hands with joy. Me! I should have known better.

Then I remembered Pa, and I turned back to tell him what was going on, but he'd followed me down into the street and now stood glaring after the wagons.

"A circus, Pa!" I said, unnecessarily.

"Follow 'em, Lizzie," he said. "See where they fetches up. And count the kids."

"Count the..."

"You heard. Count how many kids there is." I nodded, and dashed off after the wagons.

I followed them all down the road, across the bridge, up the main street and out the other side of town. All along the way, the circus picked up more and more kids trailing after it. As I walked, I looked around, counting the kids. Four hundred, at least, and more coming every step of the way. It's a big town.

At last, the steam tractor reached the waste land down by the river and turned in a wide, wide curve, drawing the wagons into a huge circle, neat as you please. I sat on the ground to rest my feet.

Just as soon as the tractor stopped, panels dropped open on the side of every wagon, facing towards the centre. Roustabouts in striped shirts jumped down and began pulling gear out of the wagons. Almost before I knew it, a big carpet of red and white canvas lay filling the circle, and they were starting to raise a tall, thick pole at the centre, pulling it up with a winch on the tractor.

After a while, sighing, I got to my feet and started back. It was dark by the time I got back to the scrap yard, but Pa had at least lit the lantern, and I found my way into the rooms without tripping over any junk.

A plate of bread and cheese was on the kitchen table, and I started to wolf it down. Pa sat there, drinking beer from the bottle. "Well?" he said sourly.

"Four hundred, fifty seven. Well, four fifty eight if you count me."

"I don't count you for nothing, Lizzie. Four hundred fifty seven. Let's see, each kid has two parents, mostly. Hmmm..."

I swallowed a chunk of bread. "But some kids only got one parent, Pa, like me."

He nodded. "And lucky you are to have me, Lizzie. How much is the tickets?"

He hadn't asked me to find that out, but I'd looked anyway. "Five dollars for grown ups, three dollars for kids. You and me could go for eight dollars," I said eagerly "They'll be in town for the next three days."

Pa rubbed his chin thoughtfully. "Might have to go. Pity. But we might have to. So, Lizzie, how much is that all up?"

That took a little longer, and I stared at the wooden ceiling, figuring it out. "If every kid and every parent goes, then pretty close on five thousand dollars, Pa."

He grunted, and then smiled, showing his missing teeth. "Five thousand dollars. Nice tidy sum, that," he said. "Be nice to have that in my pocket."

"Pa..."

"You shut your mouth. I'm thinking."

He must have thought all through the night, because in the morning he had a grin from ear to ear. "Lizzie," he said, "I've got a treat for you. You and me is going to the circus. On the last day."

So we went to the circus on the last afternoon, dressed up in our Sunday clothes. Pa in a grubby black suit and me in my white dress, the one I'd had to let out twice since Ma left. We got there nice and early to be sure of getting in and, as Pa said, "to have a bit of a look-see."

Even though we were early, a long queue waited at the little wooden ticket booth.

To one side of the big top, just behind the booth, a man was polishing one of the mechanical elephants. Looking back over it now, I think it would all have been all right if Pa hadn't spotted the elephant. Its brass and chrome shone bright in the sunshine, as the keeper applied the cloth to the plated segments of its trunk and its long brass tusks. Two other smaller elephants stood behind it.

When Pa saw the big elephant, something lit up in his eyes just as bright as the gleam of the elephant's tusks. "Lizzie," he hissed. "You see that beast? How much metal you reckon there is in that elephant?"

I had a bad feeling already, but I looked across at the mechanical elephant and thought about it. It was more than twice as high as the man, and three times as long. "Three, four tons, maybe," I said doubtfully. "But Pa..."

"Lizzie, you go over there, and talk real nice to the man. Ask him to give you a ride on the pretty elephant. Go on, you know what to do."

I did, from long practice. I talked to the man polishing the machine. I lisped. I simpered. I hated myself. Plenty of other kids stood around, open mouthed and wide eyed, but I out-persuaded them all.

"Please, mister," I said again, for maybe the tenth time. "Just let me climb up on him."

Eventually, he laughed. "All right then, little miss. Just for a minute, now. No, none of you other kids, you didn't ask nice enough."

He reached up, lifted a metal flap and pulled a small red lever in the elephant's side. With a hiss, a big section opened up and out folded a neat little set of steps. I tripped up them, quick as you please, and the elephant's keeper followed. Up on top of the elephant, set inside its back, there was a seat. I sat down in it with a plump. In front of me I could see a panel with half-a-dozen levers and dials, all nice and easy to my hand. The keeper, still standing on the steps, took a big brass key out of his pocket, put it in a hole in the panel, and turned it. It hissed and shivered, and suddenly the elephant came alive, all shuffling and shifting beneath us. The dials flickered.

"Does it all work by steam?" I asked innocently.

The keeper shook his head. "No, little miss, this here is a right new thing called the in-ter-nal com-bus-tion eng-ine. Instead of coal it uses this black stuff they discovered in Texas, kind of like lamp oil. I just have to pour it in at the start of each show."

He moved two of the levers, and the elephant picked up its feet, right dainty, and walked forward a step or two. Then he laughed, set the levers straight and took out the key. "Come on, now, that's enough. I'll get into big trouble if we're not ready for the show, and I've got two more elephants to polish." And so we climbed down again. Some of the other kids stuck out their tongues at me. I stuck mine back.

I rejoined Pa in the queue. He was now much nearer the ticket booth.

"There's a key," I whispered to him. "And it works by levers. What are you going to do?"

"You recognise that key again if you saw it?"

I nodded. My memory is as good as my number figuring. And it was an unusual key.

"Okay, now shut up while I buys our tickets."

Pa took an age to pay for the tickets. He'd brought a pocketful of pennies, nickels and dimes, and counted them out real slow while the old man at the booth fumed and tapped his fingers. But Pa did it on purpose. All the time he was looking real careful at the booth, and at the big cash tin where the money was kept. Then he dropped a dime and it bounced over the counter into the booth. Pa leaned way over then, pretending to try to grab the coin. He told me later he'd been able to see the little safe at the back where they must put the tin overnight. The old man cursed and pushed him back out, and finally gave us our tickets.

Well, the circus show was a real treat, even though Pa kept fidgeting and shuffling. His mind wasn't on the show. But it was a treat for me. Pa never took me anywhere unless there was a reason, and this was the first circus I'd ever seen.

I gasped with fright as the trapeze artists threw themselves about far above the audience, spinning in the air. The tightrope walker juggled and jumped on the wire, all without a net. Then the bareback riders danced on the backs of the steam horses as they flashed around the ring, pistons pumping and gears whirling.

Then the human cannonball. They brought out this real big steam catapult, and he climbed into the seat at the end of the big arm. They pumped up the steam and then — pow! — the arm slung forward, and the guy flew right across the tent, bounced off the canvas at the top, and then dropped into a net. I thought he'd be stone dead, but he just jumped out, took off his helmet, and bowed. Everybody cheered.

Scariest of all was the big-cat tamer, who cracked his electrical whip as the big clockwork machines crouched and roared at him, opening their mouths to show their rows of razor-sharp steel blades. I nearly fainted when the tamer put his head in the mouth of the biggest lion, pulling it out just in time before the metal jaws slammed shut.

And finally, the elephant parade.

The biggest elephant, the one I'd climbed, was in the lead, followed by a medium size one and then a baby one. The keeper rode the lead elephant, pushing and pulling the levers to make it stop, rear up and lift its metal trunk into the air. It picked up and balanced a big red ball and then tossed it to the smaller elephant behind. Its own rider, a woman in a spangly costume, repeated the trick and then tossed the ball to the baby elephant at the rear. A little midget girl rode that one, and she made the machine catch the ball, roll it on the ground and then leap up onto it to balance there while I held my breath, sure as anything that it was going to fall off. But no, she just jumped it down to the ground again.

I clapped and clapped until my hands were sore. But Pa just sat there, silent and glowering. "Eight dollars," he muttered.

We left the tent, but we didn't go home right away. We strolled off down to the river and behind a few trees. One big tree had a fork in it, and Pa clambered up and pulled out the old brass telescope he'd found in the scrap one day.

He was up there a long time, and it was starting to get dark. I was getting cold, and hungry. But that was nothing new, living with Pa. Finally, he gave a satisfied grunt. "Just like I thought," he said. "They just locks up the booth. The money'll be in that safe I saw. I was hoping it'd just stay in a tin, easy to grab, but the safe makes it harder."

He climbed down from the tree. "Come on, we need to go home and get some stuff."

We came back well after midnight. A half-moon was just starting to edge up into the sky behind the trees. Pa and me were now both dressed in black, and I pulled a little four-wheeled trolley, the kind a mechanic uses when he has to fix something underneath a carriage.

When we got close to the place where the tent was pitched, Pa made me stand behind a tree while he looked over the circus ground with his telescope again. After a while, he said: "Looks quiet enough. Come on, but keep your little trap shut and step real quiet."

Together we crept up to the tent. Just to one side, where I'd seen them first, the huge mechanical elephants stood, right pretty with the moonlight gleaming off their metal. Close by was the wooden ticket booth. The door had a big padlock on it.

"Now," Pa whispered. "The dumb thing to do would be to try to pick that padlock. I ain't dumb. I got this." And out of one leg of his pants he pulled a long, thin, flexible saw. We went around to the back of the booth and he threaded the saw between two boards and started sawing. It didn't make much of a sound. In a couple of minutes he had two boards cut, top and bottom, making a neat hole. He stuck his head in and spent a minute or two looking around.

He pulled back and blinked in the moonlight. "Dark in there. The safe's just here, bigger'n I thought," he said, patting the wooden boards to his right. He picked up the saw again and quietly set to work.

Within a half-hour he had cut away all the boards behind the safe. I could see its metal back glinting. It was just under three foot square, maybe. Pa positioned the little trolley just behind it, digging it in to the soft ground so its top was level with the bottom of the safe. Then he went back to sawing. Another board or two, and Pa could squeeze past it into the booth.

I heard him grunting and cursing softly for a long while, and the back of the safe moved, just a little. But not enough to get it onto the trolley. Pa squirmed back out. "Can't move the damn thing!"

"Can't you just open it, Pa?"

"Would I be a-shoving on it if I could open it? It's got one of them dial things, saw it this afternoon. We gotta get it back to our shed and drill it. But it's too damned heavy. Nope. This is where that elephant comes in."

"The elephant? But, Pa, we don't have the key."

"Lizzie, your Pa ain't stupid. There's a big set of hooks on the wall in there, and keys on 'em. Ten to one says they puts all the keys there. Get in here and find that key, Lizzie. Do something useful for a change."

Resentfully, I crawled through and tried to look at the keys, but it was so dark inside I couldn't make out one key from another. I felt over them, trying not to clink them against each other, thinking real hard about the key I'd seen. I picked out three of them which felt about right, and crawled out again. Under the bright moonlight, it was easy. "This one," I said.

"Took you long enough," Pa said ungratefully. "Now, this is the tricky bit." He fetched the long rope we'd brought with us, and tied it round the safe, through the big steel handle on the door.

"I figured we was gonna have to do this, Lizzie. Besides, if we can get that elephant away quiet-like, and into our big shed before sunrise, I'll have it broken down into scrap afore anyone comes a-knocking. Got to be worth at least as much as what's in the safe. Maybe more. I'm gonna be rich!"

"Don't you mean *we*, Pa? We're going to be rich?"

"Yeah, yeah. Now go and climb up on that elephant and use that key."

"But Pa, I never..."

"Just do as I says. Get on that big thing and get ready to make it move."

Well, as I sidled up to the huge elephant, Pa spooled out the rope he'd tied to the safe. Then he looped the free end high up around the elephant's back legs and made it tight.

Of all the crazy things my Pa ever did — and there was a whole lot of them — this was probably the craziest. I don't know how he thought he could get the elephant and the safe away 'quiet-like'. But he always had big ideas, my Pa.

As I stood staring, he waved his hand urgently at me, silently telling me to climb up.

I looked hard for the little flap the keeper had lifted to get to the lever for the stairs. It wasn't easy in just the moonlight, but I felt all over the elephant's side and found it at last.

I pulled the lever, and the stairs came down again real smooth, but the hiss and the thump they made sounded awful loud in the silence of the night. I stopped, sure someone would wake up and call out, and I could see Pa standing stock-still, too. But we heard nothing, and so I tip-toed up the stairs onto the elephant's back and sat down.

Which of the levers did I need to pull? I sat there in a panic. There were more of them than I remembered, and none of them had any labels. Was there a lever to pull up the steps? Maybe, but I sure didn't know which one.

"Lizzie!" hissed my Pa. "Get that danged thing a-moving!"

I took a deep breath. All I could do was try. I put in the key and turned it. The key didn't move. I turned it the other way, and suddenly the huge machine came alive again, trembling and shifting. And making more noise than I expected.

"Lizzie!"

I grabbed the two biggest levers desperately, hoping they were the ones the keeper had used, and yanked on them. The elephant began to step forward. I heard a twang as the rope pulled taut behind me.

That's when it all went wrong.

"Liz..." I heard a sudden loud, ripping crash behind me, and I jumped in fright. I looked back. The rope was pulling the safe, all right. But it hadn't pulled neatly out of the hole Pa had cut. Instead, it had shifted to one side, and torn half of the wooden wall right out of the booth. And it had missed the little trolley, and was bouncing by itself along the ground.

Lights came on in one wagon after another. A loud yell came from the nearest one, as the ring-master stumbled out in his nightgown. Other figures quickly joined him.

Next thing I knew, Pa was clambering up the steps to perch dangerously behind me.

"Quick, Lizzie, quick! You gotta get us out of here!"

Desperately, I pulled harder on the levers, and the elephant began to speed up, though it was still more like a fast walk than a run. But it steadily got quicker.

We crashed out of the pen, accidentally caught one of the tent ropes in the elephant's tusks, drew it taut, and then snapped it with a loud crack.

We were headed for some trees. How was I supposed to steer this thing? I'd never driven anything more than our little pony trap, and our old pony always knew where he was going, just needed a twitch of the reins. There weren't any reins on the elephant.

Pa was yelling, and in a panic I looked down at the levers I was holding. Two levers. Why did it need two levers, not just one? I pushed the left-hand lever forward a little, and suddenly the elephant swerved to the right. We missed the trees by a fraction, and then I pulled the lever back so that we were going straight again.

I glanced behind. Everyone in the circus was up and milling around, and I could see a couple of people heading towards the other elephants. They were all yelling. So much, I thought, for 'real-quiet like'.

The safe was bumping on the ground behind us, lurching and tumbling, but still tied to the rope. It was slowing us down, jerking back on the elephant every few bounces. If it got caught in something...

"Pa!" I yelled. "You got to cut the rope!"

Pa was wild-eyed, crazy-looking, as he tried to keep his balance behind me. "No! Never!"

"Pa, they'll catch us!"

"But... five thousand dollars, Lizzie, five thousand dollars!"

"They'll catch us, Pa! It's too late!"

"Aw, hell...!" But he lay down on the elephant's back and began to shuffle towards its tail. Meanwhile, I tried to steer the huge machine onto the road through town. Maybe, I thought, maybe if we got far enough away we could get back home and hide this thing in our shed before they saw us.

I heard a sudden snap. The elephant surged forward with a jerk. Now it was going a lot faster, almost running, striding along with heavy footsteps. I could hear Pa cursing. He told me later he'd nearly fallen right off, had just managed to hang on to the tail and climb back up.

The town loomed up in front of us. Only a few lights were on. I had lost track of the time, but it must have been around four or five in the morning. The sun would be coming up soon.

I looked back again. That wasn't a good idea. Not too far behind, I could see the middle-sized elephant racing after us, and on its back the lady rider I'd seen in the circus ring, in her night-gown, whirling a lasso. She threw it, but the loop fell way behind us. I figured that so long as we kept going, the longer legs of the bigger elephant would leave them further and further behind.

Then, in the distance behind, I saw two of the steam horses. They must have taken a while to build up steam, not like the elephant, with its magical internal combustion engine. But once they got going, they would run a whole lot faster than us.

Looking back for so long hadn't been a good idea. There was a mighty crash, and the elephant staggered to one side. We'd smashed into a sidewalk verandah. I moved levers quickly to get it straight again.

Pa was just behind me again. "Lizzie!" he gasped.

"What, Pa?" He looked pretty bad. Bewildered, I guess. Cutting loose that safe must have been the hardest thing he'd ever done.

"Nothing, nothing. Just keep going, Lizzie."

Now here came the two steam horses. As one of them came up alongside us, puffing steam, its rider yelled for us to stop. Pa just shook his fist at him. And then the man stood up on the horse's back, just like he'd done in the big top. He balanced there for a second and then jumped across at the elephant, hung on to one of the tusks like it was a trapeze bar, and then swung up to grab at Pa.

I screamed as the two struggled together, but then Pa landed a punch and the man slipped off. He can't have been hurt much, because he did a somersault or two when he hit the ground and then stood up straight.

His horse, running all by itself, veered off the road and smashed into the window of Mrs Baker's millinery store. Glass went everywhere, and the horse stopped still with a flowery hat spinning on its head, hissing steam. If I hadn't been so scared, I would have laughed.

The townspeople were leaning out of windows now, and coming to their doors, staring as the elephant thundered down the street, followed by the rest of the circus.

The rider of the second steam horse kept swerving in front of us, trying to get me to stop, or at least to turn aside, but I tried to ignore him. The make-it-go levers were pulled as far back as I could get them, but as I glanced down, I could see that one of the dials had a needle flickering on the edge of a little wedge of red. What did that mean? Was it running out of steam? Or — what was it? — that oil stuff the keeper had talked about?

We were almost at the end of the street now, nearing the little bridge over the river. But before we reached it, a loud, loud, whistle sounded behind us, almost like a mechanical scream. Pa cursed. "They got the steam tractor going. It's damn fast when it ain't hauling all them wagons. And it's pulling something behind it."

I looked back again. The tractor was pulling the steam catapult. A moment later the catapult gave out a huge puff of steam, and then came a bang. The human cannonball flew through the air, right towards us.

Pa yelled as the cannonball man thumped into him head-first, and the two of them fell forward over my back into the little seat. For a minute, all three of us were struggling together, all arms and legs. The cannonball man had on his black helmet, and he was banging it into Pa's head. Blood was streaming down Pa's face.

And then I saw Pa pull out his knife.

It was too much. There was no way we were going to get away now, and if Pa used that knife, he'd hang. I pushed my hands past them and grabbed every lever I could and pulled them all.

With a terrible jerk, the elephant stopped. Then it reared up on its hind legs, its trunk raised high in the air. Its back tilted and tilted and tilted until it was straight up like a wall. All three of us fell out and down onto the road. Luckily, I was the last and I fell on top, and wasn't hurt much. But Pa was underneath us all, and he got knocked out cold.

As I lay there on the road, dazed, the crowd of circus people caught up with us and I found myself staring up into the gleaming jaws of one of the steel tigers. I gave a little scream, but it was on a leash, and its panting keeper pulled it back and turned it off. It was all over.

Pa went to jail for a long time. In fact, he's still there. I visit him whenever we're in town. That isn't all that often, though, since we travel around so much. See, when the circus folk realised that it had all been Pa's idea, and that I was pretty much all on my own now, they took me in and kind of adopted me. That's right. I ran away with the circus!

That was more than a year ago. Since then, I've learned to do a heap of different acrobat tricks. They call me "The Amazing Leaping Lizzie" now.

But last night something real special happened. That's kind of why I've been writing all this down.

See, yesterday we arrived in a big town out west and last night we put on our show. So there I was under the big top, doing handstands on the back of Raja (that's the name of the big elephant Pa and me stole). At the end of the act, I did a somersault, leapt off his back, and spun down to a perfect landing in the sawdust. Lots of applause.

And as I straightened up, a big buxom woman in the front row stood up and shrieked "Lizzie, Lizzie!"

It was Ma.

June 2012

This story was first published in *eSteampunk Magazine* in their
February 2013 issue.

The Night Before

As Mummy tucked Katie into bed that night, she repeated yet again: "Now go to sleep, darling. If you lie awake he might not come, and then think how disappointed we would all be in the morning."

"Yes, Mummy," said Katie sleepily. But she had her fingers crossed, so it didn't really count, did it?

She did go to sleep for a while, she really did, but when she heard the gentle clatter of hoofs on the roof, she woke up immediately and clambered out of bed, being ever so quiet so as not to wake her baby brother Billy. Then she snuck out of her bedroom door and tip-toed down the hallway. When she got near to the stairs, she knelt down and then started to crawl, gently, gently, until she could just see through into the kitchen.

When they had moved into this new house, just a year ago, Katie had been really upset, and her Mummy had asked her why. "There's no chimney in this house, how will he get in?" Katie had bawled. But her Mummy had explained to her that they would leave the kitchen window open just a squeak, and he would be able to get in there.

Now Katie crawled forward a little more to look between the bars of the handrail on the landing. She couldn't quite see the kitchen window from here, but she could see the table, all loaded up.

There! There was a creaking sound, and moments later, she gave a gasp. There he was – the tall, fat figure looming over the table! She couldn't quite see him perfectly, but it was him, it really was! She had to put her hand over her mouth to stop a squeal of excitement. He mustn't know that she was here, or else he might go away without doing the presents.

The red-robed figure began to eat what had been left out for him. It was no wonder he was so fat, Katie thought, as he ate into all of the left-over turkey and ham, gulping it down greedily. Then it was the turn of the bowl of half-eaten trifle. Gulp! Gulp! It all vanished in moments. She gave a little giggle. If *she* ate like that, Daddy would growl at her so bad!

Then, at last, he came into the lounge room, and Katie crawled just a little further to see better, keeping as quiet as a mouse. As a very, very quiet mouse.

He strode into the lounge room, carrying a big sack swung over his back. She could see him better now, and he looked every bit as he did in all of the storybooks – the big, fat man in his bright red costume, with the black fur trimming his hood and sleeves, and his long black beard flowing down his chest.

He loomed over the presents all laid out under the tree. "Oh, oh, oh!" he said in a deep, booming voice. "What have we here?"

Then he pulled out a long list and consulted it. *Oh, please, please, please,* Katie thought, *I've been ever so good!*.

He bent down and picked up the awful purple sweater that Auntie Jessica had made for her, and popped it into his sack. *Yes!* thought Katie in delight. Then the tacky plastic ironing set that came from Grandma. Into the sack, as Katie giggled and hugged herself. Then it was all the extra clothing that Billy had been given – all those endless jump-suits and little cardigans and booties. Into the sack!

Then it was Mummy and Daddy's turn. The big fat man seemed to be chuckling as he picked up the book that would never be read, the CD of music which Daddy didn't like, several pairs of socks, the badly-smelling perfume, the scented bath-bombs, the ugly vase Auntie Flora had found somewhere, the digital photo-frames. Into the sack with it all! Katie clapped her hands with joy.

At that the big man looked up and gave her a wink, hefted his loaded sack onto his back, and then he was gone, in two strides into the kitchen and out of the window.

Katie gave a contented sigh and crept back to bed, happy.

At last, she had really seen him. The Anti-Claus.

November 2011

Fairy Tales

JONATHAN GRADGRIND CONCLUDED HIS SPEECH with a typical flourish.

"...and so, in conclusion, that is why the whole pernicious edifice of religion must be torn down and razed to the ground. We must raise the next generation to be free of all of this nonsense, these fabulations, these fairy tales."

He gazed around the audience, leaning forward on the lectern. "After all, how can we possibly justify telling lies to children?"

The thunderous applause, as always, was very gratifying, and he sat down with great satisfaction, a job well done. His famous great-grandfather, Thomas, would be proud of him. And in the foyer of the hall his books would be selling well. He wondered idly whether there was a market for audio-book versions. Or perhaps even a DVD of his best speeches? He would see what his agent thought. Could be a good source of additional revenue.

Then he realised with annoyance that the moderator was opening the floor to questions. *Questions?* he thought in irritation. *I'm sure that wasn't in the contract.* He would get his agent to write that explicitly into future contracts. No question time without an additional fee.

Still, he could hardly refuse now without seeming churlish. He reluctantly stood up and returned to the podium. The moderator was picking out a hand raised at the back of the hall. "Yes?"

A young woman was standing. She waited a moment for a wireless microphone to be brought to her. "Mr Gradgrind, thank you so much for your fascinating speech. I just wondered, though, about your conclusion. May I ask if you have any children yourself?"

Really? Don't these people know enough to look me up on Wikipedia?

"No, Madam," he responded briefly. He toyed for a second with the idea of quoting her the whole of that poem by Phillip Larkin, the one that ends '...and don't have kids yourself.' But he decided that it wouldn't be right for this audience.

"It's just," she went on, "that we have a two-year old ourselves. Now, of course we won't be exposing her to the Bible or anything of that sort, but you mentioned fairy tales and... and fabulations... and things like that. Do you think... is it wrong to read her story books? She does so love them."

Gradgrind smiled. It was a good question, and he had a ready answer. "There's nothing wrong with reading stories to your child provided that the stories are based on fact. Facts, facts, facts, that is what is wanted, Madam. My colleague Richard Dawkins has an excellent children's book available, dealing with the facts of evolution. I'm sure there are many other suitable books which have stories based in the real world."

Incredibly, the damned woman was continuing. Couldn't they take the mike away from her?

"But what about story books with fairies and dragons and talking animals?"

"All of them fabulations that, like God, do not exist. Fairies? Little girls with butterfly wings? Aerodynamically impossible.

What nonsense! Throw them all out in the rubbish, Madam, that is my advice." There was scattered applause from the audience, and the woman sat down meekly.

There were some other questions, none of them difficult. After all, this was an audience which had paid good money to hear him. The God-botherers usually stayed away.

As the audience shuffled out, he considered how to spend the rest of his evening. This was a provincial town, part of a tour around the country which he had been on for the last three weeks. It was gratifying and quite lucrative, but he would be glad when it was over.

He had been invited to have dinner with the moderator, the local Rotary president, but frankly he couldn't be bothered. He'd been to too many similar meals on this tour, endured far too much dull conversation. Perhaps he would just get room service back in his hotel. It couldn't be any less boring.

Just as he was stepping down from the stage, however, he felt a hand on his arm. An elderly lady, with a mass of white hair and dressed all in black. He was preparing a rude response — he didn't like to be touched — when she said:

"I'm so sorry to bother you, Mr Gradgrind. But I wondered whether you had any plans for the evening?"

Was the old hag *propositioning* him? But she went on:

"My friends and I have been so interested in what you have been saying. We have read your books, of course, and we would love to have the opportunity of discussing them with you. We feel a strong personal interest in your ideas."

Gradgrind straightened his back and smiled. "Well, of course, I'm very gratified by your interest..."

"I wondered if you would come and meet my friends? As it happens, we have a regular meeting each week — tonight, in fact — in the room behind my shop. We would just love you to join us and have something to eat."

Well, it sounded better than dinner with the Rotary president and his cronies, at least. Why not? It was always pleasing to listen to the flattering comments from his most avid readers.

"All right," he said. "Is it far?"

"Oh no," said the old lady. "My shop is just around the corner. It's never far away."

That was an odd comment, he thought, but the old woman was probably well on the way to having Alzheimers by now. Hardly knew what she was saying.

"Very good," he said, "lead the way."

Though she kept reassuring him that it wasn't far, the old woman was slow on her feet, with an odd wobbling gait, and so it took them quite a while to get there.

Along the way, she said to him: "I was particularly interested in what you said to that young mother."

"Oh yes? Quite a good question, I thought."

"Yes, it was. What would you think about *toys* for young children, then?"

It wasn't something he had ever thought about. "Well, I don't know. Nothing wrong with toy trucks and planes, I suppose. Or building blocks."

"But not soft toys like teddy bears?"

"Perfectly all right, provided the bear is realistic. There shouldn't be anything of this anthropomorphic nonsense, you know, rabbits with waistcoats and pocket watches, that sort of thing."

"Ah, I see. That's what I thought you might say. Well, here we are at last."

Gradgrind was somewhat taken aback. The shop seemed ancient, with a leaded glass window. But perhaps that was just a deliberate marketing ploy. That would make sense. Above the window, in old-fashioned red and gilt letters, were the words "The Old Curiosity Shop". Aiming at the tourist trade, no doubt.

The old woman took a long time fumbling with a bunch of large keys, but the door swung open at last and he followed her in.

It was quite dark at the front of the shop, but towards the back he could see a light. It was hard to make out in the gloom, but the shop seemed to be full of knick-knacks and second-hand jewellery, old furniture, peculiar sculptures.

"The others will be here already," said the old lady, "in the room at the back."

Gradgrind was starting to regret agreeing to come along, but he could hardly back out now without being rude. "All right," he said brusquely, "but I won't be able to stay long. Half an hour, perhaps."

The old lady smiled widely. "Oh, I'm sure that when you meet my friends you won't be able to tear yourself away."

She led the way through the dark shop to a little hallway, which was lighted by a couple of wall lamps with moulded gold-coloured brackets in the shape of cherubs, little human babies with wings. *More fantastic nonsense we should do away with*, he thought in annoyance.

"Just through here," she said, and opened a door at the back of the hallway. She politely stepped aside so that he could go through first.

He stepped through, and then stopped in astonishment.

Instead of the small back room he had been expecting, he seemed to be at the end of an astonishingly long corridor. There in front of him was a series of carved arches or door frames, one after the other, lit up by what seemed like natural light, though it was now night-time outside.

He turned to ask the old woman a question, but when he turned, she was gone, and so in fact was the door through which he had entered. There was just a stone wall, filled with carvings of fantastical figures, as were the walls to his left and right.

Gaping, he turned back in the direction in which he had first been facing, and stared along the incredible corridor. He had no choice but to stumble forward along it.

In a few steps, he passed through the first arch and entered a rough stone room which had windows to left and right, letting in daylight. Naturally he ran to one of these and looked out, trying to find a means of escape from his bewildering situation. He found that he was high above the ground, too high to jump out safely. Below was a dense forest.

As he stared in amazement, something white moved in the forest. It reached a clearing and looked up at him. A white horse. It had a long, shining horn protruding from its head.

"This is a trick," he said. "Some kind of a trick. It's nonsense!" He turned angrily away from the window.

On the other side of the room the window looked over a river bank, with more forest beyond it. At first he thought there was nothing there, but then, by the river, he spied a bearded man, playing on a set of pipes. The man's lower parts were covered with hair, and his feet...

"Nonsense!" yelled Jonathan Gradgrind, and looked away. He started to march down the corridor, refusing to look through any more windows. Up ahead there must be someone who was responsible for this trickery, this abduction. He would sue, he thought, he would get his lawyers to sue the pants off those responsible. There must have been some kind of drug he had been given. LSD, probably. Maybe in the glass of water he had been sipping from during his speech.

He strode forward, passing through room after room, arch after arch. For a long while, he didn't seem to be progressing anywhere, and he was becoming hungry and thirsty as well as more and more angry.

But as he went on, the carvings in the stone seemed to grow more and more grotesque, and the light coming in from the windows slowly became ruddy and dark. Soon there were flaming torches mounted on the walls, and no daylight.

At last he could see that the long corridor seemed to be coming to an end. The chain of arches ceased, and he stumbled at last, gasping for breath and legs aching, into a final, huge room. There were torches on the walls here, but even so the room was still quite dark. It took a while for his eyes to adjust.

There was a crowd of... creatures... beings with fantastical shapes. Huge hairy beasts with horns. Scaly lizards with leathery wings and red, forked tongues. And there... yes, little girls with butterfly wings.

There was a huge throne in the centre of the room, where it was darkest. All Gradgrind could make out was a gigantic dark figure. He realised after a moment that the attention of every being in the room was focused on the occupant of the throne.

"Greetings," came its deep, deep voice.

"Who... what..." spluttered Gradgrind.

"You may like to call me Oberon," rumbled the figure. "It is one of the many names I have been given. I am King here."

"You..." But Gradgrind's voice failed him at last. His anger was gone, replaced with a boundless terror.

"You have been telling lies," went on the dark figure. "Lies about us and our kind. We are not happy, little man."

"No, I..." was all that Gradgrind could manage.

"And so, little man, now you are going to dance for our amusement." He thumped a huge staff on the floor, sending a tremor throughout the room. "Dance!"

On his already weary legs, ludicrous in his business suit amongst this fantastic company, Jonathan Gradgrind began to dance.

And, as the old woman had predicted, he couldn't tear himself away.

November 2011

The Empire of the Sea

IT WAS HARD TO ROW THROUGH THE STREETS while the tide was going out. Rence and Kale strained against the oars, trying to avoid the eddies created as the water surged around the corners of the remaining buildings.

But their own tower was now in sight, standing separate from all the rest. Rence had been told that in the old days Harvest Tower had stood proud in the centre of its own wide plaza. Now it was an island. But proud, still proud.

There were half a dozen small fishing boats scattered around the tower, and the fishermen waved and called out greetings as Rence and Kale came up. Rence gave them a cursory wave, but his spirits were too low for him to join in any banter. He gestured to Kale instead and they rowed up to the building's lower windows.

Water sucked in and out of the empty frames, and it was dangerous to get too close. But ropes dangled down from windows two levels up. They fastened the boat fore and aft and called out to the cousins now leaning out above. The winching began, and they were slowly pulled upwards.

As Rence climbed into the building, his wife Chelle ran forward to hug him. "You've been gone for days!" she said. "I was so worried. What's the news?"

Rence shook his head. "Not very good. Let me save the details for Grandfather. Has he calmed down yet?"

Chelle smiled ruefully. "He's still doesn't believe that there is any need. We younger folk have been trying to persuade him, but all the uncles are on his side."

Just then, there was a small shudder beneath their feet. The building seemed to tremble for a moment, then was still. Rence looked grimly at Chelle, who just shrugged sadly.

"Well," he said with a sigh, "let's start up." Together, they headed for the stairwell.

Harvest Tower was 93 levels high, though the lowest levels were now well below water. Climbing it took over an hour even for people as young and fit as Rence and Chelle. As they ascended the last of the stairs, the building gave another ominous shudder. Up here it felt much worse, and the walls trembled for several seconds. Rence looked across at Chelle, who was holding tightly to the railing.

Breathing heavily, he said: "It's happening more often now."

"Yes," she agreed.

Rence gave a sigh, and wiped away the sweat from his forehead. "Grandfather will have to listen." He pulled open the battered door and went through. Into bright daylight. They were in the midst of the roof garden, the asset that had helped keep the family alive for almost two generations. Three great water tanks held precious rainwater, and green plants were everywhere, carefully tended by the cousins who worked up here. Red tomatoes, yellow peppers and deep purple aubergines were spots of colour here and there. And on one of the precious few fruit trees, orange kumquats.

In the centre of the garden, like a separate little building, was what his grandfather for some reason called The Pent House. Rence and Chelle headed for the door.

Grandfather was seated in a soft red chair on a raised plinth in the centre of the room, the uncles gathered around him. He was arguing with them, his usual state. Rence didn't know how old his grandfather was exactly, wasn't even sure how old it was possible for people to become. His bald, age-spotted head turned towards them as they came in.

"Well," he said sharply. "Have you finished wasting your time?"

"Grandfather," Rence said. "You must have felt that shaking just now. The foundations of the tower..."

"Earthquakes," snapped the old man. "Been having them for years. Natural phenomenon, nothing to worry about."

Chelle came forward. "But sir, we have seen other buildings in the city collapse. Only last year at the Drage Centre..."

"Poor construction," he said with a sneer. "I remember the Drage company. Always cutting corners. Cheap labour, poor concrete. Would have fallen down anyway. Water had nothing to do with it."

Rence's Uncle Vido nodded in agreement, and said: "Enough of this. We reluctantly allowed you to make this trip around the city, Rence. What did you find out?"

Rence sighed. "Many of the smaller buildings have been abandoned, they are in very poor shape. At most, there are only one or two people in them. Of the bigger communities... well, you know what happened to the Drage Centre. It's just rubble there now. " Rence said. "And I think the Bankhouse's foundations are going, too. You can actually see it starting to lean. We didn't bother asking them for help. The Ryan Street Brethren just drove us off. They are a little crazy, I think. The most successful of the communities... apart from ourselves," he hastily added as he saw Grandfather taking umbrage, "is the Giordano Cooperative. I spoke with them for some time, and they showed me around. They have the whole of the Southbank complex, and the buildings in the block seem to be supporting each other pretty well."

"And what did they say," said Uncle Vido, glancing at Grandfather, "when you asked them if they would offer us any assistance?"

Rence swallowed. Should he actually outline the degrading terms which Bruno Giordano had set out? To take only the prettiest young women, and those young men willing to work as serfs in his roof gardens? No, he wouldn't mention that.

"Il Capo offers to lend us boats to assist in ferrying us to the mainland, should the need arise." That had been the least offensive part of Giordano's offer.

Grandfather folded his arms. "The mainland? With no shelter? Fighting all of the people there for every scrap of food? No. Never." He spat. "I should never have allowed you to go begging to the other buildings. We can't expect any help from any of those bastards. And we don't *need* any help," he said, thumping his fist on the arm of his chair. "This tower hasn't fallen down yet and it never will."

His flat statement was belied by another shudder that made the top of the building sway for a long moment. Something was definitely going wrong down there, Rence thought. Seawater was eating away at the steel structure of the foundations.

The old man gestured dismissively. "Get out. Get back to your work. No more of this nonsense. Tell the other grandchildren to stop their chatter."

Chelle tugged on Rence's arm, and together they marched quickly out of The Pent House. Once outside, she leant close to him. "You see. We have no choice now."

He nodded sadly, then turned aside to whisper to one of the cousins weeding a row of cabbages. Chelle turned the other way to do the same to a young woman gathering carrots. They went on through the garden, speaking to a worker here and another there. Only the young people. Only the trusted ones.

That night, under the cover of darkness, a small fleet of fishing boats left the base of the tower and headed out into the open sea. Each boat carried fresh water and a small cargo of dried fish and pots of food plants they had been sneaking away from the roof over the last few weeks.

"It was time," Chelle said to Rence as she sat by his side on the leading boat, looking back at the drowned city. "Time and past time. We couldn't raise our own children there, forever living among the ruins."

"But what will we find out here? Will there be somewhere to live?" he asked.

"We'll never know," she said. "Unless we go see."

September 2012

Out Flew the Web

THE MACHINE WOVE A WEB OF SILVER AGAINST THE STARS, binding Cassiopeia, Orion, and blazing Sirius in a delicate trap.

Ariane looked on the work of the Spinner, her mechanical spider, and smiled. She sat in a tight bubble, insulated against the void, warm and safe. She felt good, creative, making something beautiful and at the same time practical. A womanly task, she thought. She smiled again, this time at the image of herself at an ancient spinning wheel, creating thread. Thread from which sails would be woven.

When this part of the web was done, Marc would move in and fill in the strands with micro-thin weave. Blocking out the view of the stars, she thought, and made a sad face.

"How goes it?" said Marc, from many miles away. The radio wave took a full minute to reach her from where Marc was. "The third quadrant's almost done," she said, and adjusted controls to tighten the work of the Spinner as she waited for his reply. It was a strange feeling, being here in the bubble in the midst of space. If she did not turn, to see the bulk of her ship behind her, she could imagine herself floating alone, without support in the endless womb of space. The machine went on weaving.

Sometimes Ariane felt like driving the Spinner to her own whim, creating fantastic abstract designs against the velvet backdrop of stars. But that would be without a practical use: a wrong thing. Still, it was nice to dream.

"That's great!" Marc's voice, back again. "I've started filling in the sail on the second quadrant. We'll have to be careful from now on: the light pressure's already starting to push the sail we've got. The faster we finish the better. John says the pod has left Earth already. Should be here in just a few days."

She made no reply: stretched out conversations generally destroyed the trivia of speech.

Alone in space. Floating in the delicious void, swimming like a new born fish in a dark and open sea. And in front of her was a net of silver, waiting to grasp her and haul her above an unseen, unknowable surface.

Ariane reached to touch the soft plastic bubble before her face, to reassure herself of its reality. Sometimes her mind seemed to go journeying on its own, beyond her control.

The web now trapped the Pleiades: they sparkled, brilliant sisters, jewels amidst the bright hair of the web.

Behind her ship was the blazing sun, blowing outwards, gusting forth a wind between the stars. A wind they planned to sail.

The shining spider wove on. Ariane, idly dreaming, neglected her instruments in the control device she held. Out in space, in one small square of the web, a streaming comet lay, its ghostly tresses tossed back by the eternal wind from the sun.

There was a red light on the control.

It was a long time before she noticed it, before she could bring her mind back from the stars. A red light. It was though her mind could not focus. Meteor warning, that was it. Meteors. She moved quickly, then, and switched on her ship's defensive shield. Immediately, the stars were filtered through a rosy shimmer: they danced like red sparks.

But before she could take any further action, two more red lights came on. The Spinner had been hit. The damage she could not tell as yet. She bit her lip, feeling frustration. The meteor warning light stayed on, and she waited long tense minutes for the shower to pass. At last, the warning light went out, a red eye closing, and she snapped off the ruddy shield. Again the stars stood out clear and white. She searched for the Spinner with her eyes.

It was coming towards her.

She could see loose mechanisms spilling out like entrails from its smashed interior. And behind it raced the wire, the silver wire. She was paralysed. The Spinner rushed up at her, loomed huge and menacing, and then was past. Ariane sat very still, wide eyed, seeing the wire stream past like an endless ticker tape. She knew, intellectually, that the Spinner had missed her by hundreds of feet. but knowing was not feeling, and she shook with fear. And the web!

The web was unwinding.

Strand by strand, it came apart. Ariane was immobilised by horror, watching the unravelling miles of wire.

She turned her ship, at last, to follow the crippled Spinner. There was the babble of Marc's voice in her ears, but she could not listen.

The Spinner was crazy. It was like a spider crazed by an hallucinogen, a manic weaver. It moved and spun as it should, but erratically; it made knots and patterns like a schizophrenic. And pulled strands across the rest of the completed sail. She could see the Spinner and its tangled web black now against the white sail, flexing it and pulling it along.

"Destruct, Ariane!" came Marc's voice. But she did not hear. Her mind had been snared by the harmony and magic in the random silver lines, by something hypnotic in the amazing network of gleaming wire.

Loops of the web spun around her ship: a thick rope wrapped around her bubble, and she saw the fine structure of it as if for the first time; the micro strands that made the cord, the cords braided to make the rope. She had never seen the wire so close before.

Then the bubble jerked suddenly, and she was thrown against the plastic surface. Again, and the ship swung, so that she could see the huge mass of the sail, and the wire that bound her to it. She could see, far off, the tugs which held the sail in place while it was being constructed: they too seemed looped with the endless thread. Like Christmas ribbon, she thought detachedly: how beautiful it seems!

The tugs had released the sail, that was it. And the Spinner, the crippled, crazy Spinner, had at last died, ran out of wire.

The sail billowed slowly, very slowly, above her, like that of a great sailing ship. And she swung below, a tiny ship beneath a vast sail.

The tugs were fouled in the wire, she could see them clearly, unable to move amidst the knots of the mad web.

There was only the gentlest of accelerations on Ariane, the softest of reminders as the sail filled with the wind from the sun and started out with her as cargo on its long voyage between the stars.

August 1975

This story was developed as part of a writer's workshop in 1975, and published in the workshop anthology The Altered Eye in 1976.

The Quickening

WE WERE WRONG, SO WRONG, ABOUT THE ZOMBIES. We'd come to treat the idea as a joke; we'd seen too many movies, too many TV shows, read too many comics, played too many games. We thought we knew all about what it would be like when the zombies came. But we were wrong. It wasn't like that at all.

I'm holed up here, as high as I can get, with the biggest shotgun I could find, and still I don't feel safe. I am lucky, very lucky, to have this gun, because I got in early. I knew what was coming, you see, when most didn't.

In fact, I was there at the very start. At the zoo.

I am... no, cancel that. I *used* to be a veterinarian, large animals my speciality. I did a lot of work for the zoo, helping out their resident vet when she needed it. They have a few on-call vets like me. But I was the one who got the call that night.

When Marissa called, she sounded worried. "Bob, it's one of our jaguars. Just seems to have keeled over in the compound. Her mate was making a terrible row, standing over her. We've brought her in to the surgery, but I can't figure out what's wrong. She's in some kind of coma, and I can't bring her round. I know it's late, but can you come and give me a second opinion?"

"Sure," I said, and set off on my motorcycle. I always loved riding the bike at night, great feeling of exhilaration.

The City Zoo is quite modern – hardly any cages are left now. The animals are kept confined by the use of deep ditches and other barriers, all the better to let the public get a good view of them in something like a natural state. It had seemed like a great advance. At the time.

I have a passkey to let myself in to the zoo when it's closed. I hurried in to the administration building and found my way to Marissa's surgery.

The huge jaguar was laid out on the examination table, a muzzle on and its legs restrained. Even if the big cat was in a coma, you couldn't take any chances. Marissa and one of the keepers were bent over the jaguar, attaching monitoring leads.

"We can't rouse her," Marissa said. "I've taken some blood samples, but it will take a while to get any results. I can't figure it out. Could she have had a stroke, do you think? Or does she have a brain tumour?"

It didn't seem likely, but it was possible, I supposed. I started examining the animal myself, not really expecting to find anything which Marissa had missed. However, I found a slight swelling at the back of the jaguar's neck, slightly warmer than the rest of her body. What did that mean? I pointed it out to Marissa, who just frowned in puzzlement. "Meningitis?" she asked. "But there's no fever."

Jamie, one of the other keepers, came in from outside. "Marissa," he said urgently. "The male jaguar... it's down, too. Same as the female. I can't wake him up. Shall we bring him here?"

"Damn," Marissa said, looking at me in alarm. We were both silent, thinking through this new development. Then she said: "Some kind of viral infection then, must be. Bob... can you and Jamie go out and look at the male? We'll need to bring him in.

Hell, we're going to have to implement a strict quarantine, make sure the other big cats don't get it."

As I walked out with Jamie, my mind was racing. Where would these animals have picked up a virus which affected their species here in the zoo? A domestic cat virus which had mutated? Brought in on the clothing of one of the keepers?

I'm not sure what I was expecting to find when we reached the jaguar compound. A very sick animal, certainly. But as we exited the wire-enclosed passage which ran behind the compounds, I saw the male jaguar stagger upright, take a few wobbly steps and then steady itself. My first reaction was relief. If only I had known what was coming...

The jaguar turned towards us, and in the dim light his eyes were glowing a fiery red. Cats often seem to have glowing eyes, a trick of the way they reflect light. But this wasn't like that. The big cat's eyes seemed to be actively generating light. It had to be an illusion, but that's what it looked like. It started to slink towards us.

"Shit," whispered Jamie. "I didn't bring the trank gun. Didn't think we'd need it. Let's get back."

We made a hasty retreat to the safety of the wire corridor, and closed the gate. The jaguar kept advancing, and then leapt, smashing into the gate with tremendous force. I stepped back in shock. The metal tubes making up the gate had actually bent. Surely the animal must have hurt itself? But no, it just paced away as if nothing had happened. It turned again and leapt, leapt an astonishing distance. Again the gate shook and deformed. I looked at Jamie, and without a word we retreated further. There were several partition gates along the corridor, and we closed and bolted them as we went back. Finally, we were out onto the public pathway.

"God," said Jamie, and I could see him shaking. "Have you ever seen anything like that? What's going on?"

I suddenly had a very ugly thought. "Marissa," I said. "If the female is reacting the same way to this thing as the male..." We started to run, but before we reached the surgery we could hear the screaming begin. And then, more horribly, it suddenly stopped. As we reached the door all we could hear from inside were smashing sounds and a feral roar.

Jamie and I looked at each other. I said, hating myself: "We can't open the door, Jamie. We can't let it out. I'll ring the police."

"Army might be more like it," he said. "Look, there are trank guns in the office. I'll go get them." He ran off.

I used my mobile to ring the emergency number. The police were frankly incredulous, and I had a lot of trouble convincing them that this wasn't a joke. "Send someone with a powerful rifle," I said. "Quickly. We think the animal has killed a vet."

Jamie came running back, carrying two tranquilliser guns, but just before he reached me, he stopped short and gave a cry, looking past me. I turned around.

The male jaguar was pacing down the pathway, its eyes gleaming red. It opened its jaws to show dripping fangs. I had time to register that something seemed to have happened to its body; it seemed larger and even more muscular than normal. How had it escaped its compound? It must have jumped the ditch. The ditch designed to be far too wide for an animal to leap.

Jamie threw one of the guns to me and together we raised them and fired darts at the jaguar. Nothing. In fact, I was sure that I saw both of the darts simply bounce off the big cat's hide.

"Jesus!" Jamie said, and turned to run. That was his big mistake, and one which saved my life. The jaguar bounded past me and after him. I fired another dart towards it, and then threw down the gun and ran in the other direction, out into the dark night, hoping to hide. Behind me, there was another scream, rapidly cut off. Jamie was dead.

Panic was only a hair's breadth away, but I fought it down. Trying to make sure that the jaguar couldn't follow my scent, I jumped a fence and into one of the waterfowl enclosures, stepping as quietly as I could into the water. A pointless precaution, as several indignant geese and herons rose quacking and honking. Still, I thought, it might be a distraction. I waded quickly to the other side of the pond, which wasn't deep.

What I found on the other side filled me with an awful dread. Until then I had been trying to rationalise what had happened. Perhaps this feline virus was triggering a kind of hysterical strength in the jaguars, I thought, extraordinary, but at least explicable.

But on the other side of the pond I could see into the rhinoceros enclosure. One of the huge animals was lying prone on the ground. But as I watched, it started to struggle upright again. And the other rhinoceros was pacing about. Its eyes gleamed as red as fire. As I watched, it snorted, turned around and, picking up speed rapidly, slammed into the concrete wall at the back of the enclosure. It was as though the wall had been hit by an armoured tank. Cracks ran through it. It should have stunned the rhinoceros, but it simply turned around unconcernedly, and prepared for another run.

No natural virus, surely, could affect species as different as a jaguar and a rhinoceros? Impossible. Could it be some kind of parasite, affecting the brains of these animals? I shook my head in disbelief.

Then I heard distant mad trumpeting. An enraged elephant. My God, what would an infected *elephant* be like? That's when the panic really hit home.

I leapt the fence and ran, ran like the devil was on my heels. Outside the zoo fence, I leapt onto my motorcycle and sped off, narrowly missing the police car which was just pulling up. I should have stopped to warn them. I feel bad that I didn't, but I was, quite frankly, terrified out of my wits.

I bought my gun at an all-night store, before the panic began. But it's been chaos in the three days since then. I have survived, but I'm not proud of it.

If it had just been the animals at the zoo, I think we could have contained this thing. The army could have used tanks and machine guns and we could probably have stopped them. But the elephants smashed down the walls of the zoo and almost all of the animals escaped. Lions, tigers, monkeys, buffalo, camels, kangaroos, you name it. All spreading the infection.

Whatever this thing is, it seems to affect all mammals. Well, all mammals except one particular species. There haven't been *any* reports of infected humans. But everything else. Cats. Dogs. Cows. Sheep. Horses. Pigs. When you think of all the animals we live with, or depend on, it's frightening. All of them with hysterical strength, nearly impermeable hides, and all of them bent on killing humans. It isn't just the random attacks of wild creatures. It seems like something is directing them, something with a very malevolent purpose.

Most people have fled the city, but I figured the city had to be safer than the countryside. I'm up here now at the top of this abandoned hotel, the stairwell door locked, furniture piled in front of it.

I was hoping to be safe, up this high. But just now I looked down out of the window and I know that I'm going to die soon.

The gibbons are coming after me.

September 2012

Ever After

ONCE UPON A TIME, there was a knock on my door.

It was late, almost midnight, and I had stayed up to correct homework from my English class at the local secondary school. I had been thinking sour thoughts as I went through the barely literate stack of essays on my desk. It was a hell of a come-down for someone like myself. At one time I had been a tenured professor at a major university. Now...

Then came the knock, and I straightened up in surprise. It was raining outside, raining hard. Who on earth would be visiting me so late on such a lousy night? It could hardly be someone collecting for a charity. And as for friends, well I didn't have any. The police? But why?

I went to the hallway and turned on the porch light. Then I opened the front door, leaving the wire security door still closed and latched. This was becoming a rough neighbourhood, and I took no chances.

It was a dwarf. Or, at least, someone very short. He had on a thin plastic raincoat, wrapped around his shoulders and dangling to his feet. No beard, but a grizzled stubble on his chin. On my covered porch he was now out of the rain, but water was still streaming down his face. He looked cold and thoroughly miserable.

"Dr Longman?" he asked in a hoarse voice. "Dr Andrew Longman?"

"Yes," I replied, completely puzzled.

But he persisted. "Dr Andrew Longman, author of *Conjectures*?"

At that, my heart sank. *That* book. That damned book, which had wrecked my career, split up my marriage, and almost completely destroyed my life. *That* book.

"What about it?" I snapped in anger. "And who the hell are you?"

"Dr Longman, I need your help. Your book... is a great work. I read it some months ago. I have travelled a long way to meet you, and I have something important to show you. I assure you that you will find it well worth your while." He coughed wetly. "Can we come in? It's damned cold out here."

"We?"

He looked up at me. "I have a... a friend with me. You might find him a little alarming at first. I assure you that he will not harm you."

By now I was thoroughly disturbed. "Let me see him," I said coldly. What on earth was going on here?

The little man called out. "Grong! Here!"

Around the corner of the house, where he must have been standing in the pouring rain, came the biggest man I had ever seen. He had an ugly, lumpy face, and was as tall as any basketball player. But unlike them he was bulky, somehow *thick* all over. He came up onto the porch wearing some kind of heavy greatcoat, streaming water. Together, the dwarf and this huge man made a ludicrous couple.

Reluctantly, I opened the security door. If there had been anyone in the house but myself, I wouldn't have done it. But my life was a mess, and the dwarf had me intrigued.

I led them into the kitchen, where they proceeded to drip water onto the tiled floor. The dwarf shucked off his raincoat and sat down at my kitchen table with a weary sigh, but the big man continued to stand. Truth to tell, he seemed too thick to be able to bend. He had ducked as he came through the door and now his head brushed the ceiling. "Food!" he said, in a deep, deep voice with a strange foreign accent. It was the first word he had spoken.

"Can you give him something?" asked the dwarf, apologetically. "He eats a lot, damn him."

I opened the refrigerator and took out a loaf of sliced bread and a one-pound chunk of cheese. Before I could set them down Grong plucked them from my hands, unwrapped and swallowed the cheese in two gulps, and then proceeded to grab handfuls of bread slices and stuff them into his mouth. I watched in amazement.

"He's an ogre," said the dwarf in a weary tone. And then, at my exclamation, he went on, "Yeah, I know, he's neither jolly nor green. He's the real thing. Acts as my bodyguard."

"*Bodyguard?* Why do you need...?"

The dwarf gave a shrug. "There are some people I'm trying to avoid. Debt collectors, you know the kind of thing."

I did, only too well. But I hadn't been able to afford a bodyguard. I noticed that despite his matter-of-fact tone the dwarf's hands were trembling on the table-top. Perhaps it was just the cold.

I shook my head. An ogre. Was this some kind of hoax? Five years ago, after the book came out, I could imagine someone trying to trick me like this, just for the laughs. But now? Now I was nothing. No-one around here even knew about the book, and I wanted to keep it that way.

"What's this all about?" I asked eventually. It sounded, and felt, weak. "Who are you two? What do you want?"

The dwarf rubbed the stubble on his chin and managed something like a smile, but it was fleeting. His eyes kept flicking nervously around the room. "You can call me Hans, if you like. You've met Grong. The reason we're here, the reason we came to find you, is that book you wrote, Dr Longman."

I was silent for a long while. "What about the book?" I said at last, when I had my anger under control.

"You wish you'd never written it," said the little man. "I can see that now. I'm surprised. It was a very good book, maybe a great book. Grong and me, we've been here for nearly a year now, without having much luck. But then I found your book in a discard bin. When I read it I knew that you were the man I had to talk to. Where I come from they would find it very interesting. You would be famous there."

"And where is that?" I was guessing somewhere in Eastern Europe. The dwarf had just the trace of an accent which could be Slavic, and the ... ogre... had sounded positively Russian.

Hans the dwarf shook his head. "Not yet. I'll tell you soon, but not yet. How would you explain your book, Doctor?" Again with the formal use of my title, one I never used myself these days. I shook my head. I was damned if I was going to give this little creep an opening to make a fool of me.

He laughed. Not a very cheerful laugh, a bitter laugh. "Very well," he said. "I'll tell you what I think it's about, and you can tell me where I'm wrong."

"*Conjectures on the Reality of Imagined Worlds*, that's the whole title, right?" I nodded, and he continued. "I didn't understand a lot of it. All that quantum stuff, I'd never heard about it before. But you said that your wiz... your scientists, they believe that there are an endless number of worlds, is that right?"

I don't understand much of the 'quantum stuff' myself. I am – or was – a psychology professor with a particular interest in literature and the creative writing process. I had picked up what I knew of quantum mechanics and cosmology from academic friends who worked in those disciplines.

"Yes," I said reluctantly. "Scientists have come to the conclusion that the universe is infinite. Some say that every possible decision, every possible random choice, is played out in every possible way in some parallel world."

"Dice," said little Hans. "I understand dice. Each time you throw a die, there are six different worlds created."

"Something like that," I said. I looked up at the huge Grong, who wasn't even listening. He had finished the entire loaf and was now looking hungry again.

"And so in your book, you say that every possible world, *even imagined worlds*, even those in your literature, your drama, must really exist somewhere, and so must every imagined event?" Hans was eager now, his eyes gleaming.

"Yes, provided those worlds and events are physically possible, of course."

Hans sat back and gave a short, harsh laugh. "You would be surprised, Doctor, about just what is physically possible." He seemed to have lost his nervousness for the moment. "And your book, it was popular?"

Popular? It had been published initially in a small run by my university's academic press, but then it was picked up by a mainstream publisher. I hadn't checked the contract closely enough and despite my protests the book was reprinted with a racy title and a lurid cover. It became an instant best-seller, and made me a laughing stock among my academic peers. As a result, soon after, I lost my job and couldn't find another. My wife left me, citing the book in the divorce papers. And I came here, to this remote rural town, where no one had heard of me or the book.

"Yes, it was popular, for a while," I said grimly. "But most people laughed at me. Said that I was trying to show that fairy tales were real."

Hans was silent, but a huge grin spread slowly across his face. I stared at him in growing astonishment, and then up at the looming form of the ogre. The ogre.

"No," I said weakly.

"No? You don't even believe in your own ideas? I am disappointed." He leaned forward. "But what if I could offer you proof, real, tangible proof, Doctor? What then?"

My throat was dry, and my head was spinning. It couldn't be true. "What kind of proof?"

"Certain... artefacts. I was a collector of sorts. Yes, a collector." He seemed pleased with the word. But then, as suddenly as a cloud passing over the sun, his face sagged and his nervousness returned. He glanced around, edgily, and then went on.

"There are ways of travelling between the worlds that you discuss in your book, Doctor. I found one of those ways, and Grong and I came here, to your world. I had hope to sell some of my collection here, but I have not been able to find a buyer who will take me seriously."

Here it comes, I thought, with a sinking feeling. The sting. The demand for money.

"Hans," I said, "I am a poor man. The book ruined me. It sold well at first, but I lost my job and all of the profit from the book went as part of the divorce settlement. I can't buy whatever it is that you are selling."

The dwarf nodded seriously. "Yes, I found that out about you. But I can make you famous, make those who laughed at you eat their words – that is the phrase, yes? I will allow you to prove your ideas. And then, when your *new* book comes out there will be a demand, a clamour for items from my world. This is why I need your help."

"What sort of proof?" I asked again. "What sort of artefacts?"

He smiled broadly. "Grong," he called out. "Go get the stuff."

It was still raining outside, but it was slackening off. Grong lumbered outside and we watched him from the front porch. Around the corner, almost out of sight of the house in a side street, was a beaten-up old panel truck, painted black. "You drive that?" I asked.

Hans shrugged. "No, my legs are too short. Grong drives. Very badly. He does not, of course, have one of your licenses. We have been lucky so far. Before the truck, we had a wagon. But the horse died."

Grong returned, carrying a huge wooden crate effortlessly under one arm. We went back inside, to my lounge room. At Hans' command, Grong said the crate down on the carpet. With his bare hands, he pulled off the nailed-down lid as though he were a child tearing open a cereal packet. Inside the crate were a dozen packages of various shapes, each wrapped in rough cloth.

I sat down, my legs suddenly weak. The dwarf leaned over the crate and pulled out one of the packages, which I now saw had labels sewn onto their wrappings, in a language I didn't know.

The dwarf struggled with the large bundle as he unwrapped it.

It was an oval mirror, with a golden frame. The reflections it made were murky and strange.

"A magic mirror," said Hans. "The very one which Snow White's step-mother had on her wall."

I laughed out loud. This was really too ludicrous for words. A hoax, then, after all. For a while I had been starting to believe this absurd little man. It was actually a disappointment.

"And if I ask it 'Who's the fairest of them all', what will it say?" I asked sarcastically.

Hans did not smile. "The enchantment has gone for now," he said. "But come now, Doctor. It is no ordinary mirror, is it?"

There *was* something very odd about the way it was reflecting the light. And the elaborate gold ornamentation was unlike anything I had ever seen before in any culture. I shook my head, though, unconvinced. "What else do you have?"

He pulled out another bundle, a smaller one this time. Unwrapped, I saw that it was a wooden harp, with an angelic figure carved into the column and crown.

"The singing harp which Jack stole from the castle he reached after climbing the beanstalk," Hans said proudly. I opened my mouth to once again express my unbelief, but Hans strummed the strings of the harp. And suddenly the harp began to play itself, and the carved figure came to life and began to sing.

It was astonishingly beautiful, and unlike any music or song I had ever heard before. The little wooden face moved smoothly as its mouth shaped the foreign words. I sat there with my mouth agape for a long while, until the beautiful music had ceased and the harp was once again still.

I started to speak, but my voice failed me. I tried again. "How did you get this?" I croaked out at last.

Hans looked sly. "Jack himself died some years ago. I... acquired... the harp from his widow."

I wasn't sure that I dared to look at the other things in the crate. I found that my hands were shaking. If these things were real... then Hans was right. I could reveal them, convince the sceptics who had laughed at my ideas. I would be famous. And Hans would make a fortune auctioning off these items. "How much... how many things do you have?"

He shrugged. "Another three crates. Lots of things, of various value. The seven-yard length of Rapunzel's hair that the witch cut off. Two pairs of seven-league boots. The belt made by the valiant little tailor, reading 'Seven With One Blow'. Cinderella's glass slippers, one of them unfortunately with a broken heel."

I could see that he was prepared to go on cataloguing his whole collection, like some shady auctioneer tallying off the lots in his sale room.

"But," I said, "people will claim that these things are just clever fakes, some kind of mechanism in the harp, for instance. Don't you have anything which *couldn't* be a fake?"

Hans shuddered a little, and gave a sigh. He was agitated again, glancing out of the window at the dark night. "I do have something," he said slowly, "but it is dramatic, and might attract unwelcome attention." He sighed again. "But I thought it might be necessary to use them." He reached into his pocket and brought out a small cloth bag. Out of it, he spilled a handful of dried beans.

"You don't mean...?"

"Yes. I tracked down the little old man who bought the cow from Jack with beans like these. We will use one of them, but you will have to be quick. We cannot allow the plant to grow tall. Do you have an axe?"

We went into my back garden and I fetched the axe I use for chopping wood. It was still raining, but lightly now. Hans held up one of the beans, paused, and then plunged it into the soil.

Almost instantly, a green shoot pushed up through the ground, twisting and thickening as it rose. It was unbelievable how quickly it was growing and how tall it was becoming. I could hear Hans yelling at me, but I was paralysed, shocked. Then, as the beanstalk rose above the roof of my house, Grong the ogre seized the axe from my limp hands and chopped hard at the stalk, blow after blow until the shaft was severed and the huge beanstalk toppled. It smashed my garden shed to pieces and broke down my back fence with a smash.

Open-mouthed, I stood looking at the wreckage, wondering bizarrely how I would explain this to my insurance company.

"I told you," said the dwarf in an angry voice, "to be *quick*. Is this proof enough?"

I could only nod, speechless. We went back inside and I poured myself a large whisky, gulped it down with shaking hands. It was true, then. All true. My book was validated. I would be famous, perhaps even rich, I remember thinking. Maybe my wife would even come back to me.

That was before we heard the thumping.

The first thumps were in the distance, and at first I thought it was thunder, but it was felt through the ground and not the air. The glasses in my bar cabinet rattled against each other.

Hans, who had been lying back in one of my armchairs, sat up in sudden alarm. "Grong!" he called out. "Go look!"

The thumping kept coming, getting stronger, getting louder. Grong stomped to my front door and pulled it open. It had been locked, but he wrenched it open regardless, without even noticing the splintering of wood as the lock tore loose.

Cursing inwardly at this further damage, I went to join the huge man at the now open door. Hans hopped off his armchair and followed us.

The thumps now shook the whole house. Down the dark street, I could see a car's alarm had been set off, heard its insistent honking and saw its lights flashing. And in the brief flashes of yellow light, I saw something like a moving tree. *Two* moving trees. Were they... could they be *legs*?

As I watched, the shape reached a street light, bending it over as it brushed by. But before it failed I could see a huge figure. A man with legs like great tree trunks, a man as tall as any dinosaur. A giant. And on his shoulders rode several smaller figures.

"Grong!" cried Hans. "It's them! They've *found* us!" He shook the big man's arm, but Grong seemed to be frozen on the spot. Hans cursed in a language I didn't know. "That damned beanstalk! I knew it was a bad idea! Grong!"

"Who... what?" I managed, as Grong finally moved, his eyes wide and rolling with a kind of ogre-ish terror.

"Who do you think?" the dwarf spat out angrily. "The people I stole the stuff from, of course! Grong! Curse you! You have to *protect* me!"

Grong finally was galvanized into action. He bent down and simply picked up Hans and shoved him under one arm. He lumbered into the lounge room, seized the open crate and tucked it under his other arm, and kept going out into the back yard.

I was stupefied, but before I could make a move, there came a great crash from out front. The giant had arrived, far quicker than I had guessed it could. The crash was the noise it made stepping on to my car, squashing it flat.

The giant spoke in a voice so deep it rattled my teeth.

"*Fee!*" it said.

"*Fo!*" it said.

"*Fie!*" it said

"*Fum!*" it said.

It stepped onto my front porch. Not into, *onto*. The porch was smashed into ruin before my eyes, and I started to run.

I ran out the back, just in time to see Grong running along the length of the fallen beanstalk, over the smashed fence, and into the woods beyond.

I would have followed them, but two steps into my yard I slipped and fell face-first onto the muddy ground.

Behind me I heard an awful noise of destruction, and then a vast foot thumped down, only inches away from my face. All I could see was an enormous boot and felt the impact in every molecule of my body. Then a second foot came down, half-way to the fence, then the first foot lifted and went on, crashing heavily through the trees, following Hans and Grong.

I lay there, quite still, for half an hour or more, as the crashing became more and more distant. I wondered, quite idly, as I lay there in some kind of shock, whether the two would escape.

Eventually, I pushed myself up and wiped off some of the mud. I looked back at the house. Not much of it was left.

As I stood there, I realised something, with a kind of dead feeling.

I wasn't going to live happily ever after.

March 2012

Nereid

Underwater, she dreams.

Her sky is made of silver, and her stars are made of foam.

She dreams.

Into the peace of her dream comes suddenly a great dark shape, cleaving the heavens above! It passes in bare moments, leaving behind it a tormented trail.

And with it a strange creature, thrashing as it falls from the sky into her domain. Into *her* domain! In her dream she remembers her outrage, tastes it anew.

She seizes it and holds it still, despite its desperate thrashing. Now she sees it is a mere mortal, a man, fallen into her realm by chance and not design. She holds its face close and gazes deeply upon it. It is dying. Dying. Such is the fate of such beings, so she is told. Shortly it will enter the long blackness that, for her, is not fated except by choice.

Dreaming of it now, she remembers the slow access of a strange emotion roused in her by the creature. Angered, half-disgusted, half-pitying, she thrusts it up, up, up into the sky from where it came. It thrashes more, but as the moments pass it seems to calm.

She returns to her realm, leaving the man embedded in the surging sky. Then comes the cleaving shape once more, and at last the invader is gone.

Underwater, she dreams beneath a sky of silver.
She dreams, and longs for his return.

November 2011

His Potent Art

The Islander

HE HAD BEEN THE LONELY KING OF THIS ISLAND before the Enemy came. All alone, the only one of his kind, but master of all that he surveyed.

The island met his every need, fed him, provided him with drinking water, gave him shelter and comfort. And it fed his inner needs as well, for the island was beautiful, and full of birdsong.

But he had been alone. Never hearing another human voice, never seeing another human face. Sometimes he imagined faces in the rocks, or in the trunks of trees, but they never spoke to him, unless it was in the splash of the waves or the creaking of tree boughs in the wind, a language he could not comprehend.

There once had been a human face: his mother's. He remembered her, but not well, for she was now long dead. Most of all he remembered her bitterness, remembered how often she had told him of the treatment she had received at the hands of her country-folk. Wise in herbal lore, knowledgeable in the ways of the human body, all she had tried to do was help others, help them heal, to gain strength. Oh, and for the young girls in trouble, she had often given special relief. And for that she had been called a witch, banished — for they dared not kill her —

marooned on this foreign shore, this island in the midst of a vast empty sea.

In lonely travail she had given birth to him, raised him as a child for a handful of years. Then she in turn marooned her child in loneliness by dying. Since then, there had only been himself.

Until the Enemy came.

They should have been alike, he and the Enemy. Like his long-dead mother, the Enemy too had been banished and cast adrift at sea.

He remembered only too well the joy he had felt when he had first seen that boat at sea, coming closer to the shore. Barely afloat, with no mast or oar, it drifted helplessly. He had run along the shore, hopping from rock to rock to keep pace with the boat. Lying inside, there was a man, holding close some kind of bundle wrapped in cloth.

When the boat had inevitably shattered on the rocks, it was he who had waded out and dragged the man and what he carried to shore. Inside the bundle, amazingly, had been a child, barely more than a baby. Unsure what to do with such a thing, he had put it down on the shore high above the waves and then waded out to fetch, one by one, the chests now floating near the wreck of the boat.

He had expected thanks. Had been full of joy at the presence of another human being — a real human face at last! Here would be a friend, a companion, someone to relieve his lonely existence.

But that was not the Enemy's way.

He had brought food and water to the castaway, tended his wounds, made a safe place for him and the child, tried to speak to him, but was not understood. Still, he had persevered, used signs to show them the isle and all its resources, done his best to help him, make of him a friend.

Yet it was not to be. Once the man had recovered his strength, he had become cold, harsh. He became the Enemy.

The Enemy had carved himself a strange staff from a tree branch. And one day the Enemy had raised the staff at him and spoken a powerful command: from that moment he had been the Enemy's slave.

In the long weary years since, he had seen the child grow, and grow. He had never seen a girl child before, seen no woman other than his long-distant mother. Now the girl, growing older, achieved a shape, a look, which threw him into vast confusion. What longing he felt!

He could not be blamed. It was not his fault that he felt this way, how could it be? Always under the Enemy's lash, forced to fetch and carry and clean, with never a friendly word. Except from her. How could he help from feeling the way he did when she spoke even a single kindly word to him?

How could he have stopped himself from reaching out...?

THE OLD MAN

THE OLD MAN LOOKED SUSPICIOUSLY AT THE SHAMBLING FIGURE coming up the path through the forest. He should have killed him years ago, put an end to the danger instead of trying to raise the creature and make him useful. Was it pity that had stayed his hand, or something else? The old man shook his head, trying to dismiss the unwelcome thought.

From the moment he had opened his eyes on the shore and seen the ugly dark face bending over him, he had been alert to the danger. He had heard stories enough of the horrors perpetrated by the natives of foreign lands on unwary strangers.

From the very first, then, he had seen the need to keep the savage under his strict control. Because, after all, there was his child to consider, his little daughter. She was all he had of his former life. Cast away on this vile shore, full of despair and anger, his child was all that kept him rooted in civilisation, all that stopped him from dashing himself from the highest peak he could find.

He had raised her as best he could in this remote place, taught her her letters, passed on what knowledge he could from his precious books.

If it hadn't been for the arts he had learned during his long studies he would never been able to supply their needs. Never been able to bend the brutish savage to his will.

Now his daughter was grown. Grown into a lovely young woman, almost the image of his long-dead wife. And he had seen the growing lust in the savage's eye, seen him turn again and again towards the girl, gaping slack-jawed at her beauty.

And then had come the attempted rape.

He should have killed the brute at that moment, he thought. If not at the start, then certainly then, when he found him pawing at his daughter.

Why had he not? The old man's hand twitched on the staff he held. There was a reason, he knew... a reason he did not want to admit, even to himself. Something he knew he enjoyed too much. No matter how hard to tried to hide it, to deny it, deep inside he knew that could not resist it.

It was the joy of having another creature completely at his command, abject.

"Caliban!" he called out, in secret pleasure. "Come here!"

July 2012

The Ancient Seed

THE DAY AFTER HER MONTHLY TIME HAD GONE, she rose in the dark morning and went to bathe in the sacred pool. Winter was barely past: she gasped as she forced herself to enter the bitter cold of the water, and her breath came in clouds of steam. When the ordeal was over, she dried herself with a piece of coarse linen.

Here, where there was none to hear, she sometimes sang soft tuneless songs to herself, her voice striking harmonies from the stone around her. But not this morning. She dressed quickly in her long white shift and went outside to meet the dawn.

It was dark still, and there were still stars. But in the north, her eye was caught by a far distant spark of red and orange. A forest fire? Surely it was still too cold for that. She frowned, and turned away.

She was called Sibyl, as all those before her had been named. Perhaps once she had been given a name of her own, but she no longer remembered what it might have been. This Sibyl had yet to pass her twentieth summer: the old Sibyl had died early.

She sat on the hard tripod between the columns of the temple, facing out over the city, shivering a little and scowling for a moment at the discomfort and the cold. From time to time she looked towards the north, still puzzled by the distant fire.

The dark of the sky became grey, and the grey became light, until at last the rays of the sun struck the tops of the shattered towers and plated them with ephemeral gold. Still Sibyl sat.

The people would just now be rising, and soon, when they found that this was the day of the Oracle, the crowds would gather.

The city elders came on age-wounded feet up the length of the main street, and stood together in grim silence before Sibyl. The people followed. She waited. When the crowd had become restless and began to shuffle its many feet, Sibyl raised a hand, and quiet descended once more. The elders looked among themselves to find who would speak first. A bald-headed ancient limped forward.

"Sibyl," he began, his voice like a trembling reed. "The winter has been hard. Can the Oracle say when the crops should be planted. and if there should be a sacrifice?"

Sibyl nodded, very slightly: "It shall be asked."

The next to stand forward was a tall man, one whom age had not yet stooped. His voice was firm. "Sibyl, there is talk of rebuilding the Tower of Signs. Can the Oracle say if this should be done, and how we must prepare for this task?"

"It shall be asked."

There was some talk between the elders before the third and final question was asked. Waiting, Sibyl sighed very softly. There would be much work to do beneath the temple before these questions could be answered. There would be little time to sit and watch the sun on the city, or the children playing outside the temple. Little time for anything.

In the north, now that the day was here, she could see no fire. But she fancied there was the faintest threadlike plume that could be smoke. She frowned again.

The Eldest was being brought forward. supported by others younger, stronger than himself. His voice was the rustling whisper of a cricket.

"Sibyl ...we have news ... news of a barbarian with a great horde ... his army. He has conquered ...many lands to the north...." The old one stopped and gathered his breath again. "Now he is sweeping south ...plundering and looting. Should he attack this country ... we would fall before him.... Can the Oracle say ... say ... what should be done?" He closed his eyes and muttered to himself.

Sibyl sat quietly, trying to absorb the meaning of the words she had heard. She glanced to the north, thinking of killings and burnings. Surely the barbarian could not be so close? She roused herself and spoke the empty words: "It shall be asked." The crowd sighed, and began to disperse.

She stood and walked to the doors of the temple. They were bronze, and worked with ancient and cryptic symbols. Inside, she strained against their weight to close them, shutting off the bright sun like an eclipse. The only light streamed down from two narrow slits above the doors, spotlighting the random movement of thousands of motes of dust. Sibyl leant against the comforting bulk of the doors. The last question had so alarmed her that the first two had almost left her mind, and she was forced to rehearse them to herself so that she would not forget. The crops, of course, and the tower. And this barbarian!

Still brooding, she walked through the empty corridors of the temple, her bare feet ringing echoes from the stone. Warm in her hand, where it had been all morning since she had retrieved it from its hiding place in the pool, was the key to the door of the Oracle.

She came to the door in the shadow of an archway. Once there had been something written on its iron face, but time and rust had hidden it. Sibyl turned the key in the lock, and swung open the door. There was a dark space, with steps leading down. She descended, closing the door and moving in thick darkness, her feet remembering the steps. Her hands met another door, always unlocked. She pushed, and went in.

The blackness was studded with firefly lights, and the silence overlaid with an endless purring like that of a cat. Sibyl waited as her eyes grew used to the dark.

The purring and the flickering lights surrounded her, and took her in. Sibyl was careful to control her breathing, careful not to make a noise. Here in the presence of God, nothing must be done that should not be done. Slowly, she moved forward, hands out, feeling her way in the dark, until she reached a point in the centre of the lights and the noise. There was a chair, and a level bench before a blank area of the wall: the Altar. She sat down, breathing faster now.

She placed her hands on the dimly seen bench. There were separate raised surfaces there, each bearing one of the symbols of the holy language. Following ritual, she pressed them in turn, and on the wall before her words appeared in letters of green fire:

"Hail Oracle, Instrument of God."

And God spoke.

Spoke with the terrible voice of the Oracle; deep, calm, and without emotion. A voice which did not echo, yet was all around, and came from no point in space. Hearing, Sibyl trembled, as she always trembled, and looked down. The Oracle had spoken but one word:

Ready.

It was usual to ask the Oracle the three questions in the order that the Elders had given, but today, such was Sibyl's distress, against her plans she found herself spelling out the question about the barbarian. The burning green words hung before her like an accusation. And then the Oracle spoke once more.

Insufficient information, it said, and Sibyl gave a silent sigh, knowing that her long hours of work now began. *Require strength of barbarian army. Require distance of barbarian army. Require location of countries occupied.* Then the silence came back into the room as Sibyl thought.

She began tapping out symbols on the panel again. On the wall, her words appeared. "O Oracle, your servant shall ask the names of the countries the barbarian has taken. Your servant does not know if it is known how many men the barbarian has in his army."

There was the briefest of pauses, and then the voice spoke again: *Require map. Require population of countries occupied.*

"It shall be done, O Oracle."

She left the room then, and emerged, blinking, into the world of light. To her darkness-accustomed eyes, everything seemed washed out, unreal. It was always this way. There were times when she thought the only real world was the one down there, with the Oracle in the dark. But she shook off these thoughts, and went to seek someone to carry a message to the Elders. She found a ragged child playing in the dust outside the temple, and gave him a paper. The child's eyes were round and fearful, but he nodded his head of tangled hair, and ran to do as he was bid.

Sibyl sat on the tripod outside the temple, waiting. It was now past noon, and her stomach complained the fast. The first day was always the worst.

She had expected the boy to return with a message from the Elders, but instead, one of the ancient ones themselves came haltingly down the street, and bowed before Sibyl. He carried a scroll under his arm. Looking down on him, Sibyl asked, "Do you have the knowledge that the Oracle has sought?"

The old man looked up. "I have brought what is known. And a later report, Sibyl. There is no doubt that the barbarian is marching on this land. He may be only days distant."

Her heart jumped within her at that, and she looked to the northern horizon. There was no sign there now, but somewhere there the barbarian rode. But the Oracle God would advise them. It had always been so.

The Elder came slowly up the steps and handed the scroll to Sibyl. She opened it, and he pointed out the marks he had made. It was a rough map of the countries surrounding them. A red line like a scar marked the progress of the barbarian, and small figures estimated the population of the countries he had overtaken. The scar drew steadily downwards toward the City. Sibyl, unable to speak, nodded, and sent the Elder back.

Suddenly she was afraid to descend into the room of the Oracle. She wanted to be here, in the light and the warming sun, so that the brightness of the day could drive away her fear. In the dark, she knew, her fear would emerge like the creatures of the night, and devour her. So she sat still on the steps, watching the sun descend towards evening.

As she sat, a dog came yapping by, followed by a crowd of dusty children chasing it with sticks and ball. And later, the women came by with their washing, talking amongst themselves and looking shyly up at Sibyl, and then away.

No one ever looks at me, thought Sibyl. It's always that brief glance, and then the averted eyes. So it is to be touched by God.

When the sun hid behind the tallest buildings, Sibyl arose, stiff from sitting, and re-entered the bronze doors, carrying the map. There was duty to be done.

Underneath the temple, the darkness of the Oracle swallowed her, and took her in. Her fingers, as she laid them on the symbols of the altar, were trembling and hesitant.

The Oracle spoke: *This represents the land surrounding the Centre. Use the stylus to show the path of the barbarian.*

The picture that came up on the wall before Sibyl was far richer than any map. The colours were sparkling blue where the sea lay, and a blending of browns and greens on the land. The mountains were outlined with the white of snow. But there were no boundaries between the nations shown on the picture. Sibyl took the stylus and pointed these out, working from the map that the Elder had brought. As she moved the stylus, yellow lines appeared on the picture. Then she marked in the path of the barbarian in bright red. The Oracle asked for the populations of the countries, and these she gave, adding that these were but guesses.

There was silence in the dark room, and Sibyl knew that the Oracle was thinking. And that was a small blasphemy, for should not God know all without thought? But the space of time was very brief, and then the calm, empty voice spoke again:

If the barbarian has conquered the northern countries, he will conquer this country. There are not enough men. There are not enough weapons. His army has many men. His army has many weapons.

Sibyl sat in silence. Then she tapped out on the Altar: "What shall we do?"

The answer came back instantly: *The Centre shall be closed, and the doors secured. Personnel will stay below ground.*

"But what about the city?" Sibyl asked.

The voice seemed cold, uncaring: *Instructions may be issued to evacuate the population of the city by sea. On no account shall the population of the city be allowed access to the Centre.*

By the Centre, the Oracle meant the temple. She knew that, and that it was the centre of Godhead in this land. It must be protected at all cost. But surely there was something she could do for the people of the city?

She thought. The other questions that the elders had asked now seemed irrelevant, trivial. She had been right after all to ask about the barbarian first. She stood up. She would have to go to warn the people, tell those that could to flee.

—

The days seemed few before the morning when Sibyl woke and looked to the north and saw again the sign she had been expecting and dreading. Smoke. Now it was black and drifting, and very close. People's homes were burning, women were being raped, and children slaughtered. And this city was next.

She went out that morning, sat on the tripod for the first time in weeks, and waited for the barbarian to come. Behind her, the great bronze doors were locked. She had taken the key, locked the doors from the outside, and tossed the key into the temple through one of the small openings above the doors.

Though the Oracle had commanded her to remain within the temple, she could not spare herself the fate of the people of the city.

Now there were no children running in the street in play. Now there were no women giggling on their way to wash. Now there was only the hot sun, and the random breeze. Many of the people had left, but many more had not. Those left were all inside the stone buildings, their doors bolted, cowering before the might of the invader.

And so the barbarian came to the city. She saw the dust first, raised by the weary feet of his great army. And in the dust there was the glinting of brass, and on the wind the sound of metal on metal, and a voice cursing.

They came, and they came, and they were legion. They came past the temple, in ranks, and they looked at Sibyl and jeered and made obscene gestures. But none approached her. That was for another to do.

The barbarian, dressed in royal purples and wearing a helmet of gold, came riding in on a dusty, tired white horse, and stopped before Sibyl. He waited, as the noise and the dust fell to earth.

In the silence then, he took off his helmet and looked straight at Sibyl, sitting on the tripod at the top of the steps of the temple.

He was not young, the barbarian. Grey touched his temples and grizzled his stubble beard. There was a tiredness about him which seemed to rest in his eyes. He looked at Sibyl and at the temple for a long time before speaking. He seemed to gaze very long at the inscription carved above the doors of the temple, words which Sibyl had been unable ever to understand.

When he spoke, a sudden shock ran through Sibyl, for the words were in the holy tongue of the Oracle. "Well," he said, "thank God! Here at last."

But his next words were those of the common people: "You, wench, priestess, whatever you are, open those doors!"

Sibyl said, "I shall not." Her voice surprised her by its calm.

One of the soldiers, pike in hand, ran up the steps towards her, but a word from the barbarian called him back.

"Girl," said the barbarian, "I've travelled further than you can know to get here. I'm not going to be stopped now. Either you open those doors, or we shall break them down."

"Then break them down you must," said Sibyl, "for the doors are locked, and the key is within."

The look on the barbarian's face was sour. He said nothing, but motioned to his ragged army. Within minutes, a group of men were ranged around a huge log of wood, the trunk of a tree. The barbarian strode up the steps to Sibyl. Still he was silent, but he took her with a firm grip and dragged her from the tripod. Though she screamed and tried to bite him, it was to no avail. The barbarian kicked the tripod clattering down the stone steps. Sibyl was suddenly quiet. There was nothing to be done.

The soldiers came up the steps with the battering ram. It was not a good place to wield such an object. They could gain no speed coming up the steps, and they were reduced to swinging the beam back and forth with all the strength they could muster. The ram hit the bronze doors with a sound like a gong. Again and again. The doors did not yield.

It was then that one of the soldiers lost his temper, and stepped forward to beat his fist against the doors. As his hand touched the metal, there was a searing flash like lightning, and the man dropped and rolled down the stairs. There was a sudden hush among the army. One of the soldiers prodded with his foot at the body of the man. The fallen one did not move. The soldier looked up at the barbarian, his foot still at the body. The barbarian was grim, but he motioned for the battering to continue. "Just don't touch that door," he said. "It's electrified." A shudder went through the men at the sound of the foreign word. Only Sibyl recognised it as a word from the holy tongue, and she did not know its meaning.

The sound of wood against metal rang again and again over the empty city. Sibyl sagged in the arms of her captors. God had struck one of their number down by lightning, but the fate He was reserving for the barbarian chief had yet to be revealed.

At last, under one final lurch of the battering ram, the doors of the temple burst open, letting light into the darkness. The barbarian lifted Sibyl up, and brought her face close to his. She could smell his breath. His eyes were reddened.

"Now, girl," he said. "Now you shall take me to the computer."

"I shall not take you to the Oracle," Sibyl said, but her voice was trembling, and her eyes turned away from his.

He shook her, as a child might shake a doll. Her head rocked painfully back. He forced her eyes to meet his.

"Do you know, girl," he said, in a hard, even voice, "I was alive when this Centre was built? Over a thousand years ago, that was. Yes," he repeated, as Sibyl's eyes showed disbelief, "a millennium ago it was, that I left this earth with the others. All dead now, except me."

Her voice was the barest whisper. "Are you then risen from the dead?"

He laughed.

He picked her up and carried her inside the temple, and kicked the twisted metal doors closed behind him.

"Einstein!" he said, as he carried her. "Einstein, that's who I've got to curse. A thousand years for you, ten for me. And another ten on this ruined planet while I built my army. Ten hard, damned years. To get here."

He set her down roughly by the pool, and stood looking around him with triumph in his eyes.

"You shall not enter the room of the Oracle," she said, making her voice as determined as she could. "Better that you kill me first than that. None but the priestess has entered the presence of the Oracle for these last twenty-five generations."

The barbarian gave a harsh laugh. "Damn your superstitions! But without them, I suppose this Centre would no longer be here. All right," he said. "I don't know how to speak to the Oracle, anyway. I'll let you find out what I want. But I shall be here with my sword and, if you do not return soon enough, I'll follow you, Oracle or not."

Sibyl looked up at him, and saw him draw his sword. It was dark with blood from the taking of the city. She nodded.

The barbarian gave a grim smile. "Then I'll tell you what I seek, and why I've come so far and killed so many to reach here. . . ." He sat down on a broken stone at the edge of the sacred pool, and spat into the water.

"Yes," said Sibyl, looking into her lap, "your path is lined with blood."

The barbarian swung his arm suddenly and pain smashed into her face, and she was knocked to the floor. The pain was like fire, and she tasted blood. The barbarian was on his feet, and she heard him through the ringing in her ears. "Damn you, you bitch!" he said. He hauled her up from her face, and shook her again. He knelt so his face was level with hers.

"Damn you! You don't know what I've gone through! To be out there ... out among the stars, my God! And then to come back, and find everything gone... everything that we'd ever striven for over the centuries, all the power, all the science... I came back, and it was all gone, forgotten. You can't know how I felt!"

Sibyl tried to speak, but her mouth was bruised, and at first she could only mumble. Her heart ran mad within her breast. She tried again. "And for this loss, you have slaughtered thousands of men and their wives and children!" Her eyes were bright, and they held his gaze fixed.

He raised his fist as though to strike her again, but stopped. His face was red with rage and passion. He shook her shoulders. "It's my destiny, can't you see that? It had to be, my coming back just now. I have the knowledge to rebuild this world, to bring back the old times!"

Wanting to keep silent, but unable to do so, Sibyl said, "And this new world you will build, will you not remember that it is founded on the dead?" Her voice was bitter, defeated.

"Damn!" he said, and pushed her, so that she fell back to lie on the stone. He leant over her, trapping her with his arms. He seemed to be trying to control himself. "Damn you!" he said and, with a quick, savage motion, he tore at the front of her shift, so that it ripped from her. She felt his rough hands on her, and saw the growing lust in his eyes. She knew, even as he fumbled at her, that she was not strong enough to resist him.

Then there was pain, and she cried out. After a moment, so did he.

—

After it was over, she lay unmoving for what seemed a long time, trying to sort out the feelings that battled within her. No more tears came, for she seemed to have exhausted their source. Her mind ran over and over what had happened to her, and again she felt herself touched and violated. She shook her head with the pain and shame, and sat herself up. She still seemed to feel the barbarian within her, and she brushed her hand against her face, trying to wipe away the non existent tears.

The barbarian sat on the other side of the pool, facing away from her. He was cleaning and polishing his sword with a bloodied rag. She must have made a noise, for he turned and looked towards her. His eyes would not meet hers. There was a long silence. "I didn't...." he said at last, and then stopped and began again. "You must ask the computer what I need to know," he said harshly, too loud. He waved his bright sword to emphasise his words. Sibyl, knowing he held her utterly in his power, nodded dumbly.

He sprang up, and began pacing back and forth across the stone. "You have to understand why I have to do this ... to rebuild things," he said, avoiding her gaze. "It's as though ... I feel as if I were a seed which has been kept stored somewhere, hidden away for a thousand years, and only brought out again into the light once everything has become a desert. Once planted, that seed can make the desert a forest again ...do you see? That is my purpose in life; that's what I've waited and worked for." He stroked his thinning hair back with an agitated

hand. "I'm telling you this because I want you to understand..."
He looked towards her and saw no acceptance. He started to
pace again, his eyes on the stone walls.

"I was lucky... No, damn it, I was meant to find it! I found a
cache of written records telling me about this Centre, and of
another place south, over the mountains. There are weapons
there, and much of the old knowledge in store." He turned to
her again, imploring her with his hands to understand. Sibyl
looked at him, and felt only hate. She hardly heard his words.

"If I hadn't come now, this Centre here, and the store of
knowledge... it might have crumbled away. But now..." He
stared fiercely at her, daring her to object, but then his eyes slid
away from hers, and a brief frown crossed his brow. "I might
need to use force at first, some of the weapons, to bring things
back under my command. There are some powerful nations
over the sea. But I shall do it."

His dreams have driven him mad, thought Sibyl. There have
been many others in our history with that madness.

The barbarian sat down beside Sibyl again. She shrank away
from him, and he put out a hand towards her as if to stop her,
but dropped it back to his side. His face was weary. He went on,
forcing his words out. "This store," he said, "it was once an army
base, I think. It may be very hard to get in. There may be
safeguards, even traps. But your computer will be able to tell
me what to do to get in. Do you understand?"

Sibyl, wearier than he, nodded. She found herself unable to
trust herself to speak. She swallowed, thought again of his
rough hands on her skin, of him thrusting within her, and
trembled. At last she said, "You wish me to ask the Oracle how
you may enter this store."

"That's it," he said.

"It shall be asked," she said, and rose.

She took off her torn shift, ignoring his gaze, for that mattered nothing now, and waded into the sacred pool. She felt about, and found the key, and stepped out dripping. She draped the shift over her still wet body, and went to the door that led to the Oracle. "You must stay here," she said, and descended into the dark. And the dark welcomed her.

In the soft dark, in the womb filled with firefly lights and the purring of an absent cat, she spoke silently to the Oracle. And the Oracle answered.

—

Each morning she rose and looked to the south, over the mountains, to where the barbarian and his army had marched. The barbarian had left carrying the scroll that the Oracle had made, bearing the plans of the store. She had pointed out to him the path he must take within the store, and the things he must do. It had been very easy. Now she waited.

She had become aware of another thing in the many days that had passed since the barbarian had entered the temple, and the Oracle had confirmed her guess. So now she waited, for a greater fulfilment of destiny than the barbarian had imagined.

She had risen early this morning, filled with a premonition. The mountains were high, and the pass was difficult. It would have taken long for the barbarian to reach the store.

She went outside to sit on the tripod, looking into the south. The mountains were blue with distance, but their peaks were gilded by the rising sun. There was a softness and a quiet in the morning, and somewhere a bird was singing.

Then it began. Another, whiter sun rose in the south, behind the mountains, swelling and growing until it became like a snow-covered tree. And it seemed to Sibyl that there were lightnings flickering about the tree. It grew and grew until it touched the clouds, and then the sound arrived. A vast crash, like heaven falling, like the sky shattering. So loud that Sibyl had to cover her ears and hold them tight against the pain of the noise. And then the earth shook, and the buildings rattled, and some stones fell.

God had spoken.

The people, running about the streets in a panic, gradually came to the steps of the temple beneath where Sibyl sat. The crowd grew, until all of the people were there, looking up, waiting for Sibyl to explain, to hear the will of God.

She turned at last, and spoke to them.

"God has taken vengeance on the barbarian. He will conquer no more."

A mutter, and then a gabble came from the crowd, and eyes were turned to the sign in the south, where the sky still glowed.

Sibyl rose. "There will be no more days of the Oracle this year. But the Oracle has spoken. Soon a new prophet will be born to you, greater than any before, and he will lead this people to greatness and might."

And she turned and went into the temple, to await the flowering of the ancient seed.

January 1978

This story was first published in an anthology called *Transmutations* edited by Rob Gerrand and published by Outback Press in 1979

Yggdrasil

Deep, deep, run the roots of this tree,
deep into three worlds.
High, high grow its branches,
winding through many heavens.

Upon its bulk rest all the worlds.

Upon this tree hung Odin, all-father,
for nine long days and nights.
Half-blind, pierced with his own spear,
sacrificed to himself.

November 2011

Repair Job

"GREAT DAY FOR IT," said Jack, grinning at his partner Davo as they pulled the van to the kerb.

"Yeah, be nice if we got a few more storms like that," Davo said. It was still raining outside, and it was a little windy still, but nothing like the lashing downpour the area had suffered through on the previous day.

They climbed out of the van and put on their fluorescent orange jackets and plastic hard-hats, looking up and down at the suburban street. "Where will we start?" Davo asked, picking up a small set of folding steps.

Jack pondered. "That one." He pointed at a house with a neat cottage garden and lace curtains. He picked up a big plastic toolbox. Together, they ran through the rain up to the door and rang the bell.

The door was opened by a man in his late eighties. "Yes?" he said, peering at them.

"Hi. We're from a local roof repair company," Jack said. "The council's asked us to come around and check on people's roofs after the storm yesterday. We just need to go up and have to look to make sure there aren't any leaks. If there are, we can fix them for you straight away."

"Oh," said the old man. "Well... Do you need to climb onto the roof, then?" He peered out into the street at the van, which had an aluminium ladder strapped to a roof rack.

"We might need to do that later, but it's quicker if we have a look inside first, spot any holes. Can we come in?"

The old man blinked, uncertain. "Yes, yes, I suppose. My wife's not here at the moment," he said. "She's with her sister, she's not well, you know."

Jack didn't reply, knowing from long experience that if he allowed an old person to start talking he would hear their whole life history before they were done. He just nodded at Davo, and they went in past the old man.

There was a flight of stairs off the hallway and Davo went up them without asking further permission, carrying the folding steps. Jack stayed with the old man for the moment, looking about, assessing the contents of the place. "Cup of tea would be nice," he said. "We've been up since five this morning. Terrible storm last night."

"Oh, yes, yes, it was bad. Yes. Never seen anything like it. Terrible."

The old man stood still, nodding to himself, until Jack prompted again, "Tea? White, two sugars, thanks. Davo won't have one."

"Oh, yes. Sorry. Won't be a minute." And he shuffled off.

As soon as he was out of sight, Jack went in to the living room. There wasn't likely to be much in here, but you never knew. He opened the drawer of a cabinet, poked through. Nothing worth while.

He scanned the knick-knacks and ornaments. Rubbish. It was always worth a look, though. He had taught himself quite a bit about antiques and art, mostly by scanning what sold well on Ebay. One time he'd spotted a Morecroft vase and popped it into his empty toolbox. Sold it for two thousand dollars.

The old man returned with the tea in a fancy little cup. Jack downed it in a couple of gulps, just as Davo came down the stairs.

"All OK up there," Davo said, winking at Jack and patting the pocket of his jacket. Jack grinned back.

"OK, then, we're all done. See you later." The old man let them out of the door, full of thanks. Jack tried not to laugh.

Sometimes they would actually have to climb onto a roof, if there were no pickings in the house. Spend fifteen minutes up there, have a smoke, thumb about a bit, then climb down and charge the householder three hundred bucks, strictly cash only. No cash? No worried, we'll drive you to an ATM. Usually worked like a charm, especially with old folk.

They climbed back into the van and drove around a couple of corners. They had a rule only to do one house in any particular street in case the owner realised something was missing, or realised no actual work had been done.

This was an older street. Jack scanned it sceptically from the driver's seat. "How about that place?" Davo said, pointing out a narrow two-storey house with an attic window.

"Sure, let's give it a try."

The door was opened by a white-haired lady who looked to be in her seventies. She was dressed in surprisingly fashionable clothes: black slacks, a deep red sweater and a pearl necklace.

Jack went through his usual routine. Roof repair firm. Sent by the council.

The lady looked at them through narrowed eyes. "Let me see some identification, please." Jack was prepared for this, but he could see that this lady wouldn't be an easy mark. He pulled out the ID that he had printed off with his computer and laminated at a neighbourhood office supplies store. He was pretty proud of it, it looked very professional.

"And this is your job, is it?" the lady asked. "You do this all the time?"

"Sure," said Jack, wondering why she was asking. "It's a pretty good business, keeps us busy."

"You had better come in, then," she said, and opened the door.

The hallway was quite small, and lined with a grey pin-striped wallpaper. "Stairs?" asked Davo.

"I'll show you the way," she said.

She led them to the back of the house. Jack looked about, but there was nothing remarkable about the furnishings, which could have come from an Ikea catalogue. There was a surprising lack of ornaments for an old lady's house. There were a few paintings on the walls which looked like originals. They could be valuable, but they were too big to carry away in his toolbox.

At the staircase, Davo started up. "Just a minute," she said sharply. "I shall show you the way."

Trying his usual ploy, Jack said, "Ah... I was wondering if you could offer me a cup of tea. Been a long morning..."

"No," the woman said firmly. "You're here to do a job, as I understand it, not to pay a social call. Up you go, I'll be right behind you." Jack shrugged, and followed Davo up the stairs as the old lady followed closely.

"Do you live here by yourself?" he asked casually as they went up.

"As it happens," she said, "I'm entertaining a couple of people at the moment, they're staying with me for a few days." Jack was sceptical. It sounded just like the kind of thing a woman living alone would say.

There was another flight of stairs, up to the attic room, presumably. "Just a moment," she said. "I'll have to unlock it. You might think I'm retired, but in fact I still run my own small business. I keep some valuable things up there." At this, Davo grinned and winked at Jack behind the old lady's back.

She went up past them and drew a key from the pocket of her slacks. "There's a trapdoor to the roof-space in here," she said, swinging open the door. "It's a little dark, watch your step."

It *was* dark. Jack realised that there was a heavy curtain drawn across the attic window. It was hard to make anything out in the room as he and Davo went in.

Behind them, the old lady closed the door, making it even darker. There was the click of a key in a lock, and then she threw the light switch.

Blinking at the sudden glare, it took Jack a moment or two to make out what was in the room. Then he realised that there were several chairs here. And in two of them, sitting as still as death, were the figures of two people, a man and a woman, their eyes staring fixedly ahead.

Dummies, he thought wildly, staring at them, *they must be wax dummies*. But then the woman's eyes gave a tremor, shifting left and right, just a fraction, and he knew that they were real. He turned to look at the old lady. "What the fuck..."

The old lady put the key away deliberately in her pocket. "Watch your language, young man. I didn't believe for a moment that you were from a roof repair company, oh dear no. I'm not easily fooled, I could see immediately that you were here to take advantage of me. That was not, you will find, such a good idea."

Jack looked across at Davo. To his horror, Davo was as still as a statue, his eyes staring ahead as fixedly as the people in the chairs.

"I have a gift, you see," went on the old lady. "Passed down to me from my mother and my grandmother. A power to control people. You will find that your legs don't work any more. But don't worry, soon I'll let you sit down with these other nice people, who are just waiting to be processed."

She smiled calmly and pointed at the seated man. "This gentleman came to my door last week, saying he was from an electricity company. He just wanted to look at my last bill, and he guaranteed to be able to save me money." She swung her finger across. "This nice young lady wanted to sell me a range of make-up. Terribly poor value. Last month there were a couple of *very* nice young men who wanted to tell me the good news conveyed by the Book of Mormon. I do get quite a few visitors, you see."

Jack couldn't believe what was happening. He tried to move, but she was right, his legs no longer worked.

"I'm sure your business is quite profitable," the old lady said. "Taking advantage of people as you do. My own business is also quite profitable in its own way." She went over to Davo and pulled the necklaces and other jewellery out of his jacket pocket. "Sell these on the black market, do you? It's so much easier these days, isn't it, with the Internet?" she said.

She pointed her finger at Jack and he found himself moving against his will to sit in one of the chairs. Davo followed. Jack found that his arms were now becoming as frozen as his legs. He was forced to stare ahead, unblinking, at the old woman.

She pulled aside a curtain on the wall to reveal a huge and complex diagram in the form of a five-pointed star. "It's a full moon tonight. A buyer will be coming along to pick up my latest shipment," she said. She traced her finger over the diagram, leaving a glowing trail.

She smiled, and it wasn't the smile of a nice old lady, but more like the smile of a tiger.

"You see, there's a good market for what I sell too. A *black* market in the truest sense. A market, you might say, for spare parts."

October 2012

A Compassionate People

IN THE TANK AT THE REAR OF THE DARKENED ROOM, there was movement.

Dr. Jacobs turned away from the window where he had been watching the sun set over the desert, and came back to gaze through the gloom at the thing in the tank. Movement of any kind had been rare in the tank of late, and he stood long moments, hoping to catch any tremor, any sign. But now there was nothing, and the creature lay as before on the bottom of the tank. After a while, Jacobs left it again and went back to the window.

Beneath him, copper-plated by the declining sun, the city ran away like a line of trees marking a river, alongside the endless highway out to the horizon. As Jacobs watched, yellow lights sparkled on one by one all over the city, in preparation for the night. Jacobs sighed.

He watched the dying day in darkness, as he had done often enough before, though it would have been less than a moment's work to turn on the electric light and banish the dark. His thoughts were more suited to the gloom this night. There had been evenings before when he had felt despair in this room, but before there had always been at least the barest glimmer of hope. Now he knew, in spite of himself, that there was none. Tonight he would receive the final order, and his dream would die. He would end his life's work.

They had been long years, the years of his burden. When Jacobs had begun his task, nearly ten years before, he had been, and felt, a young man. Now he felt older than his years told.

The door chimed. Jacobs' breath stopped, but he went, hands trembling and heart pounding madly, to answer the door. It was Drage, as he had known it would be. Drage strode in.

Drage was a soldier. His rank had long been forgotten by Jacobs, who had no head for these distinctions. At any rate, Drage was a career soldier, an officer. Devoid of his uniform and voice, it would have been obvious in his bearing, and the solid, severe lines of his face. Iron and steel, was Drage. His hair was grey and cut close to his head, combining with the hollowness of his cheeks to make his face like a skull. Drage peered into the gloom, silhouetted by the light in the hallway.

"Damn it, Carl! Don't you ever put on the lights in this place?" Jacobs, embarrassed, snapped on the lights, and then blinked with the sudden glare. Drage stepped fully into the room and closed the door.

In the harsh light, the thing in the tank was obscene. Its outlines were mercifully vague in the murky liquid in which it half floated. The colours were very, very wrong. What might have been limbs, organs and eyes, drifted limply away from the ovoid body, and the tubes expelled darker liquids into the mire. As the light came on, it moved spasmodically, once, and then lay still. Devices at the side of the tank purred and hummed and glugged, pumping fluid and nutrients, and all the time monitoring, watching over the faint life of the creature. Drage stared at the thing for an instant, looked faintly sick as usual, and then turned away.

Jacobs stood with his back to the door, feeling suddenly exhausted. "Well then," he said, "what is it to be?" Drage looked back at him for a second with something like irritation. Drage's emotions were always fleeting and vague. Jacobs supposed it had something to do with his military training.

"You know as well as I do what the answer is to be," he said. "But for the record — you have to terminate the project."

Jacobs looked sadly past the soldier, out of the window at the twinkling stars. "That's fine language," he said. "What you mean is that I have to kill it." And he nodded towards the tank.

"I shan't debate words with you, Carl. Yes, you have to kill the creature. If there had been any hope of keeping it alive without constant supervision and supplies, or of it being able to communicate, then things might have been different. As it is, there's no difference between doing this and turning off a heart-lung machine that's keeping a brain-dead human vegetable alive."

Dr. Carl Jacobs leant against the door, trying to marshal words for how he felt. All he could come out with at length was:

"It's still murder."

Drage, the soldier, shrugged.

—

There are two ways of looking at everything. From one point of view, midnight is a time: an instant recorded by the hands of a clock. From another, midnight is a place: that point on the surface of the spinning globe furthest from the sun, the very centre of the dark side of the planet. At the place called midnight, then, an object entered the atmosphere of the earth. Fast, much too fast. In its speed, it broke and burned as it hit the wall of air, and burning, cast light above the lands then at the place of midnight.

In that year, as before, the eyes of earth were everywhere. Men watched the skies with great telescopes and sweeping radar and the vast dishes of radio devices.

Some watched in order to learn more of the universe and its mystery. Others sat in rooms deep beneath the mountains, waiting for the first sign that the last war was upon mankind. And all of these saw the fire in the sky and measured it, to see if it was that for which they watched.

The falling object was that for which no man watched. It smashed, burning, into the desert, splitting in two as it fell. It was unexpected and unlooked for, but the place of midnight had not been shifted far before the desert was aswarm with men eager to see what had fallen there. And a single word went out, by official message or by rumour; *starship*.

They came for Jacobs when he was asleep and, uninterested in his protests, took him and put him on an aircraft bound for the desert. It was on the aircraft that Jacobs had first met grim-faced Drage. Drage had offered no explanation, answered no questions on the plane. He had been polite, but very military.

To Carl Jacobs, being woken at three in the morning and abducted by a couple of soldiers was a phenomenon beyond explanation. He was young then, in his late twenties, and his enthusiasm for his subject and his popularity on television were world-renowned. Jacobs had been the biologist who had examined in detail the life forms brought back to earth by the last Titan lander, and had set up a whole new theory of the properties and origins of life. He was, in effect, the world's first practising exobiologist.

Others might have been chosen by the military that night, but Jacobs was famous. His name was the one most immediately connected with his field of study. Think of life outside the earth, and you thought of Doctor Carl Jacobs. So his fate was forged.

The plane landed on the makeshift desert strip with much bumping and rattling. The soldiers let Jacobs up from his seat and led him to the door. As he stepped out of the hatchway of the plane, he stopped and looked out at the scene.

It was still black night, but out across the desert, light blazed. Floodlights stood tall, casting colour about, taking photographs, recording, probing. It was like a movie set. But at the centre of the floodlights was something huge and broken. Metal was twisted and shorn, and fluids leaked into the sand. But even half destroyed, the shape was still somehow wrong and alien to Jacobs' sight. It was partially buried in the desert, but it could be seen that although the damage to the craft was terrible, parts of it were still whole.

Jacobs was astounded and horrified. Drage, behind him, tapped him gently on the shoulder. "Go down, please, Dr. Jacobs." So Jacobs went down the ladder from the aircraft, and wandered in fascination around the colossal wreck. Drage followed him patiently, a few footsteps behind. When Jacobs stopped, just outside of the floodlights, Drage came to his side.

"It hit three or four hours ago, Doctor. On the way down, it dropped off its engines, or so we guess. They crashed about a hundred miles north of here, right in the middle of the sandy desert. We haven't been too close; they are giving out a lot of radiation. Then this part made a last attempt to slow down, using some sort of auxiliary power... it's all guesses at this stage. We are presently trying to back track on its approach path to try and work out where it came from."

Jacobs looked around at Drage, stiff-upright in his uniform, no expression on his hollow face. "But why am I here?" Drage raised his eyebrows a fraction, for a moment. "I would have thought you would have guessed, Dr. Jacobs. We think there's still some of them alive in there." Jacobs stared back at the steaming wreck, and disbelief and horror came to him. But there was also in him a renewed sense of professional dignity. This was his field. He made preparations.

There were other scientists about, sleepy-eyed from being dragged protesting from their beds. Jacobs consulted with one of them briefly and then commandeered a young soldier who had been taking photographs. Jacobs and the soldier walked forward hesitantly towards the wreck.

There was an opening, which might have been a buckled analogue of a hatchway. Jacobs bent and peered within. It was dark, and there was an acrid smell. Ammonia. He stood up and called for gas masks and a torch. Jacobs went first, with the soldier following, the light from the torch showing a narrow cylindrical passageway, sloping gently upwards. It looked wet.

Jacobs was unused to such excitement and exercise. His heart pounded alarmingly, and he was forced to stop at regular intervals to catch his breath. Fifteen feet along the passageway, they came to the first chamber. Fluid trickled from a glasslike porthole nearly the same diameter as the passageway. Jacobs' torch was insufficient to reveal anything more than something dark and vague within. He went on... The young soldier followed, sweating.

A little further along, there was another chamber. The passageway bent at right angles towards the ground a few feet beyond, apparently due to the force of the crash; the metal was split and buckled. Jacobs went more carefully.

The third chamber was burst open. and something vile lay half spilled out of the porthole, still oozing liquids. The fluid in which it had been encased had burst and poured down the passageway to the ground. The smell came even through the gasmasks. The soldier following Jacobs turned white at the sight of the thing in the chamber, retched, and crawled back rapidly.

Jacobs shone his torch down the passageway. Beyond this, all was destroyed. He backed out, after taking as many samples of the fluid and of the flesh of the creature as possible. He was covered in slime, and cut by the torn metal, but he was incapable of noticing by that time. A fearful excitement had taken hold of him and kept him moving.

The other scientists helped him analyse his samples. They worked swiftly and ran to him with the results. Piece by piece, he fitted the picture together. Methane, hydrogen, ammonia, compounds of this, and trace elements of that. Temperature? Pressure? Jacobs ordered a hole to be bored within one of the sealed chambers and the pressure taken carefully. The soldier carrying out the job was clumsy. He took the pressure reading, but allowed his bore to leak, and the fluid within jetted out like a fire-hose. The thing within that chamber jerked and then was still. Jacobs was so outraged that he struck the man, but it was an act of impotence.

They took tests of temperature, of micro-organisms present, of water vapour, of energy consumption. They probed and they measured. Jacobs was utterly possessed and driven now. At last, at the end of all their measuring, Jacobs paused for a second. and then went to Drage, a rough piece of paper in his hand.

"There's still one of them alive." Drage looked pleased, just for a moment. "How long can you keep it that way?"

"Well, it can't be kept where it is: all the seals are leaking slowly: I'd guess they've been sprung by the shock of the crash. We'll have to build a special tank for it. It's impossible at this stage to tell how badly it has been injured. I've got the list of environment specifications here." Jacobs waved the tattered paper. "But it will have to be done very quickly."

Drage took the paper to the communications unit and despatched an urgent message. He turned back to Jacobs. "I've suggested that they adapt one of the pressurised environment tanks at the space centre. It should be easy enough to fill it with these gases under pressure. And I've sent for a helicopter."

They cut the chambers loose from the starship. Inside one of them an alien being still lived. In the rest were corpses. Jacobs claimed them for his own.

The time after that passed very rapidly for Jacobs, for they were the years of his triumph. The alien lived. Preserved in a pressure tank, fed chemicals and nutrients and energy by a complex machine, it lay, still showing unmistakable signs of life, to the electronic sensors at least. In the early years, it would often thrash about and make motions with its flagella, but the waiting tape recorders heard no sound that could be deciphered. and there was none who could tell if the motions of the being had sense in them. Having journeyed across the inconceivable distances between the stars, it remained helpless to tell why it had come.

But the initial interest died down rapidly, and the alien was largely forgotten by the average man. Yet Dr. Carl Jacobs could not forget the alien. He lived by it day after day, waiting for the message he knew it must have brought.

The alien lived. The cost of keeping it alive was large and continuing. The military was paying the cost. but even the military could not support hopeless projects. One day, Drage came to Jacobs.

Jacobs had bought his years dearly. His scientific reputation had soared: he had published scores of papers on the physiology of the alien. But his once coveted public image had vanished. He no longer made television appearances or lecture tours. He wrote, ate, and slept in his room, monitoring every change in the condition of the being in the tank. Sometimes he was surprised himself that the creature managed to live on. He was obsessed, and of all of him, his eyes showed his burden the most: they had become sad and soft and wrinkled around. He wore a permanent frown.

He suffered when Drage visited him. He was no match for Drage's iron. He could only bend.

"The Special Committee is becoming concerned about the cost of the project, Carl," said Drage, pacing back and forth before the window. "It's an expense that can be less and less justified as time goes on. The defence appropriation was cut this year, you know, and that means that the special projects feel the cutbacks first."

"I know," said Jacobs, weary. "But after all, we are talking about the life of an intelligent being. How much is that worth?"

Drage pondered briefly. Jacobs had no doubt that, had he wanted, Drage would have quoted him a figure. "As for that, we have no proof that this thing is sentient at all. For all we know, the starship was a cargo vessel carrying cattle to the slaughter..."

Jacobs looked over his glasses at Drage, the barest smile on his face. Drage shrugged. "All right. I don't believe that myself. But at least that example shows the kind of argument you're up against, Carl. You know nothing at all about this thing other than how to keep it alive. Any kind of thinking about it is man-centred thinking."

"But the potential value, if the alien should eventually be able to communicate..." Jacobs trailed off, his thoughts confused.

In the tank, the creature moved feebly. Jacobs turned away from the conversation and examined the instruments for a moment. He looked back at Drage with a fixed expression. "They wouldn't have come so far for no reason. There had to be something they could tell us." Drage looked unconvinced. He took out a cigarette and lit it, glancing out of the window at the day-lit desert.

Jacobs finished with the instruments. There was so much of his own feeling that he felt incapable of communicating to Drage. There seemed to be some insubstantial barrier blocking off whole areas of ideas between them, and the worst of it was that Jacobs could never tell just where the barrier lay. He changed the subject.

"I heard a rumour recently that they finally managed to pinpoint where the starship came from," he said.

Drage looked startled, and then annoyed. He struck himself lightly on the forehead with the heel of his hand, in self reproach. "Damn! I meant to tell you about that a week ago. Yes. It took so long because of the uncertainty of the data they had to work from. But some bright type worked out a new computer program, and the answer dropped out. They think the aliens came from Procyon. It's a star about ten light years away in... damn, I've forgotten the constellation..."

"Canis Minor. That's very interesting, given what I've been finding out about the alien's physiology..." His thoughts were back to his burden again, and the enthusiasm in his voice died. Drage, not noticing, went on. "Evidently this star is not too dissimilar to our own. I'm told the radiation would be rather harder than from our sun, however."

Jacobs nodded. He was watching the inert body in the tank again, his thoughts dark. So far... Drage went on pacing backwards and forwards, his hands behind his back.

"That still leaves the question," he said, "if their star is at all different to ours, and since they clearly cannot survive unaided in our atmosphere..." Drage let his eyes flick momentarily at the obscenity in the tank and then away again, "Then why did they come here?"

Jacobs almost smiled. Even Drage, it seemed, could be caught by his curiosity. "That's a question I've been living with for a long time. The aliens are far more suited to a gas-giant planet like Jupiter than to a terrestrial world. Perhaps they came to colonise Jupiter and then noticed our radio broadcasts. We just don't know."

Drage stopped pacing and paused before he spoke again. "This discussion is futile, Carl. Things are as they are. There is no way at present we can answer your questions. And..." He paused again and then hurried on. "The Special Committee is meeting next Monday. They want you to be there."

Jacobs pulled at his lip, distressed. "All right. I'll be there."

The Chairman of the Special Committee was a balding, bejowelled man with cynicism in every line of his face: Senator Vinson. Jacobs felt like a schoolboy called to account for some atrocious act before the school principal. His knees trembled.

Drage sat to the right of Vinson, looking very formal. Vinson opened the meeting with the minimum of formality, and began.

"Doctor, we are here to decide whether or not your project should be closed down. As you know, the recent budget has both cut back our finances and our energy allocation for the next five years. Now, Doctor, your own project consumes a great deal of both money and energy, but to date has produced nothing of worth to the government." He raised his hand as Jacobs began to protest. "I grant you that much has been learnt about the biology of this creature, which is not without interest to the scientific community, but what the military was primarily concerned with when it decided to begin the project was simply this: does the crash landing of the aliens give any indication of a military threat to this country from outer space? All of our studies outside of your own project, Dr. Jacobs, have convinced us that the answer to this question is in the negative. The implications of a positive answer were so great, however, that we have allowed your project to continue for this length of time in order to confirm our conclusions. Do you now have any information to lead us to doubt these conclusions?"

Jacobs sat silently for a while, knowing that he was lost before he began. He could justify his project, but not in these terms.

"Mr. Chairman," he began slowly, "I have kept an alien being, an intelligent creature from a world other than ours, alive for many years. This has, as you point out, taken a large amount of money, and my time. But it is hard for me to stress just how much may be learnt from the alien once it regains consciousness and becomes able to communicate. Much that may be of overwhelming political, scientific and even military importance. Ending the project will mean murdering our first ambassador from another planet; something that may well be considered a hostile act if or when the second alien ship arrives here." His words were merely sounds in his throat, they seemed unconvincing to himself.

There was some low-voiced conversation among the committee, then Drage straightened in his chair and spoke, very formally:

"You speak plausibly, Doctor, but I feel there are a number of points you have not considered. Firstly, should we again be contacted by this race of alien creatures, we can have no shame: we have kept the sole survivor of the crash alive as long as our resources permitted. Our resources are limited: we have done what we could. Secondly, you have often spoken to me privately of compassion, and of murder. You have never practised as a doctor of medicine, Dr. Jacobs. If you had, perhaps you would not regard those terms as emotionally as you do. Euthanasia is now generally seen as the greatest compassion where the victim is suffering without hope of recovery, or will never be able to lead again a normal, happy life with his disability. Shall we extend less compassion to this alien creature? You can have no knowledge of how this creature suffers in being kept alive. For all you know, it is in continual agony. Our ignorance is complete."

Jacobs was stunned. Drage had never spoken so strongly or so eloquently as this in private during their frequent conversations, and in many ways he was now forced to admit the validity of what Drage suggested. But he still felt that the alien had to be kept alive at all costs.

Vinson took up the lead again. "I ask you again, Dr. Jacobs, does anything in your study give us cause to believe that we are in any military danger from these aliens?"

Jacobs shook his head.

"Then I think we are all agreed?" Nods answered. "Then the decision is this: Doctor Jacobs may continue his project only until the end of the current financial year, which ends in one month's time. He is then to prepare a final report. The meeting is adjourned."

Jacobs sat crumpled in his chair as the committee men filed out, until Drage tapped him on the shoulder. "I'm sorry, Carl," said Drage, "I'm sorry that I had to do that to you. You must know that when the aliens first crashed, I was the first to promote support for your project. But it's been ten years, Carl, ten years, and no sign of communication from the creature. Do you honestly believe that eventually it will be able to talk to us, after all this time?"

Jacobs was savage. "Yes! It must... it must."

Three weeks later, many questions were answered.

Procyon went nova.

Its white glare was visible in daylight as a brilliant diamond embedded in the sky. At night, it was bright enough to cast sharp shadows. Astronomers around the world were joyous, and their observation and measurements of the close explosion were continuous. Others, more sober, reflected how fortunate it was that the star was not of the type to go supernova. The radiation then would doubtless have killed most of the life on earth. As it was, the background radiation level was going up slowly, and some concern was felt for the cancer rate and the possibility of mutations.

Oblivious to this, his mind on one thing only, Carl Jacobs paced about his room, waiting for Drage to arrive. Every so often, he would stop at the window and look up at the fierce point in the sky. He was filled with nervous energy. He ran to the door when the chimes came at last. Drage came in, serious faced. "I received your note," he said. "What is it?"

Jacobs pointed out the window. "You know about that?" Drage looked at the destroyed star, and nodded. "It's fouling up radio communications a great deal."

But Jacobs was impatient.

"It changes everything, don't you see? Now we know why the aliens came to earth ten years ago. They knew their sun was going to go nova. Knew it that long ago. The ship that crashed was probably a scout, sounding out possible escapes for them..."

Drage nodded slowly. "Yes. That sounds plausible."

Jacobs paced in front of the tank where the alien still lay. "But can't you see... there must be an escape fleet on the way. They would still come, don't you see, even when the scout didn't report back. They would have no choice."

"But why here, and not somewhere else, more like their own world?"

"Probably they had detected our radio broadcasts, and thought that any civilisation they detected had to be on a world like their own, like Jupiter. There would be plenty of room, don't you see, on a world that big?"

Drage considered. "And if this is true, then what do you want me to do?"

"Convince the Committee to let me keep the alien alive until the fleet gets here. If we have killed their only ambassador, they may take revenge on us."

"I don't believe that."

Jacobs came up close to Drage, and looked directly into his eyes. "But you must convince them that that is possible. You will, won't you? You have to, Drage..." Drage looked grim, but picked up the telephone. When the operator came on the line, he asked for Senator Vinson. A long conversation followed. Finally, Drage turned back to Jacobs. "All right, Doctor, you have your stay of execution. Six months. If they are not here by then, they aren't likely to come at all, I think."

Jacobs nodded: "They would have to travel at a good fraction of the speed of light, and leave well before the blast."

"All right, then. You have six months."

Jacobs was victorious. But as the months passed, his victory faded to bitterness as he watched the sky from the window of his room, hoping irrationally to see the alien escape fleet arrive in a shower of sparks. He watched in vain.

Eventually, the committee sat again.

—

Edward Drage stood trying not to look at the sickening thing in the tank. It reminded him somehow of biology classes in school during his youth, of human organs preserved in a thick yellow fluid. He looked instead at Carl Jacobs, slumped over his desk, trying not to weep. Drage was slightly disgusted by Jacobs' emotionalism, though he understood the man's obsession. Ten years on one project was enough to obsess any man. At last, Jacobs looked up at him.

"So I have to kill the alien," he said thickly.

"Yes. For your sake, Carl, I would finish it as soon as possible. Now, immediately, would be best." Jacobs looked suddenly like a man condemned to execution by the electric chair: wild and afraid.

"I... I don't think I can do it..." Jacobs' look was at first pathetic and appealing, then angry and accusing. "Damn it, Drage, it's so easy for you to deliver the orders. You've never had to destroy something that meant everything to you, never seen your dreams go down the drain..." He broke then and wept.

Drage pursed his lips reflectively, and then stared out of the window into the night and the stars. At last, he spoke:

"You're wrong, Carl. I don't think I ever told you, did I, that I was once assigned to the old manned Space Exploration Authority?" Jacobs shook his head. "I was one of the team that trained for the early landings on the moon. I was very young, then, of course. Well, I didn't get there. I didn't really expect to. I hoped to get to the first moon base, or perhaps the first manned landing on Mars. But before I got anywhere at all, the first few disasters happened with the Space Shuttle. I'm sure you will remember those... And then the cutbacks began, and they decided finally that manned exploration of space was not worth the risk, and the machines took over... By that time I was pretty high up in the system, and when they made that decision, it was myself who headed the committee set up to close down the astronaut training program. But all of this is neither here nor there."

Drage turned to look at Jacobs. Jacobs was staring at him with a new expression. It made Drage feel uncomfortable. "Kill the alien now, Carl. You have no choice."

Like a man tormented, Jacobs went over to the machinery which pumped life into the creature in the tank, his expression blank and hollow-eyed. "It won't take long," he said, as though trying to find justification. "I don't think it will suffer much, even if it is still capable of pain..."

One by one he snapped off the switches. The purring machinery hummed, paused, and then stopped. For the present, the creature in the tank showed no change. But Jacobs turned away from the tank and away from Drage.

Drage left him in peace, unwilling to break into his mourning. But eventually, Jacobs turned back. His eyes red, but no more tears came. "I don't suppose," he said, "that we'll ever find out now just why they came. They sent no fleet: we'd have seen it by now, even if it were late. There will never be any way to tell."

Drage was looking out of the window again, up at the still over-bright light of Procyon. "I wonder," he said. "You know, over the last few months I've lain awake thinking a lot, Carl. Wondering. I wonder if they knew a lot more about suns than we do. They might have fled their own star years ago, taken their civilisation to somewhere else other than here. But they might have seen something funny about our sun, too, and felt that in compassion they had to try to let us know..." Drage smiled vaguely at the stars.

"And the worst of it is, we'll never know until it's too late..."

In the tank, the creature twisted in a spasm, and then stopped moving. Slowly it settled to the bottom of the tank, and was dead.

July 1978

This story was first published in *Envisaged Worlds* edited by Paul Collins and published by Void Publications in 1978

The Thorns

DEEP IN THE THICKET OF HER SLEEP, she vainly tries to reassemble the scattered pieces of her life.

They surround her like leaves caught upon thorns. One by one she picks them off and examines them. Does this one come before this other? Is there a beginning? An end? To her they seem all alike, all present at once. There is no time, only the infinite now.

She picks off one piece and looks within. She is lying on her side, wrapped in twisted metal. Centimetres from her face, there is the spinning wheel of a car, the tread of its tyre blurring past her eyes.

Somewhere there is terrible pain. Running through it all, between every piece of memory, the ghastly pain. Pain, and the memory of pain.

She picks up another piece of her life. She is in a pink party dress. Her father bends down to kiss her forehead, calling her "Princess".

Another kiss, soft and gentle on her lips. But this time her eyes are closed, she cannot see who it is.

It is her wedding day. Dressed in white she stands in the church, her heart fluttering with happiness, next to her charming husband. Over near the font, there is a disturbance... but no, that is a *different* piece of life: her mother, telling her a story, oft repeated. The baptismal font, the priest, the holy water. And the crazy mad woman, a distant relative, turning up uninvited, having to be dragged away, screaming insane curses at the baby. The shocked face of the priest.

Someone, far off, speaking a word. "Rose...". Is it a flower? She immediately sees the bright red flower in a series of static, unconnected images: the flower in full bloom, the swelling rose-hip, the bud, the loose petals withered. They are like playing cards discarded loosely onto a table, no card following or preceding another.

She sleeps, but yet this is no dream. Again comes the pain. Or the memory of pain. Like a red thread it runs through the warp and weft of her sleeping mind.

She pushes the pain aside, remembers the car again, the shattered car, the snow of broken glass in which she lies, the wheel of another vehicle almost touching her face, spinning, spinning.

Then there is a prick in her arm. How can she possibly feel that prick, a mere drop in the ocean of her pain? The face of the paramedic, murmuring something kind as the hypodermic slides in. And so the sleep begins.

The hypodermic is just the start. Somehow she knows that her flesh is pierced, penetrated, in a dozen places, by the briar thorns. Their shoots, their clear transparent shoots, flowing with liquid, are all about her, tangling her, entering and exiting the piercings of her body.

That word again. "Rose..."

A flower? Or could it be a *name*? Could it be *her* name?

At the thought, the leaves, the pieces of her life, suddenly whirl, as though a strong wind has blown up and scattered them yet again, forming another pattern. But this one is no more comprehensible than the last. She despairs of her task.

Perhaps there is no sequence, perhaps her life simply consists of these unconnected pieces. Is that what life really is? Is time an illusion? Does one thing actually follow another?

Among the litter, she picks up a discarded piece, to recognise it as one she has seen already. But it has an importance she did not see before.

The kiss.

Not her father's kiss, but a loving, gentle, kiss full on her lips, filling her with joy. Her lover's kiss. Her lover. Her husband.

Now at last she knows its place. *That* is the last piece, the end of the sequence! She has just been kissed, and he has just spoken her name. With this anchor, at last, the scattered pieces begin to fall into place, and the thorns begin to wither.

She opens her eyes and wakes. She is lying on a bed, and someone she loves is standing by her side.

It is as though a hundred years have passed.

July 2012

The Contract

"MR LUCENT HAS ARRIVED for your 7 pm meeting, Mr Forster."

Nathan Forster frowned at the intercom, started to reply, but then thought better of it and picked up his phone instead so he could speak privately to his secretary.

"I thought I was done for the day," he said irritably. "I don't recall there being another meeting in the schedule. When was the appointment made?"

"I'm really not sure, Mr Forster, " she said, then added in a low voice, "Perhaps Simon added it in at the last minute?" Simon was one of Forster's executive assistants, and the only one authorised to add appointments to Forster's busy schedule. But he had already left for the day.

Forster was annoyed not to have been briefed. He was half inclined to tell his secretary to send the man away. But then Simon wouldn't have agreed to a meeting in the first place if it wasn't potentially very profitable.

"Very well," he said finally. "Send him in."

The secretary opened the door to a tall, thin man who appeared to be in his early sixties, about the same age as Forster himself, with a sharp nose and a full head of greying hair. He was strikingly dressed, in a charcoal suit, black shirt, and a bright red tie. Made him look a little like a gangster, or a Mafia boss. Forster didn't discount that for a minute. There had been some useful deals in the past with such men.

"Mr Lucent? Pleased to make your acquaintance. Won't you take a seat?" Forster gestured to one of the armchairs arranged around a coffee table in the midst of his vast office. "Can I get you a drink?"

Lucent smiled pleasantly. "Thank you. A Bloody Mary, heavy on the tabasco, if you would be so kind." He sat down. "But we have in fact met before, some years ago."

"Oh?" said Forster, busying himself at the well-equipped mini-bar. "You will have to forgive me, I can't recollect it just now."

Lucent relaxed back into the chair. "You were just starting out, I believe. Trying to get your business off the ground."

Forster brought back the drinks. His was a straight Bourbon. "Well, that is a long while ago, quite a long while ago." He looked intently at Lucent. There *was* something familiar about that face, but he couldn't bring it to mind. He had so much to look after these days, so many deals to manage, that he could barely remember anything about those early days. He hated being reminded of those miserable times.

Lucent took the drink, sipped at it appreciatively, and then leaned forward. "That is in fact why I am here, Mr Forster. It all comes down to that early meeting."

The preliminaries over, Forster was starting to become impatient. "Forgive me, Mr Lucent, but could you get to the point? I don't have much time to spare."

"True," said Lucent. "Let me be direct, then. In those days, you were having trouble getting your business established, fighting against the big, established operators. I was able to be of some assistance, and we signed a contract. That contract involved a payment on your part which has now fallen due, and I am simply here to arrange for collection."

Forster frowned. He *did* recall borrowing some money and getting some advice from a much older man who had offered his services. But that was four decades ago. It couldn't have been *this* man.

"Well, you'll need to talk to our legal department about that, Mr Lucent. I'm sure that I'm grateful for your help, but if there's a repayment required, I'm sure Legal will sort it out for you. I don't recall the terms of the contract, exactly."

Forster sounded confident, but there was a degree of tension building in him. Had he signed away some essential rights, offered this guy a percentage? That could be expensive.

"I have a copy with me, of course" said Lucent smoothly, and brought out an envelope from an inner suit pocket but did not open it. Unexpectedly, he stood up and began to walk around the office as he spoke. "Your business has done very well, Mr Forster. You are, I understand, now extremely rich. So rich that money means almost nothing to you, am I right?"

Forster groaned inwardly, turning to watch Lucent stride up and down. *Very* expensive. But, what the heck, Legal would fight any unreasonable demands, claim the original contract was flawed, invalid, forged, even. If things didn't look good, they would probably settle out of court for a much smaller sum than demanded.

"'Rich beyond the dreams of Croesus'," Lucent murmured, flicking one of the executive toys on Forster's desk.

"I worked hard for it," Forster said, getting up himself. What *was* this all about?

Lucent turned to a side desk and leaned over the huge touchscreen there. He popped up the browser and flicked idly through some pages. "'The whole world's knowledge at your fingertips', I believe? Isn't it wonderful how technology has developed since you started out, Mr Forster?"

Forster could only nod, baffled at the way this was going.

"Is this your wife's photograph? Ah yes, so beautiful, so *young*. You have been married several times, I understand?"

"Yes," Forster said, uncomfortably. There had been a dozen mistresses along the way, too.

"'The most beautiful women in the world at your disposal', would you say?"

"Damn it, I've had enough of this," said Forster, reddening. "Tell me how much you want, and get out of here."

Lucent made a disparaging sound. "No need to become agitated, Mr Forster. I am merely ascertaining whether I have fulfilled my side of the contract. It seems that I have. And now you need to fulfill your side."

Forster was about to make an angry response when his attention was fixed on something on the desk. The little Newton's Cradle executive toy, which should have still been in active motion from the flick Lucent had given it a minute ago, was instead perfectly still, one ball raised in the air, frozen. Forster could only gape at it.

Lucent opened the envelope and took out the contract. "It is always worth reading the fine print of a contract, Mr Forster, but I believe you were a little too eager when you started out, and perhaps omitted to do so?"

Forster stared at the signature on the contract, made in red ink. He remembered now, something the old man had said at the time about it being a 'long-established tradition'.

"You declared, I believe," said Lucent, smiling, "that you would 'sell your soul' to save your business. My dear Mr Forster, you *did*."

September 2012

The Lizard-Keeper

THE RAPTORS HATED BEING MUZZLED, but the Emperor's guard had insisted, so Vecchius stroked their long snouts and muttered soothingly to them as he fitted the iron frames to their heads.

Over in the rear cell, the tyrant-lizard Augustus growled softly and dropped a pile of pungent dung. Aetius, Vecchius's assistant, hurried to clean it up with a long shovel.

In their pen, a pair of armor-heads shuffled miserably, their huge hammer-like tails chained firmly to the stone wall.

Vecchius was almost finished with the last of the three raptors. As always, he had carefully wound strips of cloth around the metal strips so that they would not chafe. Each muzzle had five leather straps, but today he didn't use them all.

Giving the raptor a final pat, he climbed off the steps and left the cell.

He limped over to where Augustus towered behind his bars.

The old lizard would once have been seen as the greatest threat here to the Emperor's safety, but now he was nearly toothless and was blind in one eye from a spear wound some years ago. He had been reduced to an almost comic role in the arena, swinging his vast head back and forth to seek out his tormentors. Mind you, he was still a powerful opponent, and only last month had smashed a bull elephant halfway across the arena, to the great delight of the crowd. Today he stood behind a massive iron grill.

Vecchius looked around. Everything was ready for the Emperor's visit.

He had only met the young Emperor once before, though he'd seem him often enough at a distance. It had been the old Emperor who had brought Vecchius and his animals here from Carthage many years before, when the Romans had destroyed the city at last.

At the start of the triumphant second war, though, it had been Vecchius' knob-heads, armor-heads and raptors that General Hannibal had marched over the Alps. They had terrified the Roman legions, as well they might, and Hannibal had gone on to conquer half the peninsula.

Hannibal would have taken the tyrant-lizards Augustus and Bithna as well, but although Vecchius had successfully bred most of the great lizards, he had failed with the tyrants. He had pleaded with the General that they were too precious to lose while the chance remained that they might breed.

Obtaining more would have required repeating that terrible journey into the dark heart of Africa to the small mountain-ringed country where they still roamed wild. Vecchius still had nightmares about that voyage. They had lost so many men and slaves. Then that long, dreadful journey back, with the slaves carrying the huge eggs on their heads. No, it could not be easily repeated, and certainly not by him.

But Hannibal had eventually lost and now Vecchius was an old man, a slave himself in his enemy's country. And his precious animals — those that remained — were mere fodder for the blood-lust of the bored populace of this city. Thinking of it, Vecchius spat with disgust. Aetius looked across and grinned, but said nothing. Aetius never said anything, never *could* say anything, since the old Emperor had had his tongue torn out. But Aetius had been with Vecchius since Carthage, and despite his lack of speech, they communicated well. Today they were in perfect harmony.

Down the corridor which came from the arena, he could hear trumpets blowing. The Emperor was coming. Vecchius looked around, checked everything again.

The old Emperor had been all right in his way, a fair man at least, one with some sense of Vecchius' achievements with his animals, and who had understood the need to preserve a breeding stock. But this young Emperor was a vain fool, whose only interest was in pleasing the crowd. Each week, he came up with new ideas for entertainments, each more gross and violent than the last. And he cared nothing for the animals.

Only last week, Vecchius had lost one of his raptors, Achilles. Pitted alone against six leopards — *six!* The brave raptor had torn apart two of the great cats, and broke the back of another, all in the first few minutes. But the other three cats had kept circling him, nipping in and making swift bites at Achilles' tail. Eventually they had worn him down, and one had leapt for his throat. He'd killed that one too, but the others finally brought him down. Vecchius had wept as he and Aetius dragged the body away.

Marching boots thundered down the corridor and the Emperor came in, swathed in his robe of imperial purple, surrounded by his spear-carrying guards. Two of the guards strode forward and threw Vecchius and Aetius to the ground.

The young man looked around, wrinkling his nose at the smell of dung and urine.

"Ah, Vecchius, there you are. Get up, get up." He smiled. "I have an idea for a new entertainment, a grand spectacle, a triumph! But first, I need to know more about how you control the lizards. Do they obey your voice? Will they do exactly what you command?"

Vecchius cleared his throat. "Not exactly, lord. The armorheads are stupid, nothing can be done with them. But the raptors are very intelligent and can readily be trained. They follow my commands on this whistle." He lifted the whistle hung on its cord around his neck. "And they can be trained to attack particular objects, or even particular shapes or colours."

"Ah, good, good." said the Emperor, "In that case..." But to his astonishment, Vecchius was interrupting him.

"For example," said Vecchius. "If I blow these three notes..." The whistle rang out three piercing notes. "...the raptors will attack anyone wearing a certain colour..."

There was a terrible crash as the unlocked gate to the raptors' pen smashed open, tossing four of the guards aside. The loose muzzles fell off and the raptors leapt forward. At the same time, Aetius pulled on a rope hidden under the straw, and the grill to Augustus' cell swung free.

"...a certain shade of purple," finished Vecchius, as the screaming began.

May 2012

Deep Freeze

IT WAS DONE. With care, yet without compassion, they laid the cold body in the tomb, and stood back. The lid of the coffin, silent and steady, closed on his face.

Carlton Mydwell was dead.

Some say that death is like a sleep without end. So then, Mydwell slept, and dreamed the long dark dream of eternity as the years passed unreckoned.

Yet Mydwell's rest was not that of the blessed, and his body did not pass into the dust from which it came. And his sleep was not without end. There came a time when he awoke.

His awakening was slow. Time after time, his mind came almost to conciousness and then drifted back into thoughtless sleep, like a cork bobbing to the surface of water and then dipping back again. But at last, his thoughts became clear.

I've cheated them.

It was his first thought, and he clung to it and used it to keep his mind afloat.

I've cheated them. All the fools, the hangers-on, the backbiters, all those wearying associates: and that hopeless bitch, my wife. Dead. Or ancient. And Mydwell is alive.

There was a dull, ruddy light, and he lay for a long time seeing only that. There was a soft strumming noise somewhere near his head. and a cold, sharp smell of chemicals. He was cold. Finally, he raised his hands before his face; they were white, and the veins stood out clearly. He raised them until they met the cold, resistant surface of glass. He pushed, and the coffin lid swung open.

He sat up. The chamber was lit with a dim red light, like the safety light in a photographic darkroom. In the crimson glow, he could see scores of glass-topped coffins stretching away from his own on either side, and in rows before and behind him. The floor was made of metal sheeting, networked with holes. Through the holes, beneath and above him, he could dimly make out other floors like this one. The chamber was stark and bare of ornament, and the bloody light disturbed him. Mydwell found himself frowning.

He swung his legs over the side of the coffin and dropped a few inches to the floor. His muscles protested and quivered. He stood shakily and realised that he would have to take things carefully now. Even Lazarus must have been wobbly on his legs when he was first raised up. It was not a common experience.

Now he noticed the thin coating of dust on everything. The airconditioning system was obviously not working as well as could be expected. The air felt dry, dead, tomb-like. Probably once this level was filled up, no one ever came down to check all was correct, and that was negligence. Mydwell had paid money and more to the company which called itself Eternity, and he decided that as one of the few customers of that organisation to be in a position to complain about the service, he might well set up a malpractice suit against them, thereby beginning his new career. The thought was amusing, and pleasant, and for the first time since he had awoken, he smiled.

His legs stronger now, he set off down the long aisle past the rows of frozen corpses. Agony and sorrow was etched deep into most of the marble-hard faces of the dead. but Mydwell passed them by. His concern was with life, not death. He had felt no pain, borne no sorrow.

At the end of the corridor was an elevator. He pressed the call-button, and then cursed when no answering light came on. It might be night-time outside, and the machinery turned off. He turned to the narrow stairwell, and began to ascend.

It had taken much of his time and money to put him here.

Years before now, he had used his wealth and his forcefulness to escape from a world which had begun to tire him.

He reached the next floor. More coffins.

It had taken ingenuity as well as money. Bribing the doctors to write the reports saying he had an inoperable, terminal cancer; using his influence to ensure that Eternity did not check those reports; paying his lawyers to set up a fund he could legally draw on when he was resurrected; and most importantly, blackmailing the technician to set the controls of his Eternity machine to awaken him a mere thirty years after he had entered the chamber.

Again, more coffins stretching way, some of them empty, with their lids standing open.

Now, thirty years later, his wife and friends dead or dying. he would be a free man. And most of all, the world would have changed enough to make life interesting again.

More and more empty coffins: they stood in rows, as though awaiting the dead. He walked slowly up one more flight of stairs, his heart pounding. He had ascended seven floors. At last the sign in the stairwell read: "Ground Floor". He walked away from the stairs. Here too were the glass coffins, most of them open and empty. The red light still prevailed. His white robe was made scarlet by the light.

At the end of the long corridor of coffins he had entered was a hatchway. Part of the information he had extracted from his blackmailed technician was the operation of this hatch. But it seemed he had no need of that information: the hatchway stood open. White daylight spilt into the corridor, making a harsh, colourful contrast against the red-lit chamber. Something was wrong.

He paused, and then walked forward rapidly towards the hatch. Just before he reached it, however, he stopped still. Above the hatch was a time-recording device marking off the years, days and minutes. The seconds moved smoothly on as he watched. But it was the figure recording the year that had halted him.

He had been betrayed.

Not thirty years, but nearly *two hundred* had passed since he entered the chamber. His blackmail victim had taken a long-delayed revenge, and Mydwell had been delivered into a dark night far longer than he had planned. Two hundred years... he stood still, his fists clenched, overcome with shock.

The hatch still stood open, and he hastened to it. Outside that doorway should have been the administrative and reception areas of Eternity. What in fact met his eyes was terribly different. He stepped outside, into the bleak sunlight.

White dazzled his eyes. reflected brightly from tumbled stone and dry, dusty earth. He shaded his face, waiting for his sight to adjust.

The sun shone harshly down on desolation. Something huge and monstrous had sat down upon the land, grinding buildings to dust and smashing the hills flat. Blocks of whitened stone, the remnants of the massive Eternity Centre, lay tumbled roughly about, shattered and split like the bones of some fossil prehistoric monster. The white glare melted into a ruddy ochre in the distance, like the colour of powdered brick. Long dead trees were fallen in lines pointing away from where the city centre had once been. The sky was blue and cloudless, and nothing stirred.

Mydwell stood stunned for a time. He felt as though he was on the shore of some great dry ocean, fearing to plunge into it lest he drown. He clung to the edge of the hatchway and shuddered.

Eternity had built well. The chamber lay massively rooted deep in the ground, and was still intact, with its stone covering peeled away from it by some cataclysm. Those within it, sleeping through the ages waiting for a cure, would sleep undisturbed until the sun grew dim. Deep under the chamber must be a power generator which kept the lights and the cooling equipment supplied. Time would not touch the frozen dead.

After the shock had subsided, he began to notice other details of the dread landscape. Grass grew yellow and straggling here and there, straining up out of the rubble towards the sun. Stunted shrubs dotted the white, and against the blue dome of the sky he could see the dark dot of a bird moving in great slow circles.

He walked back into the blood-red catacoomb in despair. and wandered aimlessly for a time around the topmost level. There were few frozen bodies here: most of the coffins were vacant. He noticed also that the dust here was disturbed and patterned. Animals of some sort had clearly been at least this far within the Centre. Mydwell leaned heavily against one of the coffins for a moment. Confusion filled his thoughts: he had not planned for this. All of the things he had worked for, all the assumptions of value of which he had based his life and the hope on which he had based his dream. had been suddenly swept away. leaving behind only desolation.

The coffin he leaned against had an occupant. Through the cold-misted glass Mydwell could see the oval face of a young girl, deathly pale and drawn, with her eyelids closed. She looked at the same time innocent and tragic, as the drowned Ophelia might. He turned away.

He came at last to an open room with lockers lining its walls. He realised that this must be where the immediate personal belongings of the dead must be kept. All the lockers carried names, and he found his own quickly. His thumbprint on the lock opened it, and he looked within. His clothes, shoes and briefcase were there, of no use to him now. But then, he looked at his bare feet, and reached into the locker and brought out the shoes and socks.

He stood again at the entrance hatch of the chamber. He stepped out, and walked cautiously through the rubble. Somewhere there must be other humans alive. Clearly, there had been a catastrophic nuclear war or something similar, but if grass and crows could survive, then men might well have done the same.

Hours passed, and the declining sun turned the tumbled blocks into a patchwork of light and shadow. Mydwell, having walked for kilometers through the rubble towards the city, returned in defeat to the chamber, sitting half-buried in the dust like a giant metallic cannister. No life, except a few scavenging crows, and the stunted, yellow-leaved shrubs climbing out of the dead land. Only the twisted, rusted metal and shattered stone stretching towards the western horizon. Hunger had begun to claw at his stomach, and there was nothing to eat.

He was about to step within the chamber again when he saw the skeleton, covered to its bony waist in sand. He went over to look at it, and scuffed some of the dust away with his foot. A woman, by the shape of the pelvis. He stood up from his examination, and glared bitterly at the setting sun. He kicked at the skeleton in anger, and the skull came loose and rolled and rattled down the dusty slope. The last rays of the sleepy sun painted the metal of the chamber in red. and he stepped inside to the darker redness of the emergency lights.

He looked out of the open hatchway and saw the sun passing down behind the great dead plain where the city had once stood, and felt anguish tear at his heart. When the light outside had gone. he shuddered and turned away.

The hatch would not close. A piece of rock had long ago become wedged in the doorway, and would not move. He ignored the door and paced back further within the chamber. He sat down on the floor.

It took him some time to identify the emotion that he felt most strongly at that moment. It was simple loneliness. As a rich man, he had been used to crowds of retainers and visitors, used to large parties in his manor, used to the overcrowded streets, filled to overflowing with the poor and starving. Now it appeared he was totally alone for the first time in his life. The feeling was unbearable.

His sudden realisation that he need not be alone was like a blow. He was surrounded by the thousands of people within the Eternity chamber, frozen in their coffins. Thinking of them as corpses had kept this idea from him before. All he need do was revive one or more of the sleeping bodies and he would have company: someone to talk to, to reason with, to help him survive in this dead world.

Mydwell stood and looked around. There were only a half-dozen or so occupied coffins on this level. He walked over to the nearest one. Again the face of the drowned Ophelia-girl stared vacantly up at him, pathetic and sad. He looked at the controls located at the bottom of the coffin, beneath the name plate. They were simple enough. He pressed a button, turned a timing control, and then stood back to wait.

The time passed slowly as the temperature inside the coffin rose gradually and the cold-misted glass became clear. Tiny needles entered the skin of the girl and forced life-arousing chemicals into her system. Her heart began to pump again and colour came back into her cheeks. Time passed. At last, she stirred and awoke, and looked into Mydwell's eyes. She was confused and empty of memories for some minutes, but at last, she spoke.

"Have they found a cure, then? Am I cured?" Mydwell's heart contracted. He had not thought of this. "No," he said, "No, they haven't found a cure." The girl was distraught and panicstricken for an instant. "Why ..." she began, and then stopped, not understanding.

"Can you stand?" he asked. Somehow, he felt concerned, responsible for the girl, and these were foreign emotions to the

Carlton Mydwell who had lived two hundred years ago. He felt almost afraid of himself.

The girl sat up cautiously, still frowning in puzzlement and peering through the dim light. He helped her to her feet, and held her as she walked unsteadily forward. He took her to the hatchway and made her look out into the darkness.

"There was a city out there," he said.

"Yes, of course..."

" I awoke some hours ago ... some malfunction of the machinery." he lied. "I came up here and looked outside. There isn't any city out there any longer."

"What? What do you mean?"

"Nuclear warhead, I'd say But the city is gone."

"And I'm not going to be cured of my cancer?"

Mydwell hesitated. "No."

"Oh God!" she bent her head and wept. Mydwell could not console her. She was young, perhaps twenty, and very beautiful. Mydwell felt himself aroused, and felt ashamed. Her sobs seemed to go on forever, and she left him and huddled in a corner as she wept. Mydwell sat on the floor again, and kept his thoughts to himself. At last, her tears stopped, and when he looked, she had fallen asleep. After some hours, he too was asleep.

In the morning, he showed her the scene outside the hatchway. She looked out for a time, and then turned away and padded on bare feet within the chamber. Mydwell, feeling helpless, left her and went out again.

His hunger was now almost unbearable. He knew that men could go for many days without food and not die, but he had been used to eating regularly each day. Hunger to Mydwell had been missing out on breakfast. Now his stomach held his attention in a relentless grip. He must find food, or die. He walked around the outside of the chamber this time. heading away from the city centre. Far enough away from the centre of the blast, things must be better.

Half an hour's walk away from the chamber, he saw the tribe.

He had come to the top of a rise overlooking a small valley. The broken blocks of stone and brick, evidently tossed many kilometres by the blast, were fewer here, and the valley showed patchy spots of grey-green grass.

On the horizon, hills filmed with the blue of distance showed themselves. And in the valley also was a ragged trail of half-naked sun-browned men, walking and chanting at the same time. They wore ragged breeches about their legs, and ornament and body paint on their torsoes. Their hair was black and bushy. Women and children trailed at the rear.

Mydwell stood still, watching. In his mind were surprise and elation, but his stomach had its own thoughts. If there were men alive, there must be food to be had, that was what his guts reminded him.

The savages had not yet seen Mydwell standing stone-still on the rise. They continued their way along a faint trail, approaching him.

At their head was a figure garbed even more strangely to the eyes of the watcher on the hill. The man was crowned with a skull-helmet, and garbed in a hairy coat. A necklace of bones was about his throat. and he led the chanting of the tribe by beating with his hand on a small drum he carried.

To Mydwell, however, the strangest thing, of all was that these savages, unlike those he had seen in his own day, were not dark-skinned African negroes or Australian aboriginals, but beneath their tan, white and thin-lipped like himself. The effect was curiously disturbing, like something obscene or out of joint. He decided to watch no longer. He yelled out something incoherent but loud, and waved his arms.

The effect was startling. All at once the savages shaman, men and women looked up at Mydwell standing there in his white hospital gown, made loud cries of panic, and turned to flee. Mydwell yelled again, and they ran all the faster. The only individual who did not run was the shaman, who walked backwards at a rapid pace, rattling his necklace and baring his teeth at the vision, his eyes showing their whites. Then he too turned and fled along the dusty track. In a moment, there was no one to be seen.

Mydwell, frustrated and worried, climbed down the slope to where the savages had been. Some of them had dropped the packages they had been carrying, and he crouched to examine one of these. Inside were a number of bone carvings, a sharp flint knife, and some strips of roasted meat. He grabbed at the meat and bit into it gratefully. It tasted odd, but welcome. Soon his stomach stopped complaining and he took all of the meat he could find in the few packages there and carried it back towards the chamber.

The girl was huddled by the door of the chamber, looking out with blank eyes. He gave her some strips of meat, and she ate slowly and in silence. Mydwell feared that the shock of her situation, together with her knowledge of her fatal illness, had turned her mind and let spill her reason. He did not press conversation, hoping she would regain normality soon.

The day passed, and Mydwell explored the nearby area for anything of value. As the sun began to sink again, she came to him inside the vault, and looked up with reddened eyes.

"What's going to happen?" she asked.

It was hard in the saying, but he said it. "I don't know." Then, as her gaze wandered, "There are savages out there. I stole the meat from them. They have a source of food ... I'd thought ... perhaps we could awaken some or all of the people here in the Centre, and then maybe together we could get something going: civilisation. Anything would he better than what those savages have."

She looked up at him pathetically for a long moment.

" No." she said. "Don't you remember? All of us are dying here. We are dead already, all of us. How can we bring life to anything?" Her voice was becoming louder, hysterical. "And me ... I'm going to die! And it's going to hurt, damn it! Why did you have to wake me up? Why me? Why couldn't you let me stay asleep and never know?" She was shouting now, and Mydwell had her by the shoulders, trying to calm her.

All of a sudden her voice dropped almost to a whisper. "Put me back, please. I want to go to sleep again. Please..." And she began to weep again.

He could think of nothing to say. He kept silent, and took her back to the coffin, helped her in, and turned the controls on once more. She closed her eyes, and the cold gradually returned and misted the glass lid. Ophelia once again allowed a Christian burial. He leant on the coffin, looking at her child's face, and wept. He had not done so for very many years.

The dawn broke over the landscape like a red, hurrying tide of light. Mydwell stood and watched the shadows of the rubble ebb away. There were clouds on the still dark western horizon, and the chance of rain. He sat and watched, alone. Somehow now he felt incomparably worse alone than he had before he had woken the girl. A heavy weight, like a great chain. seemed to hang about him, and he was forced to drag it along with him in slow, plodding steps.

The scraps of meat he had stolen from the savages were gone. He had no choice. He had to find the savages once again and try to make a friendly contact this time. They must know how to survive in this blasted world. Perhaps further away from the city animals still ran wild. Or the savages must have rediscovered husbandry and agriculture. He had to find out. The alternative of placing himself back in deep freeze he did not see as a possibility, any more than he would have seen suicide as a way out. It was not in his nature.

At last, then, Mydwell set off again, away from the desert that had been a city, and found the trail where he had seen the savage people the day before. The day was cold, and he shivered in his gown. It would rain before long. And indeed, the first heavy drops came thudding into the dust at his feet. Eventually, the downpour began, and he was soaked, but he kept walking along the trail, towards the only hope that he had left. The sun came out and dried him, and he walked on.

He came on the village suddenly. He thought of it as a village, but really it was no more than a clutter of skin tents and open campfires. Children ran about naked, and women sat sewing rough garments. The men stood around. talking in an odd tongue. Rather than walk into the village and frighten them all, Mydwell stood quietly at the edge of the crude wooden compound and waited until he was noticed.

There was general consternation then, and the women leapt up and ran around staring at him and wailing. But there was less panic this time, and eventually the nervous shaman approached Mydwell, bowing to the ground. and rattling his bones and speaking many prayers. Mydwell waited. The wizard close up was equally as odd as at a distance. He was painted garishly. and bones pierced his ears. White scars were all over his body. Mydwell could see him shaking in fear, but being forced forward by his need to uphold his reputation.

Finally, he was close enough to touch. The shaman stared wide-eyed at Mydwell's face, and then prostrated himself full-length at Mydwell's feet. Mydwell, somehow realising what was required, bent down and lifted up the wizard. A relaxed moan came from the watching crowd of primitives. Carlton smiled. The shaman grinned, and the crowd ran forward to surround Mydwell, cautiously reaching out and touching his robe, his hands.

An unorganized, wild celebration began, with much beating of sticks and atonal singing and frenzied dancing. Mydwell sat surrounded by it all, in the place of honour, feeling hungry. In a quiet moment, he made sign language at the shaman seated at his side. Food. The shaman nodded and frowned. He made a sign to one of the women. who went off and returned, minutes later, with a small bowl of wild blackberries.

The shaman made grunting noises, and waved his hands vaguely. Apparently this was all the food available in the village at this time. He must have interrupted a hunting party the day before.

Mydwell was regarded by all of the savages with awe. He could see oft-renewed astonishment in their faces as they watched him. The shaman seemed to be the most astonished and disturbed of all.

After a time, the shaman made signals indicating that they would go hunting for food again, this time with Mydwell along as a bringer of good-luck. Mydwell agreed, although he did not relish the long walk that he would probably be forced to make. His feet were already blistered with his walk out to the village. But if he expected to eat these people's food and live with them he would have to prove himself valuable in some other way than just as an object of supernatural fear.

Before the hunting party left the shaman performed a strange ceremony. He took a long, sharp flint knife, kissed it, and raised it to the sun. The primitives looked on expectantly. Then suddenly. the shaman raised the knife in both hands above his head. and with a shout, plunged it into the earth. The crowd yelled. Mydwell was merely confused.

The ceremony over, the sweating witch doctor grabbed Mydwell's arm and brought him to the head of a ragged procession of men and women. The whole tribe evidently went along on the hunting trips. They were armed only with bone clubs and knifes of flint.

They set off, Mydwell ambling along at the side of the short legged shaman, in the direction of the city. In the still cloudy sky, crows circled above them. Mydwell now was content to be led: his own resolve and control of events had disappeared. As they walked, he realised how tired he was becoming. Hope that he could rejoin human company had kept him going on the way to the village. Now, his aim at least partially achieved, his body was letting him know its complaints. And he began to think again of the sad Ophelia-girl who he had put back into her coffin the night before. He realised with a start that he had never even asked her what her name was. He felt a feeling of deep loss, and yet he did not understand why he felt so.

At some point, he must have tripped and fallen, and the shaman ordered some of the stronger savages to hoist Mydwell to their shoulders. In spite of the jolting ride, he found himself drifting off to sleep. He woke for a moment when the tribe came to the ridge beyond the little valley where Mydwell had first seen then, and he saw again the metal collossus buried in the sand that was the Eternity Chamber. And beyond, lit with the grey cloudy sky, the plain that had been a city. A fragment of poetry came into his mind then: *Look on my works, ye mighty, and despair...* The tribe raised their bone clubs high, and marched on. Mydwell dozed again on the shoulders of the sweating man.

When he again opened his eyes, the tribe was lined up in front of the entrance to the Eternity Chamber. He frowned in puzzlement. The tribe apparently regarded the object as a sort of shrine. That would explain their awe of him: he must be like a ghost to them.

The shaman marched towards the hatchway, and motioned Mydwell to follow. He got down from the shoulders of the men and did so.

It was not until they were inside the chamber, in that dim red light, and the shaman was standing next to the cold coffin where the sad girl lay, that Mydwell began to understand, and a feeling of horror began to steal over him. And when the shaman opened the glass lid and stood poised with his stone knife ready. Mydwell knew.

He leapt forward in horror and disgust to grasp the shaman by the neck and shake him, trying by his action to remove the terrible knowledge he had come to. The shaman. startled, cried out, and the men of the tribe grappled with Mydwell and tore him away from the witch-doctor, who stood coughing and spluttering for some moments before he resumed his position.

Mydwell struggled in the arms of his captors, but they seemed to have lost their awe of him after his attack. The sacrifice went on.

Food? There was plenty of food, there for the taking. Food enough to keep a small tribe alive for many years. All that meat...

The crows outside descended in a black cloud. waiting for the scraps.

January 1976

This story was originally published in *Science Fiction Monthly* magazine, January 1976

Phaedra's Thread

DEEP IN THE DARK, around this corner or the next, her monstrous brother prowls. She can hear his snuffling breath, the heavy thump of his hard, clubbed feet, the soft growling threat of his voice, muttering in a language of his own devising.

Somewhere near, too, must be the handsome stranger, sword in hand, seeking or fleeing from her brother.

Her hand is upon the thread of yarn. The yarn her sister spun, the yarn her sister wound into a ball and gave to the stranger before he entered the maze. Somewhere near the entrance to the dark complex, her sister still stands, holding one end of the yarn, awaiting the stranger's death or his triumphant return.

The thread grows slack under her hand. The stranger is moving forward, paying out the yarn behind him, his only chance of return from the terrible confusion of the darkened maze, its hundreds of passages, its endless crazy turns, its innumerable dead-ends and traps. The old artificer designed it well.

The stranger... She had only needed to set her eyes on him to know that she had to have him. She. *She*. Not her elder sister, no matter how many times her sister had kissed him, no matter that it was her sister who had devised to free him, to return his sword, to give him the ball of yarn. It wasn't fair. Her sister had had other men, or so she said. And her sister could not love the foreigner the way that *she* did.

Distracted, for a while she does not notice the approaching noise close at hand. It is her brother. More than the sound, she is alerted by his rank animal scent. Now he is so close that she can feel the warmth of his huge body. She presses herself against the cold stone of the wall, holding her breath, trying to vanish.

He has come to a halt. She hears him mutter, taking in great snuffling breaths through those vast nostrils. He knows she is there. But somehow, even in his madness, he knows that she is kin, knows her for his sister. When they were children together, before his madness forced his confinement here, they had played together, all three of their mother's children. Many was the time she had gently cradled his great misshapen head in her lap. Now, somehow, he remembers. Knowing she is not his prey, he finally turns away.

She breathes again. Why has she ventured so far into the maze, into danger? To be close to the stranger, to be near at hand if he is to die or be injured? Yes. But also because she hates the close confines of her life. The thrill of danger frees her from it. Soon she will be free forever.

Slowly, step by step, hard feet clattering against the stone, the monster, her brother, moves on. Somewhere ahead is the stranger with the sword.

So in the dark, in the twisty turns of the labyrinth, the adversaries seek each other. Soon, very soon, they must meet in bloody combat. Today one of the two must die. Her mad, deformed brother. Or the handsome young man she loves.

Her heart will break if she cannot have him. Even now, it races with fear and with longing.

She feels along the rough stone wall, reaches an edge where a new passage begins. Here. There is a rough projecting piece of stone. It is large enough. It will do.

She seizes the yarn in two places, tightens her fists upon it. She jerks her hands apart with all her strength and the thread breaks. Quickly, she takes one end – the piece her sister still holds – and ties it firmly to the knob of stone. From the top of her robe she pulls her out her own ball of yarn and knots it deftly, with touch alone, to the thread that trails ahead toward the stranger.

It is done.

Back now, following the certain guide of her sister's yarn, she retraces her steps, paying out her own thread behind her. From time to time, it grows taut and pulls, slackens and relaxes, as the hero advances or retreats. Feeling those pulls, her heart leaps with joy. Now it is *she* who is connected to him, his every move linked to her trembling hand. Her sister feels only the tug of cold stone. The girl laughs, thinking of it.

At last, far behind her, in the depths of the maze, she hears a distant, enraged bellowing, and a shout, and the clash of steel striking off stone. She stops, her heart nearly beating from her breast, as she listens to the fatal confrontation. The bellowing and the shouting reach a crescendo and is ended by a terrible scream. *His* scream? No, her brother's deeper one. There is silence then. It is over. She finds that she is crying and wipes away the tears with short angry strokes of her hand. Her brother had to die if the foreigner were to live. And he *has* to live, or she will die of grief.

Now she must be quick.

Feeling her sister's thread under her hand, she runs forward through the dark as fast as she is able. From time to time she gives the thread a tug, so that her sister will not suspect that it is no longer in the stranger's hand. Behind her trails her own yarn. Soon the stranger will wind it up as he returns.

Now. Here. Here, not so far from the entrance to the complex, with a little light leaking in from the great doors, and bouncing around the corners. This is where she turns away from her sister's thread. She takes a left turn, and then a right. She has ventured here before, counting the turns. So long as she did not go beyond into the true blackness, it was safe, just a thrill. Anything to put an edge on the monotony of her life.

Now those secret trips have found their value. She runs into the hidden room she knows of, clutching hard at the yarn in her hand. At the end of it, her love, tugging from time to time as he seeks the way out of the labyrinth.

Panting, she stands in the room, waiting for him. There is hardly any light, just enough to make out the doorway. Will he turn away from the brighter light and follow her thread?

Yes. He comes at last into the room. She smells his sweat, she smells the sharp iron tang of blood on his tunic, on his sword. Her brother's blood, but that is a grief now gone.

"It is done," he says, but she does not speak, because that would betray her. She throws her arms around him, reaches up to kiss him. Passionate, desperate kisses.

"What?" he asks, confused by her sudden vehement passion, but she puts her hand over his mouth to silence him. She pulls at his straps, tears off his tunic and his skirt, tosses aside his sword, then pulls her own gown over her head. She is naked in the almost-darkness. Taking his hands, she drops to the floor and pulls him after her.

She knows joy then, and sweet triumph. Afterwards, she lies for long minutes, disregarding the cold stone against her back, holding his head against her breast.

It cannot last. After a measureless time, a dark shadow appears in the doorway. Her sister Ariadne has found them. Her fury will know no bounds. Too late, too late!

"He is mine," Phaedra says, looking up at her sister, and laughs.

November 2012

Bone China

ROLAND BURGESS PUSHED ROUGHLY PAST HIS MOTHER'S MAID as she opened the drawing-room door to him.

"Mother..." he began.

"Sit down, Roland, and have some tea. It's just been made."

"I don't have time for tea. I need to..." He stood glowering in front of her as she sat at the antique side-table. He was a big man, and his fists were clenched.

She gazed up at him, her fine features set in that disapproving look he knew so well. How many times had he seen that look during his childhood and even throughout his adulthood? Too many times.

"You *do* have time for tea, Roland. It will help you calm down. Please sit."

Deflated, he sat in a flower-patterned armchair which was probably worth thousands. He had never been someone who understood the antiques market. It creaked a little under his weight.

"Do you like the tea set?" she asked conversationally. "It's new. Bone china. Almost transparent." She held up an empty cup, and he could see a cloudy light shining through it. "Terribly expensive, of course."

"Of course," he said sourly. "Mother, I need to talk to you about money."

"Wait for the tea, dear." She carefully poured from the elegant teapot into the cup she had just held up.

Roland's mother, her white hair tied back into a firm bun, was a perfect match for the bone china. Now in her mid-90s, she had become thinner, paler and more delicate with every passing year, and now she seemed like some semi-transparent piece of crockery herself.

"You take milk, of course. Lately I have decided that I prefer it with lemon. Strange how one's tastes change as one ages." She handed him the cup.

He sipped impatiently at the tea, annoyed by the way his large hands had to struggle with the exquisite cup. He preferred large, solid mugs.

"It's about the family trust," Roland said, putting down the cup. "I need you to transfer me a big chunk of cash. One of my manufacturing companies needs to retool its equipment, or we won't be competitive."

She frowned. "Again? It was only two months ago you needed cash to cover your financial firm's investment losses."

"You don't understand these matters, Mother. In fact..."

She looked up at him sharply. "In fact?"

He plunged on. "In fact, I think it's time for you to step down as trustee. The trust's investments have been far too conservative over the years. We could make much more by investing more aggressively."

"Like your firm did, you mean?" There was a faint smile on her thin lips. "And lost so much money?"

"That was a mistake. I sacked our investment manager over it. It won't happen again."

She sipped her tea from the fine china and shook her head sadly. "No, dear, I don't think I'm ready to step down. I'm sure your father wouldn't have approved. He placed control of the trust in my hands, after all."

"But that was forty years ago, Mother!" Roland stood up angrily. "I was only in my twenties then. And now you're..."

"In my nineties, yes, dear, I'm quite aware of that. But *you* haven't changed, have you?"

Roland said a foul swear-word. He towered over her and his face turned red.

"Language, dear," she said. "Do sit down again, you haven't finished your tea. Have one of the sandwiches."

"I don't damn well want a sandwich, or any of the damn tea. I want some money. I want *all* the money, *now*, not when you die."

"If I ever do? Is that what you are thinking?" She looked up at him with calm blue eyes.

He stood shaking with rage. "I...". He stopped and forced himself to calm down. Finally, he sat down again in the over-decorated armchair.

"Well, it doesn't matter," he said at last. "I've had my lawyers draw up the papers. You're clearly too old to be managing so much money. You'll be declared incompetent and the trust's assets will be transferred to my control."

"I see," she said quietly. She picked up the teapot again, looking thoughtful, and poured herself another cup of tea. She looked inquiringly at him, and he shook his head, his face still red, lips compressed.

She sighed. "You are a great disappointment to me, Roland. I believe I have handled the trust well over the years. I have made *some* investments with a degree of risk, but they were carefully chosen and they have all paid off. Unlike yours."

He leaned forward menacingly. "Mother, you don't..."

"Understand? But I do, dear. You should have seen the need to reorganise your manufacturing business five years ago when the Koreans entered the market. In fact, I've been talking to members of your board, and they agree with me that you have been making *most* unwise decisions recently. You will find when you return to the office that they have met and decided to remove you as Chairman and Chief Executive."

"You...! Damn you!" He stood again, and then, in a fury, stooped and picked up the delicate bone china teapot and hurled it with all his strength at the marble fireplace. A stream of tea trailed after it.

To his astonishment, the teapot simply bounced off the stone and rolled unharmed to the carpet. He stood staring at it for a moment, then strode over and kicked it again at the fireplace. The same thing happened. He stamped down it hard, trying to crush it. Instead, he hurt his foot and nearly toppled over as he lost his balance. Open-mouthed, he turned to his mother.

"It's a new ceramic, dear, incredibly strong. One of my investments was in a company developing some radical new production techniques. I believe the ceramic is going to be used for the heat-shields of the next generation of spacecraft, among other things. Very profitable."

She went on calmly, still sipping her tea, "Roland, dear, I do have my own lawyers. What judge would assess me as being incompetent once he sees how well my investments have paid off? You really must learn to think things through."

He finally spluttered "Who...?"

"Who will be the new Chief Executive? Why me, of course. Dear, dear, Roland, your blood pressure!"

May 2012

A Flash of Lightning

Despite herself, Sara flinched when the crack of thunder shook the tower. Moments before, lightning had lit up the night sky as though it were daylight. The thunder frightened the great brown bear, too, and it gave a mournful roar as it stood in its cage against the wall.

"Perfect," said Sara's master Izak, who was standing at one of the arched windows looking out at the gathering storm. He turned and snapped his fingers at his apprentice. "Jonthan! Raise the spike. Be quick about it, now!"

There was a disapproving look on the master's face as he addressed the younger man. Jonthan returned the look with a barely suppressed scowl but shuffled over to the centre of the tower and began cranking a padded handle. Gears turned, and with the shriek of metal on metal, a shaft began to move upwards through a hole in the ceiling.

Sara smiled to see the on-going discord between the two men, but next moment Izak looked across to where she was scrubbing the long stone bench. "Girl! Stop gawking and get on with your work. Make sure the bench is dry. We'll need it soon enough. And then you can mop the floor." Sara's smile vanished, and she returned to her miserable task. It was boring, but at least it left her mind free for thinking, and didn't get in the way of her observing everything that the master was doing.

All around the high tower, the storm was gathering its strength, building every moment. The wind was howling, louder and louder. There came another flash, and this time the thunder followed almost immediately. The caged bear roared again in fear.

"Is it raised?" Isak demanded of the apprentice. "All the way?" Jonthan, panting a little with the effort of cranking, nodded. "Right then, now the lever, quick, no time to lose!"

Jonthan moved over to the wall of the circular tower, where a massive lever had been erected. Thick wires ran over the ceiling to it from the central spike, and from the lever through to a complicated apparatus. From the apparatus, thinner wires ran along to dozens of huge glass bottles plated with beaten metal and part-filled with water. Sara knew those bottles well. She had been made to wash and polish every one until it gleamed, with not a single spot of grease or dirt, before the plating began.

"Now!" bellowed Izak above the storm. "Damn you, pull it!"

Jonthan hauled on the lever by its wooden handle. Outside the windows, lightning stabbed down.

And then it was inside the tower! Sara gave an involuntary gasp as sparks fountained from every connection of the metal cables. Jonthan stepped back from the lever with a curse. Lightning seemed to flicker across the array of bottles, and little arcs played around their mouths where the wires connected with them. She saw the poor bear shrinking away in its cage as far as its chains would allow it.

Izak laughed, a deep booming laugh of satisfaction. "All right, boy, throw the lever back, quick now. And lower the spike before we're hit again. We've done it."

The old man paced along the array of bottles, careful not to touch them, smiling and stroking his short grey beard.

"Very good, very good. But if we are to please the King, we must take the next step. Girl! Are you done with that bench? Is it dry? Completely dry?" Sara nodded, but Izak still came over and examined the bench carefully as though still expecting it to be filthy. Her master was like that, she knew. Everything he dealt with had to be clean beyond any reasonable standard.

Satisfied, the master donned thick leather gloves and went to the array of bottles. Each metal-clad bottle was about three handspans across, and twice as tall. Izak carefully unhooked one of them from the wires and brought it across to the bench.

"Now, you!" Izak said, looking across at Jonthan, who was still glowering. Much good it did him, Sara thought, as she picked up her pail and mop so as to look busy. "Bring the weapon and its pack. Set it down here."

Jonthan brought out from a cupboard a leather harness and a long metal pole, about the length of a long sword. He put it down on the bench and the master, despite his thick gloves, deftly strapped the bottle into the harness. "Now," he said to his apprentice, "turn your back."

Jonthan muttered something in a resentful tone, but nevertheless turned and allowed Izak to fasten the bottle in its harness to his back. He took the long pole in his hand. "Not like that, you fool," said Izak. "Put on this glove first." Once Jonthan had on the glove, the older man connected a wire from the mouth of the bottle to the end of the pole.

"Now for the bear!" Izak strode over to the cage. "By my calculations, the trapped lightning will easily be enough to kill it. What a weapon this will make for the King! How terrified his enemies will be when he and his knights wield it!" He reached up to unlock the bolt on the cage.

Sara could see Jonthan tremble with fright. "No, master! Pray you leave the beast in its cage... just in case. Perhaps the weapon will not work!"

Izak nodded grudgingly. "Perhaps you are right, though I was keen to see a real contest of man against beast. Then again, you are not much of a man, are you?" he said with a sneer.

Perhaps, thought Sara later, that was one humiliation too far for Jonthan. Or perhaps he had been plotting his revenge for a long time and just seized the opportunity when it presented itself.

Jonthan stabbed forward with the pole. Not at the bear. At his master Izak, standing next to the cage.

There was a loud *snap*, a flash from the end of the pole, and suddenly Izak jerked like a puppet and crashed back against the cage, then fell to the floor, twitching in every limb, his eyes rolled back to show only the whites. The bear shrank back in terror. Sara gave a shout of dismay and dropped her mop.

Jonthan turned to her with a mad grin on his face. "I've done it," he said in wonder. "I've killed the old bastard. I've killed him!" For a moment Sara thought he was going to break into a dance. But instead, he paused for a moment, thinking. "I have all his books, all his drawings. I'll tell the King it was a terrible accident, but I can do better. And I will, too. But..."

He looked strangely at Sara. "You mustn't tell. If you tell, I'll kill you. Better yet..." he hefted the metal pole. "I'll kill you now, why not? The accident could have killed you both. Such a pity." He began to step toward Sara, the pole outstretched.

Sara stood her ground for a moment, considering. Then she snatched up her pail and threw the water right in Jonthan's face. As it drenched him, there was a flash and another loud *snap.* Jonthan jerked just as Izak had, though not so violently. He didn't fall over, but sank to his knees, gaping with shock. Before he could regain his senses, Sara picked up her mop and swung it with all her strength at his head. He crashed over, hitting the stone floor with a thud, and did not move.

She ran to where her master lay and bent over him. He was still twitching, but his eyes had returned to their normal position and she could hear him gasping for breath. Not dead, then. She ran to fetch a cup of water and dribbled it through his lips. He choked and tried to sit up.

"Master Izak," she said. "You are in need of another apprentice. I pray you take me."

"*You?*" he gasped out. "But..."

"I was taught my letters, master. I have been reading your books when I was alone here, and I have watched everything you do."

She smiled. "And, master, unlike Jonthan, I will not try to kill you."

September 2012

The Glance

JONNY BECKS LAY BLEEDING SLOWLY into the carpet of his cheap rented room, its threadbare pattern not much improved by the bright red colour of his blood.

He was trying to summon up the strength and the breath to yell for help again when the black-haired girl opened the door and stepped into the room.

Finally! he thought, in both surprise and relief. "Help!" he managed to croak out.

She stood silently for a moment, looking at him, and then kneeled down next to him. She put out a tentative hand to gently touch the knife sticking into Jonny's chest. The touch sent a tremor of pain through him and he gasped. Her eyes narrowed, and she withdrew her hand.

He was still filled with surprise that it was *this* girl who had come to save him. Not his girlfriend Carla. Not his best friend Jimbo. Not Kevin, overcome with an unlikely remorse. But this girl who was still, really, a stranger to him, though he'd been trying to hook up with her for months.

Jonny had first seen her at the party at Jimbo's place, standing in the doorway of the hall as he swallowed down the tabs Kevin Leung had just sold him.

She had been leaning against the door-frame with a glass of wine in her hand, talking to Carla. Her long jet-black hair hung down to her waist, evenly framing her perfect, pale features. Wearing a tight black top and even tighter skirt, which accentuated her every curve. Jonny had felt a sudden strong surge of lust when he saw her. She was gorgeous. There was no doubt that poor Carla came off second-best in the comparison. Perhaps sensing his stare, the girl had given him one long, cool glance and then turned back to Carla.

He had made an effort to struggle through the crush towards them, but before he got very far the tabs had kicked in and everything became hazy. In fact, it was a pretty bad trip that night, he remembered. He'd been pretty far out of it, and Carla had nearly rung for an ambulance, she'd told him when he finally came round. He'd been as sick as a dog for days afterwards.

Eventually, though, he'd asked Carla about the girl. Cautiously. He didn't want Carla to get the wrong idea. Well, he didn't want her to get the *right* idea, really.

"I don't know," Carla had said. "She didn't say much about herself, just asked me a couple of questions. Oh, she did say her name, but I can't remember. Gail something, I think. Why?" she had ended, suspiciously. He'd just laughed it off.

But Jonny had kept on trying. He had to meet that girl, had to have her. He'd started asking others who had been at the party, but so far none of them seemed to know her. Jimbo had just shrugged. Lots of people turned up to his parties uninvited.

He saw her next one night a few weeks later when he'd been out on the road on his motorbike on his way home from the pub. He'd stopped at a set of lights when another bike pulled up next to him, big, black and gleaming. It was her, dressed in tight black leathers, wearing no helmet. She flicked a glance at him, smiled faintly, and then roared off as the lights changed, her long hair streaming in a banner behind her. He'd tried to keep up but she was fast, damned fast. He lost her when he took a corner badly and had nearly lost control of the bike, weaving it wildly to stay upright. Shaken, he'd pulled up and watched her vanish into the distance.

Then, just this very evening, he'd been walking home in a hurry for his meeting with Kevin. He'd had to sell his bike a week ago, but even with the cash from that he still owed Kevin big-time. He was hoping Kevin would wait for a bit for the rest of it. But Kevin was a pretty hot-tempered young guy.

Thinking about this, he'd spotted the girl from behind, heading away from him down the busy inner-suburban street, dodging her way along the crowded footpath. He'd actually called out, dumbly, because he still didn't know her name. Just "hey!" was all he could manage. But she had jumped up onto a tram that was just pulling away, and looked back at him, directly at him, with that long, cool stare of hers. He'd raised his hand in a kind of half-wave, realizing as he did it how stupid he must look.

And now she was here in his own room, though how she had found out where he lived Jonny couldn't imagine. But she *was* here, that's all that counted. He was getting a bit spaced out now, must have lost quite a bit of blood, ever since Kevin had stabbed him in a fury. How long had it been? A couple of hours?

Through his hazy vision, he noted idly that she was dressed in black again. A plain, well-filled, black T-shirt with black jeans.

Kneeling next to him now, she suddenly and unexpectedly leaned over and kissed him full on the mouth. Unbelieving, he responded as best he could, feeling a flood of joy.

And then she leaned back, seized the knife, twisted it hard so that he screamed in pain, and then yanked it out in one swift movement.

Jonny's life-blood gushed out onto the floor, and he was dead.

April 2012

Glorious Gold

As Lieutenant Travers began his dash across the courtyard, a cannon boomed in the distance. Just as he reached the tower doorway, a ball sped over the wall of the fort and smashed into the stonework on his right, throwing out a chip of stone to slash across his face. He staggered for a moment and then threw the door open and went through.

Major James looked up from his desk, a haggard look on his wide, florid face. "You're bleeding, Travers," he commented quietly.

"Yes, sir," said Travers, pulling out a handkerchief to ineffectually staunch the blood.

"Any news from the semaphore?"

"Yes, sir, in a way. The Frenchies have captured the nearest station on the mainland and sent us a very rude message. At least, I assume it's rude. There were several French words I didn't recognise."

"The same thing, then? They want us to lay down our arms and yield up the fort?"

"More than that, sir. They claim to have captured London itself. They... they say that King George has surrendered England to Boney and that the war is lost." Travers stopped for a moment, his young face bleak as he continued to hold the kerchief to his face. "Well, that's what they claim," he ended lamely, without much hope.

Major James grimaced. "It may be true, alas. Their flagship sent a signal this morning. They want to send their Admiral across to parley. If what you say is true, they may even have a signed order from the King, directing us to surrender."

He stared gloomily out of the narrow slit window towards the bay. In the distance, the cannons of the French fleet continued to boom, and nearer to hand, there was a continual crash and shake as the cannonballs arrived. Every so often, a man screamed.

Much less frequently, there was a louder boom as the fort replied in kind.

"Why aren't we shooting back more often, damn it? We can't be short of powder, surely? Have we lost so many gun crew?"

"No, sir..." Travers suddenly stopped, his face turning a greenish shade of white.

"Sit down, man, before you fall down."

Travers sank gratefully into the wooden chair in front of the Major's desk.

"No, sir, though it's true we have lost several crews. There's still plenty of powder in the magazine, sir, as you would expect. It's cannonballs we're short of now. I have as many men as I can shaping stone, but it's a slow process. And of course, we can't throw stone balls as far and hard as iron shot. They tend to shatter if we use too much powder."

Major James drummed his fingers on the desk. "Hmmm. If you're well enough, Lieutenant, send Captain Smithers in to see me."

Travers shook his head sadly. "Sir, I'm afraid that the Captain was killed about an hour ago by a Frenchie cannonball."

"Damn. He was a good man. All right then." He reached into his desk drawer and drew out a heavy bunch of keys. "Are you recovered? Come with me, then."

He used the keys to open the door behind his desk, and beckoned to Travers, who followed, a little wobbly.

They entered a corridor leading deeper into the fort. Reaching a set of stairs, the two men descended. On the first floor they passed, soldiers were busy rolling barrels of black powder to be passed up onto the battlements and the ranks of cannon there. There was plenty of powder still, but their supplies of iron shot had been heavily depleted to supply the ships of the fleet.

Fort Redoubtable had been established on this island as a supply post for the British Navy and Marine Corps. The Admiralty had thought it impregnable, commanding the heights above the harbour with ranks of cannon mounted behind its thick stone walls. In case of a siege, it had always been assumed that the Navy could easily relieve it. But that had been before the war went bad. The loss of Nelson and half the British fleet at the Battle of the Nile had been a disaster, and from then on things had gone from bad to worse.

The two men descended another two flights of steps, to the lowest level of the castle. They went around several corners and then the Major used his keys again to let them into a large store-room, filled with wooden crates.

"Lieutenant, I'm about to show you something that only myself and Captain Smithers knew the truth about. The war may be lost, but I'm damned if I'm going to go quietly. I'll refuse to see the French Admiral, damn his frog-eating guts. I'm not going to see what is in this room fall into their hands so easily.

They can have it, all right, by God they can have it. But they won't like it!"

He picked up a crowbar and pried the top off of one of the crates. A layer of lead sheeting covered the contents. Major James peeled it back and Travers gave a shout of astonishment. A glorious gleam of gold shone out, filling the dark room with colour. The crate was full of gold bars.

"It's from the Mint. When the French invaded and started making progress towards London, it was decided to ship half the Mint's store of gold abroad to our colony in Canada, top secret, of course. This is as far as it got before we were cut off." He looked at Travers with a smile. "What do you think?"

Travers sat down dazedly on one of the crates, suddenly understanding. "Yes, yes..."

The fort's cannons started firing again that afternoon. Major James and Travers stood behind the ramparts of the fort as ball after ball, yellow and gleaming, flew out out towards the French flagship, which had pulled incautiously close to the shore. Heavier even than lead, they wrought terrible damage, and within minutes the flagship was keeling over, masts torn away and huge holes in its side.

"We're still doomed, of course," said the Major reflectively, as the golden barrage continued. "But by God, what a way to go out!"

May 2012

Death, Who is the Key

MY WORLD IS COMING TO AN END, thought Sara as she sat in sorrow at the deathbed of her master Izak.

His breath was laboured, as he fought to retain consciousness and tried once again to speak to her. It wouldn't be long now, Sara knew. Her heart was as heavy as any of the stone blocks which made up her master's tower. He had been good to her over the years, had Izak, and she had served him to the limit of her ability as he taught her the mysteries of his art. Well, *some* of the mysteries. She suspected that the reserved old man had kept back from her much of what he had discovered. Not that she held that against him. That had been his right.

Izak's imminent death was bad enough. But within hours Sara herself could be dead, or enslaved. Or worse. Outside the walls of the castle she could hear the ongoing battle raging. King Rizzard had sent out a last desperate sortie of mounted men to try to lift the months-long siege.

Despite all of Izak's ingenuity and the seemingly magical mechanisms and weapons he had devised for the King, the forces arrayed against them were now too strong. Duke Villiers had conspired with the neighbouring kingdom to overthrow Rizzard and put himself on the throne. A dangerous piece of treachery, now about to succeed, it seemed.

"Sara..." gasped out the old man on the bed. "Sara..."

"Hush, now," she said, fussily rearranging the blanket he had thrown off. It was almost winter, and the weather was cold. Whenever he was without the blanket he shivered miserably.

But he seemed to be burdened by its weight. An unpleasant, musty smell came from Izak's body as she put back the covering. *The stink of death*, she thought sadly.

"Sara... the key." He gasped again, tried vainly to sit upright. "The door... must open it."

He was delirious, babbling. "There is no key," she said. "No door. Don't worry, don't worry, it's all right."

A small flame of determination flickered in Izak's eyes. "Must escape! You. Sara. Must... The key. Take the key... the only key."

He fell back, exhausted. A minute passed as he tried and failed to speak again. Finally, an ugly sound escaped from his throat and a shudder ran through him. Then he was still. No more gasping breaths came from the lean figure on the bed, no movement. He was gone at last.

Sara sat looking at him, tears now beginning to run down her face.

In the new silence, from outside she could now clearly hear the screams of injured men and the shouts of others, yelling out their triumph or despair. She went to the window. The King's men were fighting desperately to cover their retreat back to the gate. The sortie had failed, then.

She turned back to the bed. What had Izak been trying to tell her? There was no key on his body. She ought to know, she had been bathing and dressing the dying man for weeks now. She had never come across any unexplained keys in his rooms. For that matter, there were no locked doors in the three rooms in the tower — the bedroom, the workshop and Izak's precious library. The dying man must have been out of his wits at the end. Still... he had seemed desperate to get out those last words.

It would be doing him a disservice not to at least make some effort. And besides, what else was there to do now, except wait for Duke Villiers' forces to storm the castle, for the men to come surging up the tower, to kill, or more likely, to rape?

Moving from room to room, she opened every drawer again, though she could already have made lists of their contents from memory. Looked on every benchtop, felt on top of every cupboard, scanned every shelf in the library. No key. She could, she supposed, take down every book off every shelf to see if there was a key hidden behind it or tucked inside its pages. But there were many hundreds of books. Such a search would take hours, and she didn't have hours.

She smiled sadly at the futility and probably the folly of her quest, resigned but not despairing. She had had a long time to come to terms with her fate.

Just as she was about to leave the library and return to the workshop, her eye was caught by the glint of silver. She looked back, but her hopes were instantly dashed. It had only been the light glinting off the embossed lettering on the spines of some of the books.

She paused, though, her eye running for a moment or two over the titles of the books. So many! Izak had often talked about books being the key to knowledge. Is that what he had meant? But dying, he had talked about opening a door. Perhaps that, too was just a figure of speech.

Then, as she started to turn away, her attention was caught by the prominent title of a thick book sitting on a high shelf. *Unica Cui Clavis* . One of Izak's many old volumes, probably a transcription of some ancient Latin text. Under his tutelage, she had learned a little of the language of the long-vanished

Empire. But not very much, not enough to translate the title, let alone the contents, of such a book.

But nevertheless she frowned, thinking about the words. *Clavis*. Didn't that have something to do with the musical instrument, what was it called? The clavichord. A *keyboard* instrument. In that case, could *clavis* mean *key*? Was that, could that be the word for the same kind of key which opened a lock?

She went back to the bookcase and, standing on tiptoe, took down the book.

In the space where the book had been, she could see something. She went to fetch a chair. Standing on it, she could now see that there was a gap in the stonework, and in the gap, the bound end of a rope. In the dim light which filtered into the gap, she could faintly see that the rope ran over a pulley. Typical of Izak's clever mechanisms.

She pulled on the rope. Nothing happened, the rope didn't seem to move. Grimly she seized it in both hands and put all of her weight behind it. There was a grinding sound and then the rope went slack. The grinding sound continued, accompanied by a new sound, a whirring and clicking. Somewhere, wheels were turning. And now she could see that the bookcase next to the one where she was standing was beginning to move upwards, sliding with a slight juddering motion towards the high stone ceiling. Behind it was a dark gap.

She stepped down from the chair, picked up the thick book, and returned it to the shelf. She also moved the chair back to the table. No point in leaving clues for Duke Villiers' men.

Outside, she could hear a renewed surge of noise. It sounded as if the fighting was now at the very gate of the castle. A profound thud which seemed to shake the tower indicated that a battering ram was now in action against the gate.

In the gap revealed by the risen bookcase, she could see a flight of stairs, leading upward. But surely Izak's rooms were already at the very top of the tower? It seemed not. Sara stepped in to the gap. Another short piece of rope was visible in an opening high in the wall here. Cursing Izak's tallness and her relative shortness, Sara jumped up to catch the rope and swing from it. She felt it move. The grinding sound was renewed, and she saw the bookcase begin to descend again.

She ran up the spiral stairs.

At the top, she came out into a large dim room. An attic room, hidden under the sloping roof. One shuttered window was jammed into the short side wall. No ceiling above, just the undersides of the slate tiles. Izak must have continually been in danger of knocking his head up here, Sara thought, as she quickly went to the window and opened the shutter.

As the light spread into the room, she saw that it was cluttered with tools and parchments. On a low workbench lay a large, symmetrical construction made of folded cloth and wood, with a metallic mechanical device attached at the centre. It took Sara long moments to make sense of it. It had leather straps in several places, and it appeared to be designed to be attached to a human body. A small body, perhaps that of a child. Or a small, slight woman like herself.

From outside she heard a sound of splintering, followed by a wailing of despair from many throats. The gate had gone down, then. Not much time left.

Frantically, Sara picked up scattered drawings and tried to compare them with the mechanism on the bench. Izak's handwriting had been difficult to decipher even at the best of times, and the urgency now made it all the harder.

But then it all came together in a sudden flash of insight. Sara strode to the workbench and began turning the winding handle on the clockwork mechanism. It took all of her strength and took a long time, minutes she knew that she could not afford to waste. But there was no point leaving it only partly wound.

Then she began to strap herself into the thing.

She could hear the harsh laughing of the Duke's men as they entered the rooms below. She prayed that they would not discover the hidden door too quickly. Or at all. But they would be bent on destruction, would tear down all of the books. She couldn't rely on them not being curious about the rope in the wall.

It was done. She turned to the window, her heart thudding. *So what if I die?*, she thought.*Better this way than being forced by the soldiers and then having my throat slit.*

Moments later, standing on a ledge in the cold wind, she pressed the lever at her side. Something on her back began to spin, driven by the clockwork. Summoning all of her courage and her respect for her master's genius, she leapt out into space.

Her wings spread wide.

April 2013

View from the Top

THE BRIGHT FLASH FROM OUTSIDE ruined what had been until then a very pleasant dinner party.

Jason Dalrymple had thrown the party to celebrate moving in to his new penthouse apartment at the top of the Los Angeles skyscraper which now housed the headquarters of his media empire. Siting his offices here had raised some eyebrows – New York was supposed to be the center of the media business. But, damn it, he had been born in California and he liked the weather here.

Around the table had been a hand-picked selection of the wealthy and the powerful. Well, one went with the other, didn't it? To be wealthy in this country *meant* being powerful. And without power you had no wealth.

There were two senators, a Wall Street banker, and two business leaders. All men, with their wives. He himself had no companion present, his current wife being in the midst of messy and expensive divorce proceedings with him.

The entrée had been served efficiently by his butler, a tall elegant figure with greying hair. The silverware was elegant, to a design Dalrymple had commissioned personally. The plates were Sèvres antiques, the glasses were European crystal, filled with a variety of wines his butler had personally selected.

Around them, on the walls of the spacious dining room, were original oil paintings, including his precious Van Gogh. Dalyrmple sat in his heavy, high-backed chair facing into the room, the better to let more of his guests look out of the floor-to-ceiling picture window at the spectacular view out to Catalina and the Pacific Ocean.

The talk in the early part of the dinner, of course, had been all about the international situation.

"Got to admire how effective you've been at pushing the President over this Korea thing," had said one of the senators, who was sitting at Dalrymple's left hand. "Damn fool wouldn't have stood up to those damn Chinks if it hadn't been for your news channel and your papers hounding him night and day."

Dalrymple had smiled slightly and nodded. "Well, we need the media to keep the politicians honest, Senator."

The senator laughed aloud at that, and Dalrymple had gone on: "Besides, that maniac in North Korea is only bluffing, anyone can see that, just trying to get us to provide more food aid, as usual."

The entrée dishes were removed and replaced with dinner plates, and Dalrymple had watched approvingly as the butler shaved off slices of the beef with a razor-sharp carving knife and then delicately transferred the slices to the plates of the guests.

"Oh, Mr Dalrymple, I just *adore* your butler!" had gushed the blonde wife of the banker. "What's his name?"

"I call him Jeeves," Dalrymple had muttered in some annoyance. "He's been with me for a couple of years now."

Jeeves wasn't really the butler's name, of course. But it was something along those lines. Dalrymple could never remember it. Greaves? Treeves? Something like that. But it was close enough to Jeeves that it had become a little private joke between them. Shouldn't all butlers be called Jeeves?

One of the businessmen had started to lecture the other diners about the need for tougher sentencing laws, and a wider scope of offences with mandatory jail terms. Dalrymple smiled cynically. The man owned a string of private prisons, and there was profit to be made.

As the butler cleared the dinner plates and carried them neatly to the pantry, the senator had returned to the topic of North Korea.

"What do you say to those people on the other side who claim these goons could be a real threat? One of the Democrats was claiming in the Senate the other day that he'd seen evidence that their missile program was more advanced than we think."

The first syllable of the word 'Nonsense' had barely been out of Dalrymple's mouth when there had come the flash.

From Dalrymple's point of view, with his back to the window, what happened was that every reflective point in the dining room – the silverware, the glasses, the jewellery dangling from the ears of the trophy wives – lit up in an instant, near-blinding blaze of blue-white light. Everyone on the opposite side of the table, men and women both, screamed and threw up their hands to cover their eyes. Too late, too late.

The senator on Dalrymple's left let out a startled "What?" and rose to his feet. It was a bad move, because at that very moment the blast wave hit the picture window and sent it in a thousand deadly shards slicing through the room. The senator toppled forward onto the dining table, a huge spear of glass through his torso.

Dalrymple felt a myriad of thuds hit the back of his high wooden chair and watched in horror as all his guests were slaughtered by a torrent of deadly glass. Every painting was torn from the wall, and he felt the tower sway from the impact. But this was Los Angeles, and the building had been built to withstand earthquakes. It swayed forward, but then swung back.

Shakily, Dalrymple got to his feet. There was a lake of blood soaking into the tablecloth. The expensive crystalware, the priceless Sèvres porcelain, the artistic silverware were nowhere to be seen. The Van Gogh was ripped into shreds. A hundred daggers of glass pierced the far wall of the room.

He turned, and looked out over the sea. A huge mushroom-shaped cloud, glowing red and sparked about with lightning bolts, rose over the water some indeterminate distance away. Something insane in his head was saying: *I told you those Koreans couldn't hit the U.S. coast. Their missiles can't reach this far.* But, perhaps, close enough.

As he stood there, stupefied, he felt someone by his side. It was Jeeves. He must still have been in the butler's pantry when the blast hit. Together they watched as a black wave swept towards the coast, struck in a high surge of foam and then kept flooding onward.

"Jeeves... I..." Dalrymple shook his head. "We should call the police, the Pentagon..."

"I'm afraid, sir," said the butler, "that the telephone lines will all be out. Excuse my overhearing your conversation at dinner, sir, but do I recall you mentioning that the Koreans were bluffing?"

"Yes, yes. I... well, obviously, I... that is..."

"Do you know, sir, that my daughter lived at the ocean front? And my grandchildren? Just there, sir, where the wave is now?"

"Jeeves, I..."

"My name, sir, is not Jeeves."

And with that, the butler calmly slid the carving knife between Dalrymple's ribs.

March 2012

Babble

HELEN WALKED INTO THE TOWER for the start of her Saturday shift, a slight frown on her face. It had been a long week, and already she felt the beginnings of a headache.

"The Tower" was an ironic name because in fact the bulk of the Centre was deep underground.

Above ground, it was topped by a strange metallic forest made up of hundreds of antennas, satellite dishes, radio and microwave receivers and other electronic gear.

Below ground there were no windows of course, and little direct lighting. Instead, the huge room was lit by several dozen glowing screens mounted on the walls, each filled with a bewildering and shifting mass of text, figures, diagrams and maps. Smaller screens wrapped half-way around every workstation, of which there were hundreds.

Text flowed constantly on the workstation screens, and a peculiar soft noise filled the room. It came leaking from the headphones worn by the many operators, each set contributing only a faint whisper, but adding in total to a sound like that of a distantly heard but huge cocktail party. Speech in many different languages. For that reason, those who worked there called it "The Tower of Babel". Jokingly, perhaps, but there were few jokes here. The work was too serious.

No human being could listen directly to more than a fraction of the communications monitored here. Instead, a deeply buried battalion of computers analyzed every aspect of the electronic traffic, flagging those items of interest. A particular word in Russian spoken *here*, with *this* particular emphasis, in*this* particular context might raise such a flag. Another phrase in an email, written in Urdu, perhaps, from an individual in such-and-such a country, to another at a specific time of day, might raise another flag. Then it was up to humans to consider and make sense of it.

And those were just the communications sent "in the clear". Another, larger bank of computers even further underground worked on deciphering the encrypted messages, or else inferring conclusions simply from their traffic flow.

Helen took in the current state of play and then, rubbing the bridge of her nose, she gave a sigh, and moved towards her office to settle in for the day's work. Before she reached it, she was intercepted by her young second-in-command David Andrews.

"I want you to see something," David said. "We can't make any sense of it. It started about an hour ago."

She followed him to a workstation where a young operator sat, his fingers flashing over a keyboard as he brought up one analysis program after another on the six screens arrayed around him.

"It's a signal we've never seen before," David said. "Coming from three different locations, one of them in the mountains between Iran and Pakistan. It's encrypted, but we're applying the decryption algorithms we've had success with before on Iranian signals. So far we haven't cracked it."

Helen rubbed her temples. The headache was getting worse, and she hadn't done a thing yet. "You said three locations. Where are the others?"

"We're concentrating on the Iranian signal because it seems the most significant. The others, well, it's funny. One is in mid-Pacific. The other is in Guyana."

"Guyana? What the hell?"

David shook his head, frowning. "I told you it didn't make any sense." Usually calm and confident, today David seemed harassed and worried.

"All right," she said. "Get me all the intel we have about connections between the Iranians and South American revolutionary groups." Could Teheran be plotting some kind of terrorist attack in the Western Hemisphere? It seemed unlikely. But perhaps it wasn't them. Was it Al Qaeda, hiding in those mountains on the fringe of Afghanistan? Or...?

"You said one signal was in the Pacific? On an island?"

"No, mid-ocean. We haven't been able to get a visual fix on it from the satellite."

"Submarine, then." Couldn't be the Iranians. Had to be the Russians or the Chinese. "Any luck on the decryption?"

The desk operator shook his head. "They're using something new. I've requisitioned some time on Berkley's quantum array, but it hasn't come through yet." He sat back a moment, rubbed his neck. "Getting a damned headache," he muttered.

David grimaced. "Me, too."

Helen's own headache felt as though it were developing into a migraine. Irritably, she pushed it away and concentrated on the problem at hand. "I'm going to escalate this," she said, and turned away to call the Director, who in turn would decide whether to pass on an alert to the strategic command.

Before she had gone two steps, though, the desk operator called out.

"It's completely changed!" he said. "Now it's just a simple pattern of pulses... Well, maybe not so simple. Seems kind of random." He switched it through to external speakers and they could hear a bewildering drumming beat out.

Alarmed, Helen flashed a glance at David, who looked grim. "The start of a trigger signal, a countdown?" he suggested. With a surge of something like panic, Helen discarded the idea of going to her office. She grabbed up a phone from the operator's desk.

"Ultra priority," she snapped, taking the responsibility onto herself. "Imminent terror attack suspected. We need an immediate strategic alert."

—

Far above them, the commander of the cloaked starcraft decided that enough had been done to meet the requirements of the tribe-father's instructions. Through the three evenly spaced drones they had sent into the planet's atmosphere, they had attempted to communicate with this new species using standard telepathic means and indeed, every other known channel. Towards the end they had even tried the archaic electromagnetic spectrum just in case. As a last resort, they had used simple pulses to send the unmistakable mathematical pattern of the *Xwyzyk* sequence, which any intelligent species must recognise. Still no response.

The instructions were clear: send the ultimatum and failing any response, assume that the subject species was stubbornly rejecting the generous offer of the tribe's benign overlordship.

In which case...

With the sense of satisfaction that comes from having faithfully completed complex orders, the commander initiated the destruction sequence. On his screens, he saw the drones plunge down and began their drilling operations as they burrowed towards the planet's core with their anti-matter payloads.

Time to move the starcraft away to a safe distance, on the other side of the biggest gas giant, perhaps.

June 2012

In the Woods

THE OLD WOMAN LIVES ALONE IN A COTTAGE IN THE WOODS.

There might have been a town here once, she sometimes thinks. But all of the people seem to have left. Over time, their houses have fallen down, and trees have grown up through the ruins. Where there might once have been a busy road, now only a narrow footpath leads through the thick forest.

A young girl comes to visit her one day and brings her food. The old woman does not know her name, but she is grateful for the food and for the girl's bright and caring face.

"Thank you, my dear," she says to the strange girl. "You are very kind. Do I know you from somewhere?"

The girl smiles and laughs. "Of course, grandmother. You know me very well."

"Do I? That's good, that's good. You are very kind."

These days are bright, but at night, she can hear something slinking about in the forest. Outside her cottage it moves and mutters and growls, and she is afraid.

In the morning, her fears are gone. She looks about her. Her cottage seems smaller now. Were there not once more rooms? She thinks so, but cannot be sure. Now there seems to be just this one room, with her bed, and a window and a door.

A young man comes to the door. He must be a woodcutter, she thinks, working in the forest. Has she ever seen him before? He is tall and handsome and asks after her health.

"Oh, I'm fine, dear. There's nothing ever wrong with me." He smiles and goes away again. But he must not be working hard, because each day there seem to be more trees in the forest, and it grows a little darker outside her window.

At night, in the dark, she can hear something wild outside, something slinking amongst the trees, then brushing against her door with its long wiry fur, trying to get in. She lies as still as she can, her heart pounding in terror, praying for the morning to come.

In the morning, though, the bright light washes everything away. A young girl comes to visit and brings her food in a basket, with flowers she has picked in the wood. The old woman wonders who the girl is, and why she is so kind.

The old woman moves about the room. There is a vase of flowers here, very pretty. She picks up each flower in turn to examine it. She wonders who brought them, and why.

Something is wrong with the door to the cottage. It will not open no matter how hard she tries. But she has the water and food someone has brought, and after a while she stops trying to open the door.

A handsome woodcutter comes to see her. He asks after her health, and she tells him that she is very well, that she is never sick. Perhaps she should ask him about the door? There was something wrong about a door, she thinks.

A tree grows right outside her window now, it fills her view. The forest must be growing close, she thinks. She wants to go outside to look at it, but for some reason she cannot open her door. After a while, she sighs, and gives it up.

Then there is a terrible night.

She is in her bed when a horrible slinking thing breaks into her cottage. It climbs into bed beside her and she feels its hairiness, smells its foul breath. It paws at her. She screams and screams, and after a moment a woodcutter rushes in to her room and drags the hairy thing out from her bed. There is noise and shouting and lights, and many people crowd in, people she does not know. But at last the evil thing is taken away. She sobs in terror, but the woodcutter tells her it is gone and will not come back.

A young girl comes to see her the next day, bringing food in a basket. The old woman cannot understand why she seems so upset.

"Oh, granny," the young girl says with tears in her eyes, "you must have been so frightened. But you don't need to worry, they've moved that horrible man away to another nursing home."

"Frightened, dear?" says the old woman, admiring the girl's red coat. "Frightened by what?"

October 2012

The Twist of Fate

THERE WERE HUMAN BONES SPILLING LOOSELY from the inside of the crater, falling with the black earth in which they had been embedded to partially obscure the still-hot layer of glass that covered the bottom.

Stephen Pham Tang, standing gingerly at the crumbling edge of this utterly impossible crater, looked down at the bones, appalled. Surely there had not been so many killed by the blast? But then he remembered. Before the research institute had been built here, this had been the Melbourne General Cemetery. The catastrophic and still mysterious explosion here had killed hundreds, and thousands more were yet to die. But what he now saw were merely the relics of the long-dead.

It was hot, too hot. It was one of those blazing summer days that, as you awaken from an exhausting sleep, even at dawn greets you with the threat of its heat to come. Far too hot to be cooped up in an ill-fitting and all-enclosing radiation suit. Stephen felt as though his dripping sweat was pooling in his boots. He kept wishing vainly that he could wipe his eyes, to get rid of the blinding perspiration.

He couldn't even work out why he was here. He looked around again. The other scientists were hard at work, their bright yellow suits somehow wildly incongruous amidst this devastation. But then, the whole scene was incongruous: this landscape of shattered buildings standing like the columns of some ancient ruin in a circle around a two-hundred-metre wide crater at the centre.

There was work to be done, of course, important work. Even as he thought it, he started looking about for useful samples to pick up. But surely Samphan could have given this work to more junior workers? This was the work of laboratory assistants, not middle-aged physicists like himself.

Grumbling to himself, he bent down and picked up a piece of glass, shattered from some window. There should be particle tracks within the material which would give them some clues. He put it inside one of the plastic bags they had given him. Even that was stupid, he thought. The bulldozers whose roar now filled his ears were already removing tonnes of irradiated glass and brick from the ruins. Surely that material could be studied just as profitably as anything he could pick up. But then he gave up his internal complaints. Probably Samphan wanted to bring the researchers face to face with the reality of last week's incredible event, to shock them into a feeling of the urgency of their task, the question that they must answer, and quickly: what on earth had happened here?

For Stephen Tang, it had begun with wakening in terror, finding himself screaming with panic: "My God! What was that?" His scream had followed by the barest instant the thundering crash that had awoken him, rattling the windows.

Everyone in the crammed house where he lived had surged out of their rooms into the street, as had their neighbours, many as stark naked as they had slept in the hot night. He himself had felt the same panicky need to get out of his claustrophobic room, perhaps subconsciously fearing an earthquake, or more likely, the long-dreaded return of the missiles. They were, after all, now at war again. And, as if to fuel his fears and agonising childhood memories, from behind the night-eclipsed hills there had risen a distant glowing cloud like some mockery of the sun.

His fears had been justified, at least in part. What had that night awoken most of the millions who packed the city had indeed been a nuclear explosion, though a small one. But, though many older people had been reduced to incoherent terror by the dread that the Chaos had returned, there seemed no way that the Argentines could have delivered such a weapon without detection. And the true war was far to the frozen south. No, after the first hours of general panic, it had become clear that something, no one yet could imagine what, had gone wrong here at the Solomon Research Institute, just to the north of the city of Melbourne.

Stephen Tang saw one of the yellow-clad men waving. There was a wide red cross marked across the front of the suit, making the wearer appear somehow clown-like, certainly not the impression that he would have desired. It was Thanh Samphan, the head of the scientific team appointed by the Emergency Commission.

Like saffron sheep, the team followed Samphan over the rubble and through an arch of twisted iron girders. Out of the innermost circle of Hell, Tang thought idly, into the next most dreadful. Here the buildings were still upstanding, though burnt to skeletons and with every window gone. Beyond them was a newly thrown-up fence of cyclone wire, with a dense layer of humanity packed up against it, looking in at the scene of disaster with various degrees of wonder. Stephen hurried forward to walk next to Samphan. "Those people," he said, "aren't they still too close? The radiation..."

Samphan nodded in irritation. "Yes. yes," he said impatiently. "But what would you have me do? There are warning signs up in nine different languages and the militia continually try to move them on. But we can't block off the road, it's too busy. Do you want me to seal off half of Carlton? Evacuate a quarter of a million people? So we should, but where would we put them all? There's no room. They will have to take their risks like the rest of us. Besides," he said, perhaps made more callous by the scorching heat of the day, "the one thing we have no shortage of in Australia is people." With that, he marched ahead to the gate, where five or six militia were keeping the crowd back from the vehicle that the Commission had allocated to them.

As they passed through the gate, the crowd seemed to surge towards them, hundreds of people, faces eager or fearful, calling out, asking questions. Stephen found the crowd oppressive, even for the moment disgusting, as they pressed against him, most wearing only sweaty T-shirts and shorts. He wanted to call out: "Don't touch me! I'm radioactive! Go away!" But before he could give way to the impulse he was being shepherded into the car, yellow suit and all.

If the day outside had been hot enough, inside the car it was all but stifling. He found himself very thankful that they did not have far to go. Despite the heat, it would have been an easy walk, had it not been for the radiation suits and the jam-packed crowds lining the streets.

He was wedged into the back seat of the vehicle between two others, John Chau Nguyen and big Bill Macarthur, whose head brushed the roof. Macarthur turned to him and gave him a wink, "Bit of a change, eh, Steve? Never this much fun at ARL, is it?" Stephen shook his head with a faint smile.

The car pulled slowly away from the kerb. Its alcohol-fuelled engine was greatly under-powered, but there was no need of speed or power in driving through Melbourne's traffic-choked streets. They were forced to move at the same pace as the hundreds of cyclists, and moped drivers, in a noisy, dense and sluggish stream. Their journey was less than a kilometre, but it took nearly a quarter of an hour as the car fought its way around Cemetery Road and down Swanston Street, past the towering, barbed-wire-topped walls of the University of Melbourne, to the gates. There were militia here, too, more of them, and there was an annoying delay while the gates were unbarred and swung open, allowing the car to move into Tin Alley while the militia held back the crowd. Stephen Tang felt as though he was about to expire from heat exhaustion as the gates crashed shut behind them.

The University itself looked like a war zone. Every window had been shattered by the nearby blast, and rough sheeting had been tacked up everywhere. Piles of glass and bricks still lay around the campus where they had been swept.

There was a makeshift decontamination area set up in the old Beaurepaire Centre, and they moved into the showers still wearing their suits. A grim-faced militiaman ran a radiation detector over them before they were allowed to remove the suits. Then and only then could they wash the sweat from themselves. Stephen wondered what was being done to decontaminate the car they had ridden in.

A lecture theatre and other rooms had been set aside for them at the top of an aging mult-storey building, and Stephen and the others sat like students at the desks as Thanh Samphan addressed them. He was quite a tall man, though not as tall as a Caucasian like Macarthur, and surprisingly dark-skinned. Stephen wondered if he had some African blood in him. Samphan wore tiny spectacles which made him look somehow like a grandmother. He had pinned a large map of the Carlton area up on the board behind him.

"In many ways we were lucky," he said. "The explosion, whatever caused it, occurred on a night when there was little wind." Stephen Tang remembered the night well. It had been hot and sticky, with not a breath of a breeze to relieve it. "Because of this," Samphan went on. "the fallout from the explosion fell almost directly back down. The radiation reports indicate this as the area of potentially lethal fallout." And he went to the map and carefully drew a red loop on it, extending around the now-destroyed Solomon Research Institute and over to the east, about 800 metres from the centre of the explosion.

"It would be good if it were possible to evacuate all of this area," he said, looking directly at Stephen. "But there are enormous practical difficulties with this. However, many of the people living closest to the blast have abandoned their homes anyway because of blast damage. What we have done is to use the militia to seal off this area here... " he marked a smaller area in blue along the lines of the closer streets, "to try to prevent squatters moving in at least for the next two weeks. But we must expect cases of radiation sickness to run into the thousands."

He turned to the scientists, "Nevertheless, this is not our concern, but that of the authorities. Our concern is only to determine what caused the blast and to do everything possible to prevent a recurrence."

He turned back to the board, a marker in his hand. "Now, I think it is feasible to rank some of the more likely possibilities in order of probability." He marked up:

 * Runaway fisson in the experimental reactor.

 * Low-yield nuclear weapon assembled and detonated by saboteurs.

 * Unknown experiment going wrong.

He looked at the others over the top of his glasses. "Any disagreements?"

Chaidir Basarah, one of Stephen's colleagues from ARL, nodded vigorously. "I can't believe either number one or number two," he said.

"Nor can I," Stephen said. "Why should the reactor blow up like that? Yes, it was of an experimental design, but it was designed to be utterly fail-safe. I saw the protocols Dr Masters was using, and they were good. Besides, it had only a small amount of fissile fuel. A reaction would have to be very efficient, release almost all of the fuel's energy in one instant, to create what we saw."

"Matthews thought the reactor was safe," Samphan said with a touch of sharpness, "but he could have been wrong. So much information was lost about nuclear reactors during the Chaos. And, Stephen, the surveys of the precise centre of the explosion place it at or very near to the basement where the hybrid reactor was operating."

"Even so, I can't envisage how it could happen, unless there was some fundamental flaw in Dr Matthews design which he missed." Stephen said. There was a buzz of discussion around the table.

Samphan nodded slowly, without it signalling agreement. "Then possibility number two? A terrorist incident?"

Basarah folded his arms in annoyance. "No. Look, building a nuclear weapon isn't something to be done in your backyard, or even in a forgotten basement lab at Solomon. Someone would notice you. And even if the Argies wanted to blow up Melbourne, why such a little firecracker? And if it was sabotage, I can think of many more useful places to blow up than Solomon."

Samphan shrugged. "Perhaps it was intended to be a multi-megaton device, but it didn't work properly. Or perhaps it was just intended to disrupt our research program, which is certainly has. Or perhaps it was intended as a warning, to show us what could be done: 'Get out of Antarctica, or else'."

Bill Macarthur spoke up. "Not very likely. Besides, we'd have had an ultimatum by now. And I think the Argentines feel the same way about nuclear weapons as we do. They suffered just as badly after the Chaos as we did. I just don't think they would do it. But look, we're not here to debate politics, but physics and technology. I agree with Chaidir. It would be impossible to build such a thing undetected, particularly if you intended it to be a big one."

"Which leaves us with possibility number three — something unknown. Which is hardly helpful," Samphan said.

He opened up the meeting to discussion, and ideas, probable or improbable, began to be thrown around.

After an hour or so, Samphan called a halt.

"Gentlemen," he said, "we have to begin some serious science, not just bandy about speculation. We can begin studying materials taken from the blast site to rule out various possibilities we have so far discussed. I propose to break up this team into sub-groups studying various possibilities. Myself and Ji Zhen will look at the feasibility of a smuggled-in weapon, which I personally still feel the most likely possibility. William Macarthur, John Chau Nguyen and Chaidir Basarah will study the hybrid reactor... a terrible loss, that. We need that energy. But I am going astray. Stephen Pham Tang will look at the other research which had been going on at Solomon, to investigate any other possibilities, no matter how remote."

Stephen felt a sudden pang of anger. It was typical of Samphan to stick him at the bottom of the list and to give him the least useful job. He had no idea why Samphan disliked him. But there was always this suppressed hostility between them. Stephen gritted his teeth and nodded.

Thanh Samphan shook his head sadly. "At present, I agree, nothing seems very likely. But the Commission has been given every resource possible, The terrible loss of life and destruction of irreplaceable research information must never happen again. I propose that we each map out a plan of attack, and meet here again tomorrow, at 10. If you need information from other people, the militia is at your disposal should you meet any resistance. You have the highest authority to enter premises and demand papers and other information." He looked over his glasses at them again. "You are privileged, gentlemen. No other scientists have ever had such power, I think. All right. Let us get moving."

John Nguyen was a senior lecturer in physics at the University, a small, painfully thin man in his late forties who always seemed ill, perhaps because of childhood exposure to the radiation from the Chaos. He walked out of the theatre with Stephen. "I have a pretty fair idea of some of the work that went on at the Institute," he said. "So I can give you a start. But a lot of the research was kept tightly under wraps because of valuable commercial or military applications. The money and the State's support is why the University ran the Institute, of course. Trouble was, a lot of secretive bods managed to work there doing pure science they claimed had commercial applications but which was just their own pet hobby."

Stephen nodded. "The biggest problem as I see it is that the blast itself has managed to destroy all of the evidence about what caused it. I take it that because of security reasons, there wouldn't be copies of research information kept here in the University itself?"

Nguyen shook his head. "Not unless there were papers published. The library would hold those. But look, let's go over to Admin and have a look at what the people working at Solomon claimed they were about. It'll be as vague as hell, but it'll be a start."

The campus grounds were full of students as the two worked their way across to the administration building. There was little recreation space left now. Every square metre of space was desperately needed. Stephen had rarely been back here since his own studies were completed over fifteen years ago, and he was startled at the number of new buildings that had been squeezed in, or older buildings razed to make way for skyscraper-like structures. A lot of the need was for residential space, of course. Almost all the students chose to live within the safety of the high walls. The few who lived outside had to put up with twice-daily pass checks at the gates.

In the administration centre they quickly found the records they wanted on the computer system. The list, though, was dauntingly long. "I should be able to rule some of the work out simply on common-sense grounds," Stephen said. "None of the genetic engineering work is likely to have led to a nuclear explosion, for example."

Nguyen smiled. "Not unless there are genes for nuclear fission. All right. I'll leave you to it. I'd better catch up with Bill and Chaidir."

Stephen began cutting down the list. It took him an hour to reduce it to a list of six projects which, however unlikely, might conceivably have had something to do with the explosion.

Stephen took a hard copy from the machine and looked gloomily at it. He couldn't help feeling he was pissing at the stars. Surely, no matter how improbable it was, it had to have been something going wrong with the hybrid reactor. These other things ... He shook his head, wondering still why Samphan had wanted him on the team in the first place. His studies at ARL were relevant, of course, but there were other, younger men now, keenly at work on things Stephen Tang barely understood. Perhaps that was it, he thought. Perhaps it was simply that I could be spared, that my work was not so important that it couldn't be left for several weeks. He sighed, and stood up. Despite his pessimism, he would do the work he had been given.

Listed on the sheet together with the name of the researcher, his topic of study, and any published papers, were the names of assistants who had been working under his control. Some of these people would be dead, he supposed, killed in the blast. But then, the blast had happened late at night. It was likely that at least some of these assistants had been sent home earlier. He sat back down at the screen and started to methodically work through the personnel records, hoping that the data had been brought up to date on the deaths the previous week. Fortunately, it seemed that they had. If nothing else, he thought cynically, the administration would want to stop the salaries of those killed as soon as possible.

At the end of another half hour, he had made a number of ticks and crosses on his list. Somewhat to his surprise and dismay, most of them were crosses, indicating that the people were dead. It seemed that working late at night was common at Solomon.

He sat back and looked at his list. He ran a marker through the entries where there had been no published papers and were no researchers or assistants left alive. He could see no way of making any progress at all on those, and the description of work was so unhelpful that, if the blast had eventuated from that research, no one would ever be able to prove it. That left him with only three possibilities.

Dr Choe Dong Ju had been working on "Nuclear transitions as a source of lasing phenomena at gamma-ray frequencies." Two assistants were still alive.

He noted the number of their room in the residential colleges.

Dr Michael Cruickshank had been studying something he called "Local induced deformations in the space-time matrix".

That didn't sound very hopeful. One assistant alive. He noted that she lived outside the University.

Finally, Dr Qing Xu was still alive herself. She had been working on "Nuclear reaction rate pathways in supernovae and applications to fusion research." That could be promising. Could she have induced a small-scale supernova? After a second, he shook his head. It sounded preposterous. Still, he would see her first.

He looked at his watch. It was in the middle of the peak hour, and millions of people would be out on the footpaths and the roads surging home.

And it was still fiercely hot. It would be intolerable trying to get all the way out to his room now. Better to wait until a little later. He looked up Qing Xu's telephone number, and rang her. Would she see him now?

She would.

—

Later that evening, he left the foyer of the new Trinity College. Although the sun was setting, the heat was still intolerable, and he could feel himself starting to sweat the moment he left the shaded college. Qing's room had been air-conditioned, an incredible luxury. It appeared she was quite wealthy.

But after two hours talking to her, he had convinced himself that her work had not been the cause of the explosion. Her studies of reaction rates had been done with the aid of the Institute's linear accelerator, buried in a kilometres-long tunnel beneath the Institute and now destroyed by the blast. But the accelerator had been no match for the huge devices built overseas before the Chaos, and it involved very simple, well-understood technology. Qing's work had involved careful computer studies of nuclear reactions, but on a tiny scale, and in small inert pieces of material. The supposed fusion applications had just been bait to obtain funding. Besides, her work had not been scheduled to go on the accelerator that night, which was the reason she had survived. He crossed her work off his list.

He had left his moped in the parking tower near the southern gates of the University. He climbed in, lay back, closed down the flimsy transparent hood — rather like closing a coffin lid on himself, he always thought — and grasped the control stick between his legs. This was the one luxury he had permitted himself after the breakup of his marriage. Dr Qing Xu had her air-conditioning, he had his moped. Tonight, he thought that he would let the engine do most of the work. He felt bone-weary. Besides, he could probably get the cost of the alcohol refunded by the Commission as a necessary travel expense.

He drove down to the gate, showed his special pass, and was permitted to pass out into the torrent of humanity that still surged along the streets. Hundreds of bicycles, many of them in the energy-saving recumbent design, dozens of mopeds like his own, the occasional automobile. And thousands upon thousands of people plodding along on foot along the widened footpaths.

He fought his way through the choked streets, seemingly little less densely trafficked than at the peak hour. He still found it amazing that so many people still had to travel. Most people, after all, elected to live close to their workplace, if they had one. It was not as if there was any public transport left.

Once, there had been electric-powered trams and trains in this city. But that was before the Chaos-induced energy shortage had gripped Australia like a maniac bent on strangulation.

Thinking these dismal thoughts, he at last reached the freeway. As he steered the moped around the slightly slower-moving cyclists, Stephen looked up grimly at the disgusting slums jammed onto the sides of the freeway and over where the parks had been, makeshift shanties packing every jot of space with hopeless humanity. That was where you ended up if there was no work for you, shitting into a tin can with a piece of plastic over your head to keep off the weather.

At last, he reached the rooming house where he lived, only a couple of kilometres from the Australian Radiation Labs. What had once been a garden was now packed with roughly-built extension rooms. He climbed out of the moped and wheeled it inside and through the narrow corridor to his room. With the hood collapsed, it fitted fairly well under the bed. He drank some of his water ration, and then, exhausted, dropped on to the bed and fell quickly asleep.

—

At the meeting the next day at the University, there was a lot more discussion. Some of the preliminary results had come in on the materials they had collected, and Bill Macarthur had begun a detailed engineering analysis of Dr Matthew's experimental reactor. Using a mathematical analysis, he had identified a possible design flaw which could have been overlooked. It sounded quite plausible. More and more Stephen felt that his own task was make-work, unimportant, a dead-end. The explosion must have something to do with the hybrid reactor after all. But still, not all the leads had been followed up.

After the meeting broke up about lunchtime, Stephen again consulted his list. Dr Choe Dong Ju's two surviving assistants lived on the campus. He would visit them next.

It turned out that the two assistants, both male, were on detachment from the militia. They lived in the same room in Newman Tower, and sat like mass-produced dolls together on the edge of one of the beds as Stephen sat on the other, asking them questions. Their hair was identically cropped short, they were of about the same height and colouring, and each was as reticent as the other. The only thing that distinguished between the two was that one was a Caucasian. Stephen almost felt that, if it had been possible, David Carnegie would have had his round eyes and longer nose altered by surgery to look more like his room-mate, Charles Hoang. The two had survived the blast simply because they had been rostered off together that night. They seemed to show little emotion or sense of loss that their professor and other colleagues had died in the mysterious blast.

For the first time, Stephen had to use the threat of his emergency powers in order to make the two talk at all. But after a while, he fully understood their reticence. Dr Choe's work had been on the feasibility of creating a graser - a gamma-ray laser. A weapon which would be appallingly lethal if it were possible. Given an appropriate power source, you could use one to carve your initials on the Moon. Stephen's skin pricked with anger and disgust. Does this madness never end? he thought.

"How far away from success do you think Dr Choe was?" he asked the two, fearing the answer.

"A long way," said David.

"Years, maybe decades," said Charles.

"A weapon like this, you'd need a small nuclear explosion to power it, isn't that right?"

"Possibly," said David.

"Probably," said Charles.

Stephen sighed. "Then you must tell me whether Dr Choe had access to such power sources. That might be the reason the Institute, and all his work, was destroyed, isn't that obvious?"

David Carnegie shook his head. "Out of the question. Anyway, the old man wasn't anywhere near actually building a graser. All he was doing was pottering about, mainly with theory, trying to work out if the thing was feasible."

"Besides," said Charles, "you don't think the State would just hand him a nuclear weapon to use in his basement, just like that, do you?"

"Even if the State admitted that Australia has developed such weapons, which it doesn't," said David.

"After all," said Charles, with the first hint of a cynical smile, "we don't want the Chaos back again, do we?"

After an hour of this, and a close examination of some working papers that the youths had kept, Stephen finally decided that he was getting nowhere. If the two militarists were telling the truth — and how could he determine that? — then Dr Choe's work was still very much at the theoretical stage. Stephen gave up, and left the two still sitting as they were, militarily upright and tight-lipped.

Outside the tower, he again looked at his list and pondered. It was yet another damnably hot day, and the humidity was high. Probably by that night a cool change would sweep in, heralded by a sharp-edged thunderstorm and crackling lightning. He hoped so. He looked at his watch. He would have to drive out to one of the inner suburbs if he was to see Elli Wirruna, the sole surviving assistant of Dr Michael Cruickshank. But the address he had was not far from the beginning of the freeway, almost on his way home. And the sooner he got this farce over with, the better.

—

He pulled the moped up outside four crumbling towers, and looked up in disgust. It was obvious immediately that these ancient buildings were merely vertical slums, twenty storeys high. He looked again at the address. No mistake. And the room number was on the nineteenth storey. Evidently Elli Wirruna, despite having a job, was in poor circumstances. Perhaps she was still repaying a grant that had allowed her to attend University. She certainly could not have had wealthy parents like most students, or she would be living on the campus.

What had once been a recreation area at the foot of the towers was now filled with a rambling dole-market, where the poor traded scraps of vegetables, hand-made goods and other junk. The smell almost made him gag. But he forced his way through the crowds of hopeless, dirty people, ignoring the jeers of the myriads of yelling children who ran naked in the narrow aisles between the tents and stalls, to eventually reach the foyer of the building he wanted.

The lifts were out of order. In fact, it looked as though they had not worked for many years. The door to the stairwell was propped open, and the stairs were worn away in shallow curves by constant use. For a moment, Stephen was tempted to give up here and now. The thought of climbing nineteen flights of stairs on a hot day like this could not have been less appealing. Still, he had a job to do. Once he had seen this Wirruna woman, he had done what he had been asked to do. Samphan could either involve him with the more interesting work on the reactor flaw, or let him go back to ARL in peace. He began to climb.

Gasping desperately for breath and soaked in sweat, he managed to reach the nineteenth storey at last. He had had to fight his way past dozens of people coming up and down the stairs, though there had been many less people the further up he climbed. Time and again he had been forced to stop and regain his breath. His legs were trembling and weak. Why would anyone chose to live all the way up here with no lifts? Housing was desperately scarce, of course, as the shanty-dwellers attested. But he would almost rather live along the freeways than be forced to climb up those stairs every day. Evidently he must expect Elli Wirruna to be athletic.

Piles of rubble were stacked on the crumbling concrete balcony outside the doors. Some of the doors had been broken open, and revealed narrow, deserted, rubbish-filled rooms. Stephen found it very hard to reconcile the idea of someone who worked at the research institute living here except because of the direst necessity.

He found Wirruna's door at last, and knocked. For a long time there was no answer, and he was just turning away in exasperation when the door came open, secured from opening further by a thick chain, and someone looked out.

Stephen Tang stepped back, startled by a face that did not at first seem human. It was pitch black, for a start, with a flattened nose. That was unusual enough, but the woman whose face it was looked as though she were desperately ill. Her eyes were bloodshot and her lips dry and cracked. From behind her came the sour stench of vomit.

But these unfavourable impressions were modified somewhat after Stephen had a moment to overcome his surprise. The woman was quite young, and neatly and cleanly dressed in a green blouse and pants. "Who are you?" she asked in a weak but well-educated voice. "What do you want up here?"

Stephen explained, and showed his authority. He hoped he wouldn't have to go back down to fetch the militia. But the young black woman just nodded, and attempted a smile. "You don't think Cruickshank's work blew up the Institute, do you? Not bloody likely. Still, you'd better come in." And she unhooked the chain.

Inside, the room was small and cheaply furnished, almost filled by a bed that had its head to the windows opposite the door. But it was clean and obviously well-kept. There were attractive posters stuck up on the walls, mostly engravings by Maurits Escher. "Sit down," said Elli Wirruna, bringing out a wooden chair from the tiny kitchen. She herself stood shaking with her back to the wall, hands clasped before her. Above her head was an Escher engraving of ants crawling over the surface of a wooden-framed Mobius strip.

"I'm sorry for the stink," she said after a moment. "I've been crook the last week, keep on having to throw up. Could be shock, I suppose. Dr Cruickshank and I were quite close." She stopped for a moment, and her hand made a spastic gesture towards her face as if to wipe away familiar tears. Seeing his glance, she suddenly snapped. "Not like you're thinking, I wouldn't have slept with him. Too old, for a start. But I respected him, respected his brain. respected what he was doing, even if he wasn't practical about it."

"How did you come to survive the explosion?" Stephen asked.

"Blind luck. I'd gone across the footbridge to the University to fetch him a book. He lived in Ormond, did you know that? I was halfway across the bridge when I was knocked down by the blast, knocked unconscious. They told me afterwards I was lucky the bridge didn't collapse underneath me. They had to tear it down the next day."

Stephen gave an inward curse at himself. He should have checked whether there were any relevant papers in the personal rooms of those killed by the blast. Taking such materials out of the security of the Institute would have been against the rules, of course, but it would have to be followed up nonetheless. More time-consuming and probably useless work.

He looked down at his list. "This work of Dr Cruickshank's. What can you tell me about it?"

She shook her head sadly. "It was the most important, most incredibly important and original work for decades. And now most of it's gone. Cruickshank was another Einstein, do you know that? I mean, really. Most of the other scientists are just catching up with what was lost during the Chaos and the years afterward. We're barely getting beyond what was known forty years ago. But Cruickshank's work, mostly in his head, theoretical work... it was as though the Chaos didn't exist for him. He just ignored it, and kept on thinking. He was way beyond anything they thought they understood about general relativity before the Chaos. I know that hundreds died in the blast, but there was only one of them who was important. Michael Cruickshank."

Stephen listened to this song of praise with some impatience. "Yes, yes, but I need some details. Do you have any papers, published or unpublished, about what he was doing?"

She gave him a sly look. "I might have, I might not. Oh, don't threaten me again with the militia. I don't give a damn. What's important is that Cruickshank's work be carried on by someone who understands it, who knows the potential it had. And I don't think it would be helped by letting the details out too soon. Next thing we'd know, the State would have grabbed it up and given it to some half-wit whose uncle is on the Council, and we'd never hear any more. Or they'd appoint a bloody committee to look into it. No bloody fear."

"Look here," said Stephen sharply. "I'm not interested in who continues Dr Cruickshank's work. You can keep it to yourself to work on for all I care. But I must know whether his work could possibly have led to that blast, the blast that killed him, and has killed hundreds of others. Thousands, when you look at those who will die from the after-effects. You must tell me, or I will have no hesitation about calling in the militia. And I can also arrange it that you are never able to work in science ever again."

That was the threat which unnerved her. She sat down on the bed, looking very ill again. "All right. Michael was working on the theory of space-time, and had developed a practical means to create small-scale deformations in the space-time matrix."

"So his project description says. But what does that mean?" It was hot in the room. There was no air-conditioning here, of course. And Stephen was becoming impatient to get this over with and set off home. He was also worried about the safety of his moped, parked near the market below. A determined thief wouldn't take long to cut through the lock.

She hesitated, and then stood up. "Hang on a sec," she muttered through a clenched mouth, and staggered over to a door. Beyond it was the toilet. She started to dry-retch, and, wishing he could stop his ears, Stephen looked away, up at the Escher print. How curiously simple and yet weird a Mobius strip is, he forced himself to think, unable to bear the sounds of misery. Take a thin strip of paper, give one end a half-twist, and join the ends. *Don't listen!* And then you have an object with only one edge and only one side.

The noises stopped. In a few minutes, Elli returned. "Nothing there," she said weakly. "Sorry." Then she sat in silence for a while, obviously working out what to say. Despite himself, Stephen was becoming curious.

"Cruickshank had developed a complex theory, going well beyond the Einstein-Hawking formulation of general relativity that was the accepted wisdom before the Chaos. In simple terms, he was fascinated by the curvature of space, and the various four-dimensional topologies that the universe might have. Cruickshank believed that the topology of space might be very complex indeed. And he wasn't just a theoretician. He was a brilliant experimentalist, too. What he'd done was to work out a way to experimentally create small deformed regions of space-time which could be examined in the laboratory, by seeing how they bent light, that sort of thing. Very small scale: the first regions he worked on had microscopic dimensions. But I encouraged him to work on larger-size regions, so that different types of experiment could be carried out, sending solid particles into the region and so on. That's about it, unless you're interested in the mathematics."

Stephen was a little disappointed. "And how were these regions created? Did they involve the use of nuclear energy?"

She almost laughed at the naivety of the question. "No. It involved the use of the electromagnetic force converted via Cruickshank's equations into gravitic curvature. The energy involved depended on the dimensions of the deformed region, but was really surprisingly modest. Gravity is, of course, the weakest of the known forces."

He pondered, tapping his notepad with his marker. "And were these regions stable?"

"In a sense, no. Left alone, the deformation would reduce out and the space in the region would become normal. Again, the time taken for the deformation to flatten out depended on the dimensions of the region. But I..." She stopped.

"Yes?" he prompted. "But you...?"

Somewhat reluctantly, she said: "I was responsible for showing that, in the larger regions, the deformation could be maintained indefinitely by the insertion of a specially-designed framework of rigid material. But, look, when we're talking about these regions of space being unstable, we're not talking about nuclear explosions. There was nothing dramatic about it. The deformation just gradually faded out, that's all. No bangs."

He sat still for a while with a slightly puzzled expression. Elli Wirruna was also silent, but then she burst out: "Look, I've told you more than I wanted to. You're right, I want to keep on working on Cruickshank's work myself. And there's no way that the explosion could have come from our lab. It was probably that bloody hybrid reactor of Matthews', damned expensive toy that it was. Can't you keep Cruickshank out of it, leave his work to me?"

Her hands were open, making grasping motions. Slightly repelled, Stephen Tang stood up. "All right," he said. "I'll do what I can. But I'll need copies of whatever papers you have, mathematics and all. I promise that I'll keep them secure."

"Okay," she said slowly. "But, look, do you mind waiting outside while I find them? This place is a mess, I don't know where I've left them. And there's hardly room for two people in here while I rummage about. Please?"

Frowning slightly in puzzlement, he could find no reason to refuse. He stepped outside onto the balcony while Elli closed the door. He heard it lock, and his frowns became deeper. But instead of worrying about it, he looked out over the edge of the balcony. It was a long way down to the squalid children-filled yard below, and the concrete parapet was clearly deteriorating with age. He wondered how long it would be before the balcony itself fell into the yard. That was an unpleasant thought.

Just when he thought that he would have to fetch the militia up to break open Elli Wirruna's door, it opened, and her black face looked out again. "Sorry. Here they are." And she passed out a couple of sheets of paper, covered in equations which meant nothing to him.

But now he felt that she owed him something. "I wonder whether you would answer a personal question?" he said.

She gave him a suspicious look. "Depends."

"Why do you live up here?"

White teeth flashed again. "Because nobody else wants to. Good enough?" As it obviously wasn't enough, she went on: "It's cheap. And I don't like visitors. Don't like crowds in general. Maybe I just like the view, all right? Is there any crime in that?"

He could see her hostility increasing, so he shook his head and went off, carrying the papers, and thinking hard. There was something in what she had told him that gripped him deeply. The science itself was fascinating, that could be it. And certainly there seemed to be no connection with the bomb blast. He gave it up, and started down the endless stairs.

—

The next few days were spent in communal discussions in the old psychology lecture room. Samphan had now come down on the side of Bill Macarthur and was supporting the consensus view that the hybrid reactor designed by Dr Matthews had been at fault. Macarthur had shown that if certain controls had been operated in a certain way, the flaw he had identified could have led to a swift, catastrophic chain reaction.

Stephen Tang felt unsatisfied. It all sounded so very unlikely. He had known Dr Matthews well, and couldn't accept that he would have missed such a flaw, subtle though it was. But nevertheless, he wasn't going to attract any ill-feeling by submitting a minority report. If Macarthur's theory was good enough for Thanh Samphan, then it better be good enough for Stephen Tang as well.

But John Nguyen came up to Stephen at the end of one of the sessions, a couple of charts in his hand. "Have a look at these: they're the results on the irradiated samples we picked up. What do you think?"

Stephen studied the graphs carefully, and then looked up, puzzled. "There don't seem to be enough heavy particle tracks. It looks..."

"Yes?"

"Well,, I'm no expert, but I'd say that it looks more like what you'd expect from particle-antiparticle collisions. Lots of gamma rays."

"Hmmm. That's what I thought. But Bill says it depends on the exact nature of the fissionable material Matthews was using. We know that he was trying different isotopes. We'll not convince him, so I suppose we'd better shut up."

After another few days of heated discussion, Stephen was becoming weary of it all, longing to be back in his own office at ARL, doing mediocre but useful research. A footnote scientist, that's what I am, he thought. He had made the wrong decisions too long ago to change himself now. And next year, he turned 40. Too late, too late.

Dozens of assistants and clerical workers had been called in by now. and the top floor of the Redmond Barry was beginning to look like the centre of some new industry, an industry whose entire output would be one report that would explain the explosion to everyone's satisfaction. It would carefully recommend severe restrictions and oversight of any research involving fissionable materials in future. Stephen found that he was distanced from it all. The scientific team didn't really need him, and he felt that he was just marking time.

Sitting one morning at the desk they had given him, the telephone rang. "Excuse me, sir," came the voice, "Ngoc Khieu here, the Room Allocations Officer from Admin."

"Yes?" said Stephen, bewildered.

"Well, we're very short of accommodation room in the colleges, as you'd know. And we're still holding open the rooms which used to belong to the unfortunate people killed in the blast two weeks ago. You asked us to do that, sir, according to our records. I was wondering if we could clear them out now. sir, and let some new people in?"

Now he remembered. After visiting Elli Wirruna, he'd asked that those rooms be left as they were. But he'd never got around to looking through them. Now he hesitated. He had the scientists' inbuilt reluctance to destroy information.

"I'm sorry," he said at last. "I should have gotten to it sooner. You can clear out the rooms as of tomorrow. I'll spend the rest of today looking quickly through them. All right?"

"Fine, sir," said Khieu, clearly happy to have a problem resolved.

Stephen also felt irrationally happy. He had no hope now of finding anything to overthrow the conclusions of the Commission, but he would have something to occupy him, get him out of his chair. He dug out the list with the names of those killed in the explosion. There were a lot there. No wonder Admin was fretting about the dormitory space.

—

He spent very little time on each room. The sleeping rooms at the colleges were small of necessity. The morning blurred together into an amalgam of various bedrooms and he found himself looking not so much for evidence about the explosion as for signs of how each person individualised their rooms, put their mark on it to make it their own. A poster here, a stuffed childhood toy there, a vase of flowers, now dead and stinking. These things had reminded the inhabitants of the rooms of their own existence, their own individuality among the millions of others who lived in this ant-nest of a city.

Then he came to Dr Michael Cruickshank's room, and somehow the blur stopped and he found himself looking through it with new interest. Elli Wirruna had been on her way here to fetch Cruickshank a book when the explosion knocked her down. He looked around, thinking again about that remarkable interview he had had with her.

The room was slightly larger than that allocated to students or research assistants, but not much. It was dominated by the bed, of course. But there was at least room for a small desk, with a couple of bookshelves propped on top of it.

There were no working papers to be found. The only thing on the desk was an odd piece of glasswork that Cruickshank had apparently used as a paperweight. Stephen picked it up. It was a model of a Klein bottle, a kind of vase-shape with the bottom tapering out into a tube which was then passed through the side to connect with the mouth inside. Obviously part of Cruickshank's fascination with topology.

He skimmed through the books quickly. Mostly physics. No light reading, no thrillers, no poetry. Cruickshank must have been obsessed with his theory to the exclusion of everything else. There were no posters here either, no marks of individuality, except a small silver ornament on top of the bookcase, hardly big enough to catch the eye.

Stephen sighed. There was nothing here of any interest. He was wasting his time.

But as he went to the door, he turned around for one last look, and the silver ornament gleamed. He frowned. Possessing something like that seemed to be out of character for Cruickshank. He went back into the room and picked the tiny thing up.

It seemed to be nothing more than a small sphere of glass cupped in a fine silver lattice which enclosed barely more than half its surface. But it was surprisingly light if the material were glass. Maybe it was just plastic. He poked his finger at it.

Once, long ago, as a child growing up in the crowded, hungry streets of Melbourne, Stephen Tang had had a weird experience. He had been walking towards a cyclone-wire fence across an alley, beyond which were playing some of his friends, when he had suddenly had the overwhelming conviction that he could walk through the fence as though it were not there. And, centimetres away from the wire, he had been forced to stop, dry-mouthed and trembling. Not from the fear that he would hit himself on the wire and look stupid, but from the terrible fear of what would have followed *if he had indeed* walked effortlessly through the wire. It was unbearable to contemplate. His whole sense of what was possible would have collapsed, and his world with it. And so, still trembling, he had turned away from the wire and sat down.

Now, in the tiny bedroom of Dr Michael Cruickshank, Stephen Tang's mental universe collapsed just as it would have if he had walked through that wire fence.

His finger passed straight through the sphere in the ornament and did not come out on the other side.

Giving an inarticulate cry, he sat down suddenly on the floor, his left hand still grasping, as if in a vice, the ornament that seemed to have swallowed the index finger of his right hand. Desperately trying to retain his sanity, Stephen closed his eyes for a second, feeling dizzy and trying to think sensibly. He had felt no pain, and he wiggled his invisible finger to be sure it was still there. He opened his eyes. Then, very carefully, as though he were moving it through a maze of razor blades, he withdrew his finger. It was unharmed. Trembling a little, he held up the amazing object to the light.

It still seemed as it had before, a small glass sphere, acting as a kind of lens and inverting images of what lay beyond it. Trying to regain his sense of reality, Stephen fumbled for his marker. You're a scientist, he told himself. Facts, observations, objectivity. Test, experiment, discover. Repeating this litany over and over again in his mind, he pushed the marker point first into the sphere.

He noted, first, that an image of the marker was now visible within the sphere, but diminished in size, shortened and distorted. There seemed to be no resistance, nothing solid within the sphere. But the sphere was only a centimetre in diameter and he had easily pushed four centimetres of marker into it without the tip emerging. He kept moving the marker forward.

Finally, when he only held onto the marker by its very end, he met a resistance. Gingerly turning the sphere and marker together, he saw that the very tip of the marker had now emerged on the other side and was wedged in the silver lattice. The marker, which was at least ten centimetres long, had been almost entirely swallowed up within a sphere many times smaller.

"Local induced deformations in the space-time matrix"! That was what Cruickshank had been working on. And now Stephen held in his hands the reality of what those words had hidden. Somehow Cruickshank had found a way to pack ten centimetres of space — no, in terms of volume, a thousand cubic centimetres — into the space of one. He shook his head. The very language didn't cope with such a concept. What did he mean by "space"? All he knew was, there was far more room within that small sphere of space than there ought to be.

Still barely able to believe what he had seen, he stood up. His legs were wobbly, and he had to support himself on the desk. There was one more test he wanted to try. Carefully hiding the sphere inside his hand, he left Cruickshank's room and walked down to the communal bathroom. He put a couple of coins in the meter, ran a basin full of water and then slowly lowered the sphere into it.

It was like immersing a sponge. Air bubbled constantly out of the tiny object and the water level in the basin shrank away as though the plug had been removed. When the bubbles stopped, with only a thin layer of water above the submerged sphere, Stephen tried to move it. It felt as heavy as lead. He pulled it out of the basin, and water streamed out of the object as if from a tap.

He looked at the thing again, still amazed and confounded. So this was what Elli Wirruna had been so concerned to conceal from him. He had to see her again.

—

The nineteen flights of stairs dimmed his curiosity somewhat. Gasping, he found his way to her door and thumped on it. This time, there was a kind of croak, and then a slow shuffle of feet, before the door came open.

He had been startled and shocked the first time he had seen Elli Wirruna. Now he was shocked again, but for a different reason. The young woman's dark face was marked with patches of flaking white skin, and her lips were cracked and bleeding openly. And she seemed to be losing her hair.

She stood silently regarding him for a long time. "So," she said. "And what did you find?"

Stephen silently brought out the weird sphere from his pocket. The silver lattice gleamed. "The idiot!" she said bitterly. "I suppose you found that in his room. When he was working, he could never think about anything sensible, never worry about security. I used to be on at him all the time." Then she was silent again, looking at the unnatural object in Stephen's palm. Finally, she unhooked the security chain.

"It doesn't matter, anyway, not now," she said, and her voice held secret agonies. "Look at me!" And she grasped her hair with one hand and pulled out a patch of it without effort. She moved to the bed and sat down, looking out of the window. "Radiation sickness. I think I knew, really, deep down, from the moment I woke up and they told me what had happened. I was too close, too exposed, there on the bridge. And so I'm going to die." These last words were spaced out, each one held for a second and then let go. Tears began to fall from her eyes as she stared blindly out of the window. Stephen, embarrassed and shocked, sat down on a chair, not knowing what to say. He had not expected this.

After a while, she said: "I'm glad that you came. I can't get up and down the stairs anymore, for one thing. And now I'm not going to be able to continue Michael's work. And someone must. It mustn't be lost." She turned to him, a feverish light in her eyes. "You found one of the small spheres, you know it's something incredible. Can't you see the potential? Room, that's what it means! Room to live! Away from these damned crowds."

Stephen shook his head a little, not yet following her completely. "What do you mean, room to live?"

She gave him an angry glare. "You fool! You're as bad as Michael was. He couldn't see anything except his precious theory, he had no sense of practicality, no sense of the *applications* of what he had found. Theory, theory! My God!" On unsteady feet, she forced herself to stand. "You don't know what I mean by room to live? Come here, then, and see!"

She staggered, almost toppled, towards a small wardrobe built into the wall of the tiny room, and threw open its door. Immediately under a long, thick belt tied to the clothes rod was an ordinary-looking cardboard box, with a power cord leading into it. Triumphantly, she pulled open the flaps at the top. From inside came the faint gleam of silver.

Slowly, hardly able to believe what she was showing him, Stephen moved forward.

Inside the box was another sphere and lattice. But this sphere of distorted space was almost half a metre across. He stood looking at it, thoughts whirling. "How big is it inside?" he asked at last.

She laughed, unpleasantly, the laugh of a sick and doomed person. "That's a tricky question to answer. The volume is about 72 cubic metres. But, another way to look at it, if you were to push a stick through it, the stick would have to be nearly nine metres long before it came out the other side. Put yet another way, the 4-space diameter of the bloody thing is only about three metres. Are you any the wiser?"

Stephen could only shake his head.

"You still don't understand what it is, do you?" she said in an angry, agonised tone. "Damn it, I don't ask for another Einstein, another Cruickshank, but I need someone with some sense! The bloody thing's a bubble in space-time, a miniature universe, a 4-sphere, an unbounded but finite volume of space! Oh, for God's sake, go down into it and have a look. Here, I'll go first and turn on the light." And, weak as she was, Elli Wirruna stepped into the weird sphere in the cardboard box and let herself down into it by means of the leather belt. It was like watching a conjuring trick.

Suddenly, the sphere lit up from inside, and he could see a miniature image of the woman inside the thing. Refusing to allow himself to think, Stephen grabbed hold of the belt and followed her into the sphere.

The first thing that happened was that his stomach revolted, and he suddenly panicked. He was falling! Falling endlessly without going anywhere.

"Don't have kittens," came Elli Wirruna's voice. "Should have warned you. You're in free-fall in here. Steady, wait till you're used to it."

It took him a while, and he closed his eyes until his sense organs had righted themselves. Then at last, he felt able to look about.

He seemed to be floating inside a large spherical room whose walls were made of some kind of canvas, apparently tacked onto a wooden frame. Ropes criss-crossed the area from wall to wall. Floating inside this region were himself, the woman, and a varied assortment of objects like books, lights and sound equipment secured to the ropes. Together with the weightlessness, the large space came as a sudden release from the confines of Wirruna's cramped bed-sitter. It was as though he had been suddenly, effortlessly transported to a roomy spaceship hanging above the Earth.

Cautiously, he turned his body. He was still hanging onto the leather strap, which now seemed to be embedded within a sphere just like the one he had entered to get into this place. He let go, and drifted out into the room, his mind almost as unfixed now as his body.

Elli Wirruna hung limply, like a corpse immersed in the sea. A trickle of tiny red bubbles of blood was floating from her mouth. But she roused herself as he looked at her. "Do you see? Tell me! I need to know you understand."

Stephen looked about, only now beginning to realise how weird this space was. The ropes were taut to the touch, yet to the eye they followed obvious curves. He moved to one, looked along it. It seemed perfectly straight now, but the other ropes were even more strongly curved. There was a hole in the canvas wall near the end of the rope, and he pulled himself towards it and looked through.

On the other side of the wall was what seemed to be another spherical room, also lined with canvas, though this time with the wooden framework inwards. But then, suddenly, he understood. The canvas he was now looking at was exactly the same as that which enclosed the first room, except that he was now looking at the back of it. A single wall, which bounded a sphere inside, and another sphere "outside". The wall was in fact, in a sense, flat, cutting Elli Wirruna's private universe exactly in half. And it had obviously been erected to keep her sane. Otherwise, wherever she looked, she would be seeing the back of her own head.

Two-dimensional analogies were the only way for Stephen's mind to cope. Imagine the universe to be two-dimensional, like a flat sheet of plastic. Now soften a small circular area of this plastic, and blow onto it, blow a bubble into three-dimensional space ... To any two-dimensional creatures, such a region would contain far more area than its outside appearance would indicate. It would be anomalous, weird. And yet that was what Cruickshank had done with three-dimensional space: blown a bubble of it up into the fourth dimension. And he, Stephen Tang, was now moving around on the surface of that bubble, that fourth-dimensional sphere.

He turned to Elli. "Yes," he said. "Now I understand."

She looked at him triumphantly, her thinning hair floating in a halo around her head. "There's no apparent gravity because the curvature is constant in every direction. You get used to weightlessness very quickly. There's no better way to sleep. Now do you see what I mean by room? Make eighty million of these 4-spheres, and every man, woman and child in this country can have as much room as they like to themselves. Or create ones with bigger volume. My God, you could put an entire office block in one of these."

That was all a bit much for Stephen, who was overloaded with wonder and speculation. "Let's get out," he muttered, and grasped for the leather belt within the latticed sphere at the centre of the room. Moments later, he was outside, hauling himself up on the belt. He had to help Elli Wirruna out of the weird region of space, she was so weakened and ill.

He lay her on the bed. Her body was clearly near exhaustion, but her mind was incredibly active.

"How did you get that thing here?" he asked.

"Made it at Solomon, then smuggled it out." Her voice came in gasps, each sentence punctuated by long silences. "You can move them easily, that was a surprise. There's no inherent resistance from space-time to moving the bubble, except that you have to move the mass that's inside the region. I had to pump my universe full of helium and make it airtight before I could carry it. Ordinary air would have weighed far too much. Imagine, though, carrying a universe with you inside a cardboard box! Think of the possibilities! Think of the potential!"

Stephen saw the potential all right, and he saw also that Elli Wirruna had wanted to keep the glory of the discovery to herself once Cruickshank had died. Leave it a few years, and she could present the creation of the 4-spheres as her own triumph. But now she was dying, and it was too late. And there was something else that was worrying at him, nibbling at the edges of his mind, but he couldn't quite identify it just yet.

He brought his attention back to reality. The woman was talking, almost incoherently now, gasping and spitting blood. "All those damn people out there... three hundred years ago, this land was empty apart from my people. Just a few of us in all this wide land. We belonged to the land, and the land was us. And room! My God, the room! Plenty of room, plenty of space, room to breathe. But then the white people came, and it was bad enough. And then the Chaos, and all you bloody Chinks flooded in! My God! You asked me why I lived up here? So I could breathe, so I could breathe!"

And then she subsided into a feverish muttering. The exertion of climbing into and out of the 4-sphere and expounding its nature to him had been too much.

"Can I get you a doctor?" he asked, but she shook her head violently.

"Leave me alone, just leave me to die."

But after what he had seen it was impossible for him to go. And he was thinking something through, something that was still irritatingly just below the consciousness of his mind. He looked up and found himself staring at the Escher print on the wall. Ants crawling over a Mobius strip. The Klein bottle that had been on Cruickshank's desk was another example of the same kind of thing, an object with no inside and no outside.

He had been forced to use two-dimensional analogies just minutes before, to grasp the nature of the 4-sphere, and his mind was still running along in the same vein. If you were a flat, two-dimensional creature, and you lived within the surface of a Mobius strip...

Elli Wirruna had almost gone off into an exhausted sleep. Now he shook her awake. "Elli! You said Cruickshank was experimenting with strange topologies for the universe! Could he have been trying to create a space-time bubble connected like a Klein bottle? Answer me!"

Her eyes blinked open. They were the colour of blood. "Yes, yes, something like that. Theories, his damn theories..."

And Cruickshank had had no head for practicalities! Suddenly it came perfectly clear to Stephen in one astounding stroke of insight. If you were a two-dimensional creature living within a Mobius strip and you made a trip once around the surface, when you returned to the point of departure, you would have undergone a mirror-reversal. Twice around, and you would be back to normal.

And mirror-reversed matter was anti-matter!

He stood up with a shout. It was Dr Michael Cruickshank who had caused the explosion at Solomon!

Intent only on his theories of the topology of the universe, Cruickshank had created one of his regions of deformed space-time with a half-twist in its topology, a four-dimensional analogue of a Klein bottle or of a Mobius strip. And once air had rushed into the newly created region, some of the molecules had moved off in a "straight" line within the region, gone once around the miniature universe, and returned to where they had started. Mirror-reversed, as molecules of anti-matter. And there they had met molecules which were still ordinary matter. The resulting annihilation of mass had resulted in an enormous explosion of energy. Less than a gram of mass destroyed would have been enough to do the damage at Solomon.

He looked down suddenly. In his excitement, he had crushed the fine silver lattice of the small 4-sphere he held in his hand. As he watched, the strange sphere began to gradually fade as the distortion of light it caused became less and less, until there was nothing left. It was gone.

He looked round at the bed. Elli Wirruna was lost in some inner mental world of her own. She could not have understood anything of what he had just discovered. But she seemed to rouse herself as he looked, and she whispered:

"Papers. I have all his papers. In the 4-sphere. In the blue box. You must publish them, get his work turned to use. Give us all some damn room. Room to breathe..."

He left her and went back into the anomalous region of space, the private universe that Elli Wirruna kept in a cardboard box in her wardrobe. The sense of unreality still filled him.

Floating and pulling himself along the ropes, he found the blue box and opened it. In the weightless state, it was all but impossible to properly look through the papers inside. But she seemed to have made photocopies of every one of Cruickshank's working papers, right up until a few days before the explosion. It was all here, the whole theory, the whole discovery of how to create space-time bubbles.

With this treasure, he hauled himself up out of the 4-sphere. As he stepped out, he heard the sound of choking.

Dropping the box, he ran to the bed. Elli Wirruna was unconscious, her lips blue, choking to death, her mouth wide open to reveal the dozens of bleeding sores that filled it. She was drowning in her own blood. He hauled her over the bed so that her head hung downwards, trying to drain the blood from her lungs. She was jerking spasmodically, and he felt utterly helpless. He should attempt some kind of artificial respiration, he knew, but he recoiled from putting his own mouth into contact with that bleeding, toothless mess. And even if he were able to save her now, within days her death would be as certain as the sunset.

In a minute the spasms had stopped, and the woman was still. A pool of bright red blood lay soaking into the cheap carpet at the side of the bed, reflecting the light like some gory mirror.

He looked away, and sat down. It was all too much, too much to bear.

On the floor lay spilled the copies of Cruickshank's papers. He knelt down and mechanically began to pick them up, one by one.

Now, both Cruickshank and Wirruna were dead, both of them killed by the discovery that had obsessed them. And only Stephen Pham Tang was left to triumphantly announce the discovery to the world. He could go back and demonstrate that the Commission was utterly wrong about the explosion at the Solomon Institute, shatter that expression of smug superiority on Thanh Samphan's face. He could be famous, a saviour, bringing to the world, even if he had not created it himself, a means of salvation from overcrowding, and a means of salvation from the desperate lack of energy. For, given the right safeguards, there was no doubt that one of Cruickshank's Klein-bottle regions would be an endless source of cheap energy, a region of space that by its mere geometry was capable of continually converting mass into energy. Kept in a vacuum and fed small amounts of matter, such a thing would provide enough energy for all the world.

But there was another side to it. He found it impossible to keep the image of the devastation at Solomon out of his mind, the image of human bones falling loosely down onto the radioactive glass. It would be all too easy to enclose a Cruickshank region within a vacuum and place it inside a bomb casing. The bigger the volume within the region, the larger would be the resulting explosion when air or water rushed into it. He could see no upper limit. A tonne of water flooding into a suitable region would provide an explosion equivalent, not to megatonnes, but to gigatonnes of TNT. It was unimaginable.

And he thought also of David Carnegie and Charles Hoang sitting telling him calmly about the graser. A Cruickshank region would be an ideal power supply for such a device.

Instead of mere picosecond pulses of unbelievably lethal power, you would be able to operate the weapon continuously. Wielded from space, such a weapon could cut open whole planets.

What was he to do?

He was a scientist, not a militarist. And he would not be responsible for how the discovery was used. His hands would be clean. And the world needed space, and energy.

But he was also a human being who was once a child, and he remembered his childhood terrors of the Chaos that had killed three-quarters of the world.

He stood up in anguish, the papers in his hand. He couldn't decide! How could he be responsible for releasing such a potentially lethal invention onto the world? But how could he be responsible for suppressing such a potentially valuable invention needed by the world? It was too much for one man to bear.

He wished that Elli had not died. It could have been her responsibility, not his. She would have released it, no doubt about it. But she was dead.

He went to the door, opened it, and stood outside on the aging balcony. The weather was changing, and a thunderstorm was coming. A wild, hot wind was whipping by. He looked down over the balcony. A mass of screaming children ran about in the yard, oblivious to Stephen Tang high above their heads.

He stared at the papers. There were many individual sections, each bound together by a single staple at the top left hand corner. Somehow, he found himself being obsessed by the staple of the first section. He tugged at the top sheet, and ripped it away from the staple. He held out the sheet of paper, and the wind took it.

One by one, he released the sheets, letting the wind take them where it might. Like a flock of birds, they flew far and wide, high, high above the crowded city.

August 1985, modified June 2014

The original story was published in the collection *Urban Fantasies* edited by David King and Russell Blackford, published by Ebony Books in 1985.

Paradise Lost

THE DAY BEGAN WITH A BLOOD-RED SKY that lit up the interior of the cave with a ruddy glow. Waking up and finding Josh missing, Ellie got up and went to find him.

She didn't have to go very far. There he was, sitting on a sand-dune, staring out to sea, silhouetted against the spectacular sky. Her dilemma.

She came up and sat down beside him. He was still a head shorter than her, and she put her arm around his shoulders. She could tell that he had been crying. Barely acknowledging her presence, he said thickly "I miss my Dad."

"I miss my Mom and Dad, too," she said softly. "And everyone else."

It was harder on Josh right now, though. They had buried Josh's father only about a week ago. Ellie, on the other hand, had had two or three months to reconcile herself to the loss of her parents. It was hard to be definite about the lapse of time here, Ellie thought to herself. She had better start making some kind of calendar – scratches on the wall of the cave, perhaps, or a pile of white stones. She should have done it sooner.

The sun began to emerge from amidst the flaming clouds. "'Red sky in the morning, sailor's warning'" she said. A pointless remark, really, but it was something to say.

Josh shrugged off her arm in a sudden angry gesture. "Why did we get into that boat, then? There were lots of red skies before we left! We shouldn't... We should never have gotten in that boat! We should have stayed at home!" And he stalked away from her, trying to hide his sudden tears. Ellie forgave him those tears. He had been through a lot, and he was only half her age. She was twenty-two. He was only eleven. Only eleven.

But they couldn't have stayed at home. Not with all the chaos going on. Millions were dying, and the group had counted themselves lucky, very lucky indeed, to have the chance of escape on the charter boat. Trying to reach somewhere cooler, somewhere where the wars weren't happening, somewhere beyond the reach of the fallout.

It was easy now, in retrospect, to see that their voyage had been hopeless, a fool's quest. But perhaps if they had stayed it would have been worse. It might have been a quicker end, though. Sometimes hope was the most treacherous of emotions.

Their hopes had been wrecked, literally, on the shore of this island.

It had been the middle of the night, and Ellie remembered the horror only too well. The crowded boat, barely enough room to move about. Everyone with their pathetic belongings clutched tightly to them. The wild winds and the huge waves. The crying and the stench of vomit. And then the sudden terrible shock as the boat struck the unseen reef, the dizzying spin as Ellie was thrown from the deck into the cold salt water, her desperate struggle to stay afloat even with the precious life-jacket her father had paid a fortune to obtain for her before they left. The screams, and the awful cracking sound as the boat broke up. Floundering in the water, spitting out gulps of brine, half-choking. And then the blessed feel of something solid beneath her feet, and stumbling up the beach to lie exhausted until the sun had come up.

So very few of them had survived. Her parents had both drowned, along with all but a handful of those who had been aboard. Ellie, Josh and his father Derek, and Mrs Goldberg. Mrs Goldberg hadn't lasted long, poor old lady. And Josh's father had died of what was probably a heart attack last week. But he hadn't been well for weeks before that, deprived of the half-dozen medications he was supposed to take every day. His lips had been constantly a shade of light blue for days before he died, but there was nothing that Ellie could do for him.

Josh walked back to Ellie. "What do you want me to do today?" he asked sulkily. He wasn't a bad kid, and Ellie had grown quite fond of him, but he'd been spoiled by his former life, had been one of those overweight kids who would rather have played a video football game than dream of actually going outside and kicking a ball about. All that was gone now, of course, and on their meagre diet Josh had slimmed down and was starting to become fit. Eventually his mind would catch up with that and he might even grow up into a nice young man. If only...

"Go and collect some gull eggs," she said briskly to him.

"But the birds peck at me, I don't like it."

"Use your stick and hit them hard. If you kill any of the birds, all the better, bring them back. Come on, Josh, you've done this dozens of times before. You don't want to starve, do you?" He shook his head and set off compliantly enough to climb up the cliff toward the gull nests, wearing one of the back-packs they had rescued from the surf.

Ellie returned to the cave to check on the driftwood fire. She didn't want it to go out, though she had no great fear that she couldn't light a new one if she had to. On a rough shelf in the cave she had stacked a dozen cigarette-lighters they had scooped up from the waves, and their precious reserves of butane all seemed intact.

She looked around the cave, checking their supplies. Considering how many bodies had sunk beneath the sea after they struck the reef, it was stunning how many cases and packs had floated and come to shore. She had long since mentally catalogued all their contents. She and Josh had enough clothing to keep them warm for the rest of their lives, if they were careful not to wear anything out unnecessarily. There were several bottles of multi-vitamins stacked in a pile, though how long their potency would last was anyone's guess. And she smiled sardonically at the rows of useless cell-phones she had arranged on ledges. She wasn't sure why she kept them, except for decoration.

Time to go out gathering. There were rock-pools on the shore with limpets and crabs, easy to gather if you didn't mind the odd nip on your fingers. She had tried eating some of the seaweed, but it was nasty stuff. Nevertheless it stayed down and maybe did them some good. The lack of vegetables was her biggest concern, and she was cautiously trying various plants around the island to discover what might be edible. A lot of this island, she supposed, would have been covered with ice at one time, but with the warming over the last few decades, areas of reasonably rich soil were being exposed, and new plants were sprouting up, probably from wind-borne seeds or bird droppings.

Bringing back her harvest, she stood looking for a while at Josh, now starting to climb down the cliff-face.

She sighed. There was no hope of rescue, none at all. The world had been busy destroying itself when they left. If anything like civilization still remained on the mainland, it would be centuries before it got back onto its feet. And even then, why would they come exploring up here? It would hardly be a priority.

Josh was her biggest problem. It was nice to have some sort of companionship, she supposed. In his best moments, he was quite a nice kid. But in a year or two he would reach puberty. And then he would start looking at Ellie with a different eye. He'd turn into a big man, too. Derek, his father, had looked as if he had been a tall, beefy man in his prime. There would be no way she could fend off a fully-grown Josh, no way to resist his inevitable desires.

Ellie had always been a practical, down-to-earth person. While it was nice to dream of her and Josh as an unlikely sort of Adam and Eve, repopulating the world with their children, the practicalities were hopeless.

She had found a few packets of the contraceptive pill in the luggage, but the sum total of their daily dosages didn't add up to more than a year or two, and then they would be gone. Without them, she would be likely to give birth every second year. In a place with no medical facilities and no midwives. Her odds of dying during childbirth or its aftermath were frighteningly high. Leaving Josh with a gaggle of babies or toddlers to look after in this desolate place. And then what? No, she simply couldn't let that happen.

She eyed Josh as he reached the base of the cliff and started towards her.

He was a nice enough kid, but sometime soon she was going to have to kill him.

November 2011

The Other Side

GLADYS WAS ALMOST TOO LATE FOR THE SÉANCE. Well, no, not 'almost'. She *was* late. It had already begun when she arrived. The room was darkened, lit only by the small candles in the centre of the table. Gladys moved quietly into the shadows at the back so as not to disturb matters.

The medium, Mrs Horatio Bottomley, was a stocky woman in her fifties, clothed in a voluminous flowery dress covered with lace and postively dripping with beads. She sat at the head of the table, clasping hands with those on either side of her. Her eyes were closed, and she was calling on the spirit world in a tremulous voice.

The woman was a fraud, of course. Gladys knew that. They were all frauds. She ought to know, she had visited enough of them, always hoping to find someone with a true talent, the talent it took to really communicate with the spirit world, to speak to those long dead and bring back their thoughts to those still living. If only it *were* possible to talk again to her beloved father, to say how sorry she was for what had happened. That was what drove Gladys to keep coming to these events.

"Oh hear me, White Feather of the Blackfoot tribe!" called Mrs Bottomley.

Gladys had to supress a laugh. Spiritualists like this one always seemed to have a 'spirit guide' who was either a native American or from the Far East somewhere. Chinese guides with ludicrous names like 'How Long Chee' were becoming popular.

The table shook and a loud 'crack' sounded. Gladys was prepared to bet that beneath her arms in those loose sleeves Mrs Bottomley had hooks extending under the table. And between her knees, a metal tin or some such arrangement which let out an alarming noise when squeezed. Some of these people were more convincing than others, though. Mrs Bottomley wasn't the worst that Gladys had encountered.

The medium's voice shifted down a register. "Me here. Who want pow-wow with White Feather?" Gladys did laugh out loud then, and only barely managed to turn it into something like a cough at the last minute.

Mrs Bottomley's eyes fluttered open and she turned toward the sound with an annoyed expression. "Silence, please," she said crossly in her normal voice. Gladys stepped a little further back into the shadows.

The medium closed her eyes again and went on to speak to her guide. "It is I, Matilda Bottomley, White Feather. We have spoken before."

"Hum. Speak on," she answered herself in a deep voice.

"We have those present here who wish to speak with their loved ones on the Other Side. Can you help us, White Feather?"

"Yes. Who seeks?" Really, Gladys thought, this woman was quite good as frauds went. Entertaining, at least, which was more than you could say for some of them.

"Mr Frank Jenkins is here and seeks to speak to his beloved wife Dora. Is she there?"

"Yes, she here."

Mrs Bottomley's voice shifted again, now to a high and reedy register, as she impersonated 'Dora', apparently to Frank's complete and tear-filled satisfaction. Gladys didn't pay much attention to the words spoken, but looked hard at the medium's face as she spoke in the character of the dead woman. Either she was a great actress or there was a sense of some real empathy there. While the words she spoke were invented, perhaps she was channelling some real emotion from the spirit she impersonated? Gladys felt a flicker of hope.

There *was* something different about this woman, Gladys thought. It was barely there, mostly covered up by flim-flam and misdirection, but it was there nonetheless. Just the faintest hint of a real talent.

Can that be how it works? Gladys wondered. You start with a faint but genuine sense of someone being present alongside you when you are alone. A tentative feeling that someone dead has returned to give you reassurance. But then, sparked by the huge popular enthusiasm for spirituality and the prospect of making money, you spin up that genuine feeling into something more than it is. You bolster it with all sorts of tricks. You magnify that 'still small voice' into a crude bellow as though using a megaphone. Perhaps you manage to convince yourself that you have contacted 'White Feather' or someone like him in order to protect yourself from the awful fear of *actually* being in contact with the ghostly multitudes — with the 'numberless infinities of dead', as Donne had put it.

Dora had left now and Mrs Bottomley was moving on. She was going through a routine of having lost contact with her spirit guide and having to seek him again. It all spun out the length of the séance and gave extra value for money, Gladys supposed.

'White Feather' returned at last, however, to the relief of those around the table though not to Gladys.

A weeping elderly woman called Mrs Keithley asked, between sobs, to speak to her son, who had died in the recent conflict in the Crimea. In a gruff, soldierly voice, Mrs Bottomley passed on some anodyne expressions of love.

One of the other guests at the table was an elderly man with a full head of silver hair. He looked up hopefully as Mrs Bottomley opened her eyes again and scanned the table. The medium caught his gaze and nodded slightly.

Now, then, Gladys thought. She could at least try. Silently, she moved around the table, keeping to the shadows, until she stood behind the medium.

Mrs Bottomley was speaking once more. "Oh White Feather, hear me! Colonel Masterton is here. He wishes fervently to speak with his only child, who died in a sad accident a few years ago. I... oh!"

Gladys had stepped forward and placed her hands on the medium's shoulders from behind. A sudden violent shiver ran through the woman, and her voice ceased abruptly.

Gazing across the table into the old man's sad eyes, Gladys spoke for the first time that night, and to her joy, the medium's mouth now repeated her words.

"Yes, father," Gladys said. "I am here."

May 2013

About the Author

David Grigg is a retired software developer who lives in Melbourne, Australia. He worked in the field of interactive multimedia for over two decades, and has also worked in public relations and as a journalist and sub-editor. He is married, with one grown-up daughter and two grand-children.

Born in the north of England, he emigrated to Australia with his parents at the age of 13. He has lived in Australia ever since.

During the 1970s and 1980s, David was deeply involved in the science fiction fan community in Australia, publishing fanzines and helping organize SF conventions, eventually becoming Chairman of the 43rd World SF Convention held in Melbourne in 1985.

He is the author of a number of professionally published short stories and two short fantasy novels for teens, "Halfway House" and "Shadows".

Rightword

Editing, proofing, book design and publication services

---

*Your new book is your baby; it's precious to you. We understand that.
Let us help you to deliver it safe and well into the hands of your readers.*

Rightword offers a range of services to help you put your book together:

Copy-editing; proof-reading; typesetting and formatting; book design and layout; cover design; ebook production; assistance in working with printers and retailers.

For more information and to see samples of our work, please visit our website at *www.rightword.com.au*, or send an email to *book.publishing@rightword.com.au*.

www.ingramcontent.com/pod-product-compliance
Lightning Source LLC
Chambersburg PA
CBHW050546260626
47157CB00002B/459